MEGAN
BUTTON

and the Dragon Keeper

Megan Button and the Dragon Keeper

A new novel by M. T. BOULTON

MEGAN BUTTON

BUTTON

and the Dragon Keeper

M. T. BOULTON

 New Generation Publishing

To thy dim past that ye tide of which
with filters discarded hath ebbed, A

Tribulation first makes you realise who you are - Marie Antoinette

Chapter One

Doll

Megan Button's neighbours of Marlberry Mews were most all unmerrily not amused. Again.

It was generally agreed upon that it had been, and perhaps sometimes still was, a little row of snoozing houses napping in the tippytoe village of Baxley-upon-Beau, but the tranquil district of Snitterden had been crashed apart yonks ago, out of its lullaby hushed slumbering, by the arrival of the Button's.

Now, it ought to be pointed out that, on the whole, each of the twelve grown-up residents positively thought the rest of the Button family were rather divine: 'Beth - cor, a right cracker, smarts, and gorgeous pins... a broad,' had gushed Mr. Earl Monteygoose, of number Six, from the neighbour's first brush with them, many moons past, as they moved into their chessboard-like townhouse.

'That Jeremy, a jolly fine fellow! Upstanding! Thoroughly dotes on his wife and children!' boomed Mrs. Joyce Kurren, cooing from number Two, after her third tipple of sherry and feeling rather free with her favours, rabbiting on in a hiccup about the starting stalls horse fixtures in that day's *Racing Post* newspaper.

'Megan, aww, what a stonkingly well-mannered child: but very quiet. Quite owlish,' Miss Liza Partridge, of number Eleven, had summarized, swinging a book about championing her, then returned to her biography on King Henry V.

The one bone of contention that stuck in their throats, like an irksome chicken leg, was that concerning the youngest daughter of the Button brood, and especially the last escapade administered by her:

Five weeks ago, Putz was minding his own business, haughtily sat by the lamppost with his lazy eyes lounging at nothing in particular. Putz (or, to give him his correct show name, Putzwilliam Saint Bartemus The Fourth. Who was not, as perhaps guessed, a human. But rather a cat - a big cat. In fact, so big that as he hefted himself around he somehow, with the impression of not wanting too, pivoted in one direction then another. Though, the fluffed-up look did not nothing to dispel his engorged size; he looked as if he had been electrified, and by doing so, had used up eight of his lives) was then rudely interrupted out of his daily inactivity, of leaning against the unlighted streetlight, by someone booting him up the backside. In a yelped meow and a *hiss*, Putz barged round to see a hornswoggle vision of fleet-footed purple with a dash of blond cackle over him, certainly looking very pleased with herself.

In several mews, Putz's wail complained in strength the longer he hissed his warble.

His owner, Mrs. Hardfly, of number Five, who maintained a well kept clipped front lawn, that she liked to think was perfectly perfect as ever a manicured lawn could be (and took quite prideful relish in, with looking down her perfectly powdered nose at those lawns, which weren't up to what she judged as scratch), and had been providentially dusting near the front living rooms net curtain - incidentally, all knew that Mrs. Hardfly would stand by the net curtain, and 'dust' all day - she came storming out, suddenly, with ill-disguised agitation, grabbed Lucy by the top of her ear, frog-marching her over the street in a furious waddle, and then hammered on the door of number Nine.

As Lucy's mum opened the yelling front door from the hullabalou of the unsolicited visitor, she found her youngest child doing a hurly-burly nettlesome dropkick with her thick, chewing mouth grindingly set in not giving up with her loud chomping (Lucy had maintained hold on the candy pack of sugared Carol's Cola Bottles), whilst Mrs. Hardfly held on barely, and looked as if she were about to blow her Tweed coat off from screaming.

Mrs. Hardfly had, sometime later still, knocked on every single door and gave blow-by-blow accounts of the horrid drama. Everyone petted her knee, nodded sympathetically and the general feeling was summed up by Mr. Monteygoose, the elderly gentleman of number Six, who was that hard of hearing he took to using a brass trumpet (he thought the modern equivalent being far too "progressive"), and had sagely drooled, 'Fine family. But by Bertie they let the side down with that terror of a child.'

Mrs. Hardfly pronounced one afternoon - by route of an issued typed note that she circulated:

Dear _____ [she ever-so-politely embedded the name that corresponded to the addressee on her distribution list] *I am off for a few days - to visit my sister.*

Muriel owns a delightfully adequate, quaint cottage by the seaside, and having spoken to her, I have taken the advice that, as certain events are not helping my nerves, it would be best for me to take a short rest.

I shall bring you back a pasty.

With fond goodbyes, your respectful neighbour

Betty Hardfly.

And off she went.

Mrs. Hardfly had came back from her restful days with a miaowing Putz in a brand-new cat carrier, and upon opening her reeking house, advancing past the collection of post, she then slipped on a pond of something smelly and bellowing 'What the Dickens!', she squashed her sponge, that, as luck would have it, had almost gone in a trajectory out of her luggage-case-handled, iron-grip, not three seconds before. Such was the rank driveling intensity, of the four putrid bananas, they had squirted through the shagpiles, slobbering in splodged, fat rivulets that bled into the floorboards.

In a galled and early-morning look, she swung a caged mewing Putz in one hand, and in the other a mushed-up pulverizing specimen of the polluted harvest (ladled up by the use of the local county paper, the weekly-printed gazette of the *Chathouston Bugle*), and pounded across the way in a hodgepodged walk with her legs spattered in Victoria sponge, looking even more glum.

Beth Button had wrung her hands (once more, not for the first time, standing on her front-step over her youngest daughter), and troweled some fingers through her long brown hair, but was most firm that she, or no-one in her household, knew of the perpetrator.

Unsatisfied, but with no evident proof, Mrs. Hardfly had stormed off, leaving Lucy's mum wearing a weak smile, camouflaging the troubled look of knowing that as far as she was concerned, she had not taken delivery of any note that detonated Mrs. Hardfly's outlined holiday.

Two passers-by, one beefy-necked and the other weedy-looking, were trundling down the road and commenting on this very matter.

'But she has been extremely quiet of late,' said Mrs. Lurrve-Hamilton, of number Three, who had just dropped her thirteen-year-old daughter, Fortuna, at horse practice (such was Fortuna's love of all things colt-crazed, that all she banged on about were gymkhanas, and coincidentally, also happened to be horse-faced), and was now off out with Mrs. Jungling - for a spot of tea, fruitcake and backgammon at The Bridge Club.

'Quiet? Pah!' Mrs. Jungling whipped a ham-sized fist; she recalled Lucy stating quite clearly her opinion that she took her to be a mad old hag, knifing off bats heads, boiling them in a cauldron stew and brewing the lay of the stars. 'We all know that is because the queen bee is hatching her next deadly plan - it could be either of us, next.'

'She wouldn't,' twittered Mrs. Lurrve-Hamilton.

'She would,' nodded Mrs. Jungling, pulling on the leash roped to the ratty-looking dog, forced into wearing a canary-yellow plastic overcoat - Mrs. Jungling had briefly seen the news forecaster mention the possibility of the drizzle of rain, and so not wanting Jasper drowned in a flash downpour, thought it prudent to take precautions; even if they included gross mistakes in doggy chic wares.

'Maybe she just needs more time in a naughty space' prattled Mrs. Lurrve-Hamilton, as if Lucy were a bothersome toddler.

'Oh that thingamajig! Naughty space? Don't be a donkey, dearie. Naughty space,' repeated Mrs. Jungling. 'What that little jackanapes needs is too be thrown in the naughty dungeon!' she prescribed.

'Oh, Maud!'

'Oh Maud nothing, Floela! Nine-hundred years this area was as it were, and now too see what has happened!' Mrs. Jungling shook her hardy-faced head. 'She's the proverbial enfant terrible. She always ensues arguments. And always windmilling about!

'No wonder that poor child always like she'd wet herself if a ghost said boo to her. Oh that reminds me: when the Button's moved in, I watched their removal van being unloaded, and I didn't see any Aga! Can you fathom it!' she reported, tittle-tattling.

'Well, really! No Aga?' Mrs. Lurrve-Hamilton stopped short,

shocked.

'No Aga,' nodded Mrs. Jungling wisely, feeling proud in her chin-wagging, she put her clasped hands in front of her ample waist. 'Mind, I have heard they have easels in their house. *Easels*, I tell you!'

'Hmm, I don't know about any easels, but as for the older child, she is awfully introverted.'

'As I say - no wonder. Can you imagine growing up in a household with that as your sibling,' thundered Mrs. Jungling.

'It must be terrifically hard for her.'

Stroking her blue rinse, Mrs. Jungling looked distinctly disgruntled. 'And we all know…' and shaking her broad-shoulders, rambled on about what've happened to Lucy in her day, and certainly would not have been spending eight contemplative minutes in a designated naughty space.

Mrs. Jungling's words on being

argumentative, were, at the precise moment, being proved true: inside the black-and-white, checkered-front home of number Nine, Lucy pulled the doll's head off, and as it went *pop*, her bedroom door banged closed; which abruptly cut the sound from downstairs of their dad attempting to tinkle on the piano (just after ladling a day's old chilli-con-carne in a casserole pan in the oven), while their mum worked on a very difficult jigsaw puzzle from a charity shop of The Shropshire Welsh Marches, but which, upon nearing completion, was frustratingly discovered to be missing three of the one-hundred pieces in the Corndon Hill section, and upstairs, in amidst a flurry of ruffled auburn hair, in hustled her eldest daughter.

Spotting what she was doing, she said exasperatingly, 'What do you think you're doing?'

Lucy flexed her fingers as if she

had talons.

'What does it *look* like, Megan?' she trilled back selfishly, as she continued along her toy shelf, yanking out arms and legs.

'But they're very expensive, and you're *only* doing this because Mum asked you to tidy the mess downstairs - that *you* made!'

'Is not!'

'Is so.'

Each Sister glared, and Megan pointlessly asked. 'Then why are you spoiling your dolls - you used to always like them?'

Lucy continued without really listening. 'I'm older now, and anyway, these are like *so* yesterday.'

Lucy was prone to *so* enjoying channeling a miss diva.

Megan balled her hands. 'What?'

Lucy gossiped. 'Well I overheard Millie say Roy's Toys has these,' she waved a doll, attired in the rather fierce outfit of a puce ra-ra skirt, paired with a vest top with a skull and crossbones printed fancifully on the front, and sporting clumpy boots on its dainty doll feet, and rounded off with florescent-green braids in her blond locks, 'on a two-for-one *offer*.'

'And?' Megan asked blankly.

Lucy's top lip puckered.

'Err, hello Megan! On offer!' she derided in a blistering tone, with no sentimentality for her poor dolls.

'Did you say... Millicent?' Megan grilled, in a stricken voice.

She realised to whom Lucy had mentioned in passing with her named reference.

'Mille. Yes.'

There was a gasp of disbelief from Megan.

'H-how do you know Millicent?' she asked, with her heart thumping in fear.

Lucy showed a polished sneer.

Megan frowned. Lucy smiled.

'Everyone knows Millie,' she blabbed tersely in spite, adding in such an unnecessary, acidic comment.

Megan felt defensive.

'You don't... *obviously.'*

Megan was gobsmacked. 'That's outrageous, Lucy!'

'Excuse *moi?'*

'Pft.' Megan mumbled.

Lucy gave a short, clipped titter.

Megan sadly looked very hurt. Terribly hurt.

'Hum.' Lucy grunted.

Megan sighed, staying quiet.

'Idiot!' Lucy said, savagely.

Unsurprisingly, Megan oftentimes felt as if she wanted complete isolation from Lucy.

Chapter Two

Rainbow, Wordy Raindrops And Blackness

Two days later dribbled on into the third, and found Megan's windowpane having dappled sunshine beaming down against it.

The day before Megan had, with permission, raided her mum and dad's big, treacle-brown coloured haberdashery basket in the larder (which, on the shelving unit, had glass ketchup bottles, a couple of jars of brown pickle, coffee granules in canisters and tea-bags inside Tupperware containers, cased drill bits, spanners and screwdrivers, a white packet of Murdoch's Mint Imperials, two buy-one-get-one-free elderflower cordial bottles, bought yesterday, from her dad's shopping spree in the local corner shop, old used toothbrushes, a squirty mustard bottle and three packed bloomer loaves, with a full butter tray. The haberdashery wicker basket was also concealing a selection of bath plugs, smaller basin stoppers, fuses, a rolled-up yellow and grey tape measure in inches and centimetres, two washed-out pots but now were handling curtain rail hooks instead of Eaton Mess and apricot-and-rhubarb yoghurts, a spare white apron and mitts, oven advertisement leaflets and the company's accompanying small microwave brochures), and over the afternoon, by utilizing a long, rectangle strip of cardboard, and with painstaking care, she'd sealed some material over it, to create a rather nifty pink felt bookmark. This hand-sewn marker was stuck at page two of her school Science manual - she couldn't make head-nor-tail of any of the muchly dreaded Chemistry words.

She'd given the directory the once-over and then left it at the back of her unbalanced-looking desk.

Megan's mind felt then congested with something about a Periodic Table.

Though this baffled feeling didn't last long, thankfully. A more altogether nicer nightly sound salved Megan into feeling a tad more at ease. Last night Megan was serenaded sleepily by an owl tooting *terwit-terwoo... terwit-terwoo.*

At that precise moment, Megan was holding the rim of her most cherished pink hat.

The weather had been uncommonly warm of late, and a spiffing straw bonnet was called for, to shade herself with for the current and coming season.

Megan took a sip of pink lemonade.

After draining her drink, she set the tumbler back on her desk, near to the freshly-roasted, buttered and strawberry-jammed Devonshire scone on a pink paper plate, then Megan dug a magenta-bright ruler out of the right pocket, from her pink fluffy dressing gown. She'd retrieved the angle art appliance from her school bag not five minutes ago, and was going to use this for her drawings later - she wanted the right shade of all pinks, too best know which to colour-in some of her wonderful pictures.

Megan was also attempting to decide betwixt wardrobe choices: a pink sundress and white wool cardigan with three-quarter length sleeves, or a pink-and-white gingham pleated dress, a cream-and-hazel sundress, or, lastly, pink corduroy trousers, a cream t-shirt with a sequined rainbow streaming upon the material, and a pale pink, full-length jersey cardigan.

Megan dithered on the spot for a spell.

After gazing at the sparkly rainbow design, she opted for the latter ensemble.

As she was getting changed into the selection, she looked to the radius of her new souvenir, that only had one eye and looked generally sad for himself.

Megan had, just a short time ago, received top-marks, A +, for an Art assignment. She was snidely bullied over the results, and was pushed into corner walls when a teacher or dinnertime person wasn't around (Megan tended to really not like having the spotlight torched on her). The school code on bullying was to tell a family member or teacher, so as then to crackdown on the maggot-like children with their bludgeoning words and actions, though Megan kept ever schtum - because of not wanting to distress her mum and dad, bring more limelight to herself, and she always hoped they'd stop. Should she say anything to her mum and dad, or teacher, then Megan longed suspected that afterward, the bullies would get only worse.

Her mum and dad had remembered Megan mentioning in passing about her Art reward: that came about by her mum making sure Lucy and herself were occupied at an ice-cream stall; as her dad had then clandestinely bought the raggedly battered teddy bear.

Humphrey (as Megan now named him) was now sat on her desk, looking like an annex to Megan's latest copy of her biweekly pony magazine - of which he was roosting on top of, and was a handy pier for a perforated pouch of half-eaten Shirley's Sherbet Dip.

A little later on in the hour, Megan was doctoring a picture of a spiffing Unicorn until the mane was the right shade of exquisite silver, then reviewing the next element, she started the revising work on its tail. She was remembering her Unicorn friend, and how Prince Tumble looked like a massive white shire horse, only with a horn in the middle of his forebrows, and he could talk!

Megan turned the bands up on the sleeves, then rolled both up to give her room to move and draw; as her hands flew over the page, the inserted panelings on her cardigan jangled from the pink and studded clear crystal pillates dancing about.

Megan paused.

She smoothed the page down tenderly with the back of her left hand.

Megan used the end of the silver-tipped pencil to scratch an itch on the right-side of her cheek. She was reflecting back on a recollection to do with Prince Tumble and the congregation of Unicorns. She was recalling with a smile how she very nearly fell head-over-knees when dismounting from the wonderfully aromatic, vanilla-smelling Volkener.

Megan examined the next picture.

She scrutinized the point-of-view of each facet of her tremendous drawing.

She divested more pinks and yellows were needed to be pronounced, and some merging of a riot of colours. Then she could begin on drawing more pictures of Prince Tumble and after, the other Unicorns.

All of a sudden, Megan heard a sarcastic laugh out on the landing.

Megan sighed.

She wouldn't? Megan thought.

And yes, poor she was right, as her bedroom door swung open to show a tyrannical mini-madam in its wooden threshold.

The colour drained from Megan's face.

Lucy was still laughing unpleasantly at something.

'Get out,' Megan suddenly cried.

'No!'

Megan was fuming. 'Mum and Dad told you before to always knock. I would!'

Lucy looked at her contemptuously.

Megan was tired of Lucy's meddling.

Lucy carelessly gained entry.

She was scoffing the last leg of a gingerbread man; her mouth was also full with creamy-marzipan and chilled caramel syrup.

Lucy had a hat on her head. It was lilac, tall, with a long gauzy-white veil spuming in froths of out from the pointy top. She looked about her sister's room.

Megan gritted her teeth.

'Not much has... changed,' Lucy said callously, still eating.

Megan felt cross. 'I-I like the way my room is.'

'Of course you *do*.' Lucy said, in such a cauterized worded tone.

'Stop this. We don't need to fight.' Megan demanded.

'No! I don't want to.' Lucy leaned against the left-side of the doorjamb.

Megan's face looked incredulous.

'Just please go back to your room, or downstairs. I'm drawing,' Megan explained, quite needlessly.

Lucy took a step boldly into Megan's space.

Megan shook her head silently.

Lucy nodded her head back in a lofty manner.

Megan's hands protectively flitted round the pink rose she had etched yesterday.

Lucy's eyes tightened as her purple-socked, intruding foot, punted at the stacks of comics piled on the pink carpet.

Megan felt rising incandescence. Her anger was like a gurgling cauldron about to blow its lid off.

Lucy's answer was to carry on digging by Megan's cuddly toys, then turning her foot on to the open, tatty-looking, medium-sized hardback Dictionary turned at a page, for words beginning with the letter I.

Megan glared.

Lucy airily raised her right hand, snapped her fingers then examined the cuticles on her nails.

Megan bristled.

I'm sick of this, she thought defiantly.

Megan shook her spiraled hair.

Lucy did not attempt to make amends.

Megan bit her tongue in self-restraint.

Again, they were sparring spiky words in one of their bedrooms.

Tears were standing in Megan's eyes.

Lucy trod away, bored.

Megan stewed.

Chapter Three

Smegan

Megan's pink clock twiddled a chiming *cuck-ooo-cuu-ckooo*.

Megan shot up from her bed.

She made sure her drawing equipment and papers were carefully laid down.

Megan stood with a start.

Frowning, she straightened her back, then her pink-socked feet followed her waltzing sister, hot-on-her-heels, as she exited to cross her bedroom.

Megan felt as if an electric current *zapped* through her.

'I still can't believe you spoke of Millicent like that. As if you were best friends.'

Megan had pattered to Lucy's room.

'Oh, just shut up Megan,' Lucy said severely.

Not for the first time, an unavoidable argument was going to begin. Or rather, Lucy would be ranting, whilst Megan listened.

Megan butted the door closed of Lucy's bedroom.

A corner of Megan's mouth twitched. 'She-stuck-another-sticker-on-my-school satchel... screaming words... of... Barmy Button!' shouted Megan.

'So?' Lucy asked flatly, most uncaringly, in a cold, high voice, as her features darkened.

Megan took her face out of her hands.

'I-I... d-don't you think that's plain *wrong?*' Megan pleaded.

Lucy's top lip curled.

'Whatever. At least it's one-up from Boring, Bookworm Button. Anyway, you are barmy,' Lucy said impassively, as she took her cone-like hat off, she unloosed the long, thin elastic band under her chin that ran in a strand, on both sides, to the tops of her ears, then she spritzed a can of some hair solution into her clean locks.

Megan took a step back, protectively. 'I... B-pardon?'

'You are a little *odd*.'

Megan stared blankly.

'Barmy Button suits you.' Lucy said, renaming Megan.

Megan turned a bit red.

'Stop it.'

'I mean, you may as well be called, oh, I don't know... Blanche Bland.' Lucy said, crinkling her nose.

'Who?' Megan said blankly.

'No idea. But a good name for you. Blanche Bland! Megan Bland!' Lucy taunted.

This was severe for Megan.

'Stop it!' Megan cried, pleading.

'Button Bland!' persisted Lucy.

'Stop being so nasty!'

'Stop being *so* bland!' she shot back.

'S-I-Lucy!' Megan hissed, stunned, in a slip of the tongue.

Lucy shook with unsuppressed giggles.

'He h-e-e!'

A very annoyed Megan yelled, 'Stop now!'

'Smeg Megan.'

'WHAT?' Megan shouted.

'Smegy Megan.'

'Stop it.'

'Smegan!'

This was sufficiently painful to greatly hurt Megan.

Lucy just wouldn't cease.

Megan implored again loudly, 'Stop it!'

'No!' Lucy replied tartly.

She looked at Megan with a feline silence, quite fit for a tomcat surveying a particularly plump sparrow.

Megan's face purpled.

Lucy's lips were bared over her teeth.

The atmosphere was extremely close.

Lucy looked as if she really was enjoying the cruel amusement.

'SMEGAN.'

Megan looked liked she had been hit in the face with a tennis ball.

Lucy was laughing nastily.

'S-S-M-MEGAN... SMEGAN.'

'Stop!'

Lucy would not let up verbally lampooning her sister.

'SMEGAN.'

'Stop, please.' Megan said, quietly.

'No!'

'Sto - '

Megan could tell she was only going to offer a one-word answer.

' - No!.. No!' Lucy's roaring tone

indicated rising irritability.

Megan pressed her lips together.

Lucy had spoken as though this settled the matter.

Megan sighed.

Lucy looked satisfied.

Megan was too stunned to bite back.

Lucy's green eyes flashed.

Megan shrank back.

'I - ' Lucy was talking, dully, but she noticed her sister's face.

Megan's eyes had became alerted instantly.

She felt unnerved, and she knew that something was extraordinarily awry within that room. ' - Lucy, where precisely is Abraxus?'

'Over there,' she divulged nonchalantly and flipped her head yonder, indicating to the bedside cabinet.

'No, he's not.' Megan replied darkly.

'Oh, yes *it* is,' she snapped archly, and went to turn around and as she did so, the leaf in her left pocket scratched slightly painfully against her leg. Lucy pulled it out, and Megan roared at the altogether shocking appearance, 'So, you have that in your pocket and carry it around, but you lose Abraxus?'

'So?' Lucy's blond framed face snapped, waving the doll's head in one hand and the dimly, multi-coloured leaf in the other.

'Why do you carry that round then?'

'Because I like the colours,' Megan folded her arms as Lucy spouted, 'I bet you do.'

Megan looked at her reproachfully.

'I don't. My Brim-Tree leaf is safe in my room. Anyway, never mind that, where is Abraxus?' Megan's tone matched Lucy's, but she reigned in her voice, as she didn't want her Mum or Dad to hear, but her voice strained at each word.

'I don't know where it is.'

'You don't know?'

'No, I cant remember. Don't you look at me like that! I've been busy.'

'Busy?' Megan almost mocked, from sheer confoundedness.

'Yes, some of us have *actual* friends,' Lucy said disparagingly back, spoiling for a fight, 'and I've been busy.'

'Do you have to be so nasty?'

'Do you have to be *so* boring?'

'What have you been doing then, if you're so busy?'

'Being pretty.'

'And?' Megan simplified and rehashed her original probing.

Lucy pouted.

'Playing, and stuff.'

Megan's eyes sharpened.

'This is your responsibility, do you even know how important it is?'

Megan was about to blow the roof off, when her eyes darted to the doll's head - as its hair was moving. Megan mentally said sorry to her about being ripped apart, and then her gaze rested upon the leaf.

Lucy stared at her sister's appearance with a troubled look; it would usually be a prologue to fear.

Lucy gasped, and Megan knew her face to be in genuine utter terror.

Megan felt a familiar surge of horror. As her brown hair spilled over her shoulder, Megan registered just in time to see that Lucy's doorway was black, with out-stretching tentacles that were dead centre, dartingly swirling.

Megan felt her stomach sink.

They snapped out and wrapped around Megan, and in one quick tug, they had snatched her into the yawning abyss.

Lucy didn't even realise that they

had also gotten hold of her: the black shards had sparked themselves around her mouth and as she was towed in, a frozen scream was carried with her, along with the doll's head and black shimmering leaf.

Chapter Four

Alone

Lucy awoke to find gushes of cutting wind rushing in streams against her chapped face.

She snapped her head round and got a crick in her neck. Looking about at her surroundings, snow-capped crags rose up high into the skyline like twenty-ton boats being birthed high on waves, bashed about as nothing mere than toys.

Gaping, Lucy gasped.

Through the clouds a great rainbow stabbed the air, but whereas a rainbow would be bright and have seven pleasing colours, the lines in this particular one were varying shades of grey, and hung in the sky like a dirty flannel.

The wind nipped at Lucy's red cheeks.

She scanned around, looking for her sister, of which there was no sign, and she coughed and then stood up. Crackles of whining thunder came overhead; her wavering eyes shot up and felt slightly more calm knowing they were far off, over distant Lands.

Flecks of white lined her hands and when she looked more closely, she gasped as she realised that it was snow!

Lucy's face looked anxious.

Snow covered the stone ground she was on and she looked right up, fighting back the biting wind as it flogged down: she gasped again as this time she saw that above her, lining the horizon, was a mountain peak, topped by snow, and other wind-blasted rocks littered the mountains which shot to craggy heights. She batted her eyelashes -

something she did often - to get rid of the snowflakes, and her mind reeled, *if that's a mountain, then that would mean…*thought Lucy, but she didn't get to form that thought, as when she looked down she nearly fell, for she was rested on a precarious mountain ledge, with its bottom yawning far below and its summit way up above.

Lucy had been shunted on to a magnificent mountainside!

So many resplendent grey blazing peaks. Too many blue-black ranges she couldn't count them all.

They would have been splendidly breathtaking, had Lucy not wanted to scream at each one.

Clearing her eyes she now realised that between the crags, other thunderous mountains dawned up, like teeth awaiting fresh prey.

'Where is this is?' Lucy said urgently with a hollow voice, drenched in uncertainty.

She heard swooping far from above; she ducked, half-expecting the murky clouds too part and to screamingly spy Abraxus swooshing down on her. She imagined feverishly that there were unstable incessant chattering and bane-filled eyes all about her.

Lucy suffered an acute sickening spell.

Feeling an ache, she hadn't realised that she must have been holding on too tightly to the objects in her palms, as when she opened them, red imprints of the leafs stalk and the doll's head were impressed into her skin.

Her movements caused rubble to fall off the pebbly ledge; she peered down to see how far it landed, but heard nor saw nothing.

She huddled into her purple jumper and propelled herself to and fro.

Small accelerated lines of tears

froze on her cheeks, and in her mind she screamed at Megan for bringing her here, then she shouted that somebody should be saving her right about now.

In between her racked sobs and the flights of the high, gusty wind, she was sure that the doll's head in her hand actually blinked!

But rubbing at her raw eyes, she told herself that the wind and tears had caused her to imagine it.

Lucy had planned on chomping her way through a fist-sized, lime-green lollipop, and yet, instead of doing just that, she was here... wherever *here* was....

Lucy's insides felt like wibbly-wobbly jelly.

She resolved herself that something just had to be done, and as heard her Mum say to her Dad once, "If you want something doing right, then do it yourself," and so with that it mind, she backed to the mountainside, squished herself against it, and telling herself not to look down over the ledge. Ever.

Lucy had a fully formed means-of-action: she would walk down the mountain.

Snow flecks swayed down, causing her to blow them off her nose; she scrunched the leaf up and put it into her pocket, along with the dolls head in the other. The ledge wound round the mountain like a train track, she then said aloud, to no-one in particular, 'I wonder if I goes all the way to the top?' then realised that was in the opposite direction, and that this was not the time for an adventure. She began to edge, ever so slowly, down the ledge's descent; she felt lightheaded and knew that if she stopped, she might not have the strength to get going again.

A vivid image of her toppling over

made Lucy knuckle her forehead desperately.

'Hu-uuam.' Lucy whispered.

She drew back suddenly.

The ledge in front was almost missing, as though a giant had bitten it off; she looked back and noticed she hadn't moved far: the wisps of clouds were still squidged, mingling around her head. Attempting not to spy down, she knew that the only thing to be done was to jump for it!

Sports was her thing at school, but this quite different. She backtracked slightly just as much as she dared to, then realised that if she ran, thus bearing her weight down, would the ledge give way?

So, instead, she used the techniques taught in her Dance and Ballet Class: she was an expert at pirouetting and spinning, so she gingerly circumnavigated her way over to the ledges mouthed edge, and executed a leap over where blasts of wind shouted through the missing join.

I can't believe I'm about to do this, Lucy thought...

And yet... and yet... she was...

She hitched up her pyjama bottoms.

Lucy took a running leap.

'Ah!'

She sprang up, attempting a cat-like motion. As she vaulted over the hole, she glanced down slightly and started to lose her hold on her motive, and in one *'HUMPH,'* which knocked the wind out of her lungs, she scrambled on to the other side of the broken ledge.

Her legs dangled below, the wind raced up her trousers and gravel fell between her finger-holds.

The twisting mountain offered no footholds and so inch by deathly inch, she clawed her way to the rim of the ledge, using her top weight to lean over.

In one lug she scrambled her knees over the edge and heard a rip, *great*, she thought, *these are my favourite jeans, and, oh, I don't do crawling* - but there she was, literally crawling for her life.

Chapter Five

She'll Be Coming Down The Mountain

Lucy squeamishly stuck a foot out.

She tried with all her might to procure a steady hold; and telling herself quite sternly not look over the teetering edge.

Panting and swallowing huge lung-fills of air, her mind raced at what almost just happened.

Her sprawled right hand found its way on to the mountain and she waited until her vision was more level, feeling the rustling of the leaf and the bulge of the head in her pockets, she stood tall, wishing that her legs not to give way. The weeping wind coming through the edge's gap frothed her hair up and so she slowly inched away, her back, once again, to the wall of the mountain. In her slow circumvented movements, she glanced straight ahead, attempting to see anything far below, but the clouds and the wind made it so all that was visible were the unsteady hands in front of her.

Crazy thoughts plagued her and intruded: *why did this have to happen to me?*

Desolately, Lucy raised her eyes. *I can't believe Megan dumped me here*, she thought furiously, not grasping, one little bit, that it were she who was to take all the slices of the blame cake.

At some points she shouted out her sister's name, but her crackly voice was lost into the gale. Creaks, whimpers and windy bellows made Lucy move quicker than ever: she couldn't tell which direction they came, but she sure didn't like the sound of them.

She found she didn't feel as lightheaded and the air seemed to be more breathable, and as the ledge snaked down the mountainsides, thunder rumbled far above, where once she had been thrown.

Like a battering-ram the wind flew at her.

'This just *won't* do,' Lucy ordered, to no-one but herself.

Hurriedly the air tore down.

The shock still stunned her and Lucy felt some pain, and a more than a tincture of discomfort.

Lucy walked on, disembarking lower.

The rock-face was helping Lucy to propping herself up.

The wind would not let up, and Lucy felt feeble in the very face of such harsh currents.

Lucy attempted to maintain a

graceful gait.

But this failed.

She darted a look at the rock; all the while making sure she didn't look down.

The wind was streaming in harmonizing rhapsodizes. There seemed to be a slight scream as it contuinally flew by Lucy.

She just narrowly avoided plummenting over, by aiming a hand along the lip-like formation of the rock-face.

Lucy's own was squashed up against it.

She felt bone-tired and as her sleepy eyes tried to close, she saw slightly darkened lines in parallel swirling shadows.

Lucy shook her head.

Her nose touched the rock.

Lucy looked diagonally along the grainy-feeling granite.

She had stopped, and taking a

dissecting moment, she desisted with pausing her progress.

'Curpmf.' Lucy said, sighing.

Lucy hesitated.

Her expression did not change by a shade.

Lucy tried to acclimate herself.

She consulted the rock; taking in the greys of the stone.

Lucy sailed on.

She knew it was imperative and categorically only her who could get herself down the mountain.

Now, right at this point, Lucy was taking a reflection.

She asserted this was her sister's fault.

Lucy felt along the platoon of rock; as he hand went out, her foot copied its same movement.

Oh! This is a complete... Lucy's thoughts broke off into her shouting, 'How *dare* Megan put me here!'

She kept a secure footing, and

didn't want to loiter any more than she had too.

With compulsion and feverish eyes Lucy edged on.

This was such an insufferable calamity.

Lucy was doing her utmost to cling on.

Scarcely could she have ever imagined she'd ever be on such a mountain.

Lucy took advantage of the pigeon-hole in the rock.

Her fingers held the bulbous crystal stone that was sticking out of the rocky-surface.

The landing of the ledge came quicker than she had imagined it too, thinking this would go on forever.

When eventually stable, firm ground was in sight, her footing tripped on a small rock, there she found her balance wavered and she splayed and bounced willy-nilly down the last bevel slope, and her legs and arms flailed out akimbo, coming to a stop in a mess on hard gravel.

Landing like an upended tortoise, she lifted her head up and pushing away stray strands of hair, which had come loose from her ponytail. She said to herself what she really wanted was a hot, steaming pudding.

Instead, all that was offered were vast boulders, rocks and countless snow heaped mountains which looked like they were peaked far in the sky, and topped with whipped cream.

Lucy, out of the corner of her blinking eye, saw a line of white on the ground near her foot; she went to scream, thinking some vile worm was working its way up her leg, then clicking her teeth in a tutting way, she squatted down, and re-tied the loose lace on her dirty-looking purple trainer. Standing straight, she rocked her left foot back and forth, blew her cheeks out resignedly, and tapped a couple of fingers on her chin.

Lucy fanned her face operatically with her hands.

In her fallings, she saw that her pockets must have been spewed open, as resting and being stirred by the wind, lay the leaf and next to it was the doll's head, looking blank, almost accusingly.

She totteled over to them, grabbing the head and placing it back into the depths of her jeans pocket, making sure it was firm, and she then bowed down again and handled The Brim-Tree's leaf: a memory came quickly of the last time when she was here... with Megan.

Lucy hiccuped slightly and scratched her nose.

Her eyes burned and she swallowed; holding the stalk of the leaf, she carefully held it as the top half uncurled itself, whilst the lower remained crumpled up.

Ignoring the pain of her scrapped knees and gravel-impressed hands, she hung her head.

She hadn't a clue where she was; none of the creatures of The Enchanted Kingdom had mentioned a place such as this: so barren and desolate, where every hope was driven mad by the searing wind and ominous mountains.

A particularly painful cramp tore through Lucy's stomach, and her knees started to buckle, so she limped over to rest against a rough-hewn boulder.

Gaining her breath, her face, suddenly, became alighted by the top half of the leaf!

Bubbling sparks roamed around; it then burned in brilliance and chased away all threatening lengthening shadows, casting arcs of light in front of her.

What is this? Is... it... me? Lucy wondered.

Lucy was piloting the leaf this way and that.

She wheeled forwards, marveling at how the light banished the dark, driving them into all corners and crannies: or, whatever manner of homes that dark patches and shadows live grisly in.

The dollops of rubble had obligingly fallen in such a way that a clear path was laid out for Lucy's escape, and as she waded in different directions, the light from the leaf remained still and would not budge: the flaring only occurred when she moved in a precise progress.

As she moved both her hands to the leaf, it burned its brightest, and the thought snapped in her mind: *it's finding its home.*

Like a homing device, it was navigating the safe way for her; only being devoid of colour in Lucy's hand.

And when, eventually, she the crossed the stretching path that led to its brethren of leaves, Lucy hoped hers could find them all... and hopefully The Brim-Tree.

Chapter Six

Despair

As the leaf gained in radiance, its luminescence seemed to pull her, until Lucy found herself almost running over rocks and debris, and as dust sprayed up, she narrowly missed boulders and the outskirts of mountains.

She glanced down, expecting too see smoke rising from her purple and dirt-stained, casual trainers, and in jerky hand-movements, she pulled back like pulling tight on reins, as she needed to rest; the leaf almost impelled out of her grip - but she managed to hold on to it just in time.

Lucy stood still. Hearing the beat of her heart in her ears.

The wind had picked up, as though it was rising in a notch that would explode.

The stones and rock splinters crunched as she plodded slowly.

She knew from what Megan had said that Abraxus had gotten free, *but how, and where is he now?*

Every sound nibbled in shards at her imagination, she expected to see him, or something: but nothing came, just the steady rumbles of thunder and the flashes from the forks of lightning.

If only I could see something I know, or find someone, thought Lucy: she almost willed the rocks to talk to her, just so she could find out where she was, but, then what?

No, the best course of action was to trust in her and the leaf, it knew where it was going, *but what if the dark side of the leaf is maneuvering the good half?*

Her mind asked questions, spinning such gruesome scenarios, that in the end she told herself to promptly shut up.

As the horizon was black, she was almost consumed with all that happened to her: just some time ago she was arguing with her sister, a favourite pastime, and then an uncharacteristic wave of sorrow came upon her and she nearly cried out with its force... how can all this righted to she could get back home...

She didn't like the answer, for there wasn't one.

Lucy's feet were hurting.

She firmly pulled her jumper down for good measure, and cursed inwardly with clicking her tongue for not having a kerchief: she was forced to wipe her runny nose on the edge of her top, and then put one foot in front of the other. She gulped, held the leaf once more and followed its pull: from her bleakness she wanted to fall to the ground, but she didn't, something within her abated such action.

Lucy loped and with the leaf arching out in front of her, she suddenly heard the noise of choppy waves.

The sound she knew grew in immensity, the rolling matching her aching feet. From the streaks of light, beaming out like jumbo headlamps, she knew to slow her chase: it was as though The Brim-Tree's leaf was controlling her feet!

A sickening smell then invaded her; she went to gag and as she waved the leaf to her mouth, this caused the scene below to come into a full heart wrenching openness.

A giant river caused the sound; its torrent had mouthed itself between two-faced cliffs, where she now stood, atop a white edge. She slowly peeled her hands down and dared to actually look: she trembled as the true horror of the river presented itself. She scanned right to left, seeming to see where the river started, or ended, but of that there was no sign: it flowed in windy-wounding then carried on, with no shore, *out to Ocean Land?* she mused.

The river was not as smooth as glass like the good waters of Ocean Land had been left in!

A film of black gobs like tar and oil spread its evilness over the surface of the river, causing black, gorged belches to spew as the river dossed over rocks that were projected out from beneath the rolling waves. The rocks were being hit with such force she was surprised some of them didn't blast and bust away, to be sunk far below the billowy waters. The points of the rocks were slicked in all the slime, and as Lucy blinked in the full spectacle, cries slowly drifted up with the rivers gush. The noises of the storm disrupted a bit. She knew them to be screams, coming from women, men and children: all sounded anguish in their own voices, until they rose in one big clang of a torturous howl.

The light rove up into the murky sky as she shut her hands to her ears, tears welled and in one leap she ran away, away from the cliff's edge, the now evil lucking river, and screams of those that could not be saved.

*

Lucy trekked on.

Even though she knew time worked so differently in The Enchanted Kingdom, she had with no notion if time ticked by slowly, nor any clue if it tocked on startlingly fast.

As the light from the steering leaf fanned onwards, she wound through a deep gully, and as she glanced down to the long depressions and the bowled effect, she just knew that she would have to entre this, only to rise on the other side.

Dead grass smoothed down as she stepped upon it.

Lucy didn't stray.

Down she went, the waves of the wind rushing to meet her: the blocks of air kissed witchingly at her cheeks, sniped at her clothes, but not once did she lose the leaf.

As she found herself in the deep low of the valley, she threw a quick glance over her shoulders; the white-tipped, cloud-skewing mountains still bulked far above the other side of the vale, in such an open expanse, she felt confined and unbearably claustrophobic.

Picking her way skittishly through the dark and the dead strands of grass in the dell, the light ahead banished the creeping shadows, and in a rare moment when the clouds must have parted, shafts of grey light streaked down.

Lucy clucked her tongue.

She climbed the rise, this time the wind rushing up behind her, her tied hair streaked like a Venetian fan opening itself and as she rounded the lip, at the pinnacle of the valley's rise, she gasped, for as the light from the leaf shone out, it lit up a sight she never thought she would ever see.

She knew that more must be beyond the lights sighting, and so now on high ground she edged further, and more did came into an upsetting view; all around laid a forest of dead trees: all black and smoldering that were not Fairy dust-silked, like the big ones in Unicorn Land, which Lucy remembered escaping into, before, in a marathon run out of a cave's wall of fire.

The ashen smoke rose and mist danced into the air; she coughed it back and placed a foot upon the crisp soil, the wind rushed through the trees but yet they stood upright, elegant in their charcoaled bark crumbled death.

Lucy couldn't go any further: she had no idea how far this dense jungle of death slopped on for, but she knew it would all be like this.

She turned away, the light arcing back as she did so: the torch left the trees in their wakeful right.

Chapter Seven

Answers

Borne in the air came a faint familiar sound, rising in tone until a clopping against stone rang in her ears.

She scurried almost head-over-heels with all her pluckiness and as she frantically looked about, the light followed her movements, so soon, all she saw, was the black of the shadowed surroundings, and the unbalancing light from the leaf.

The sound grew. Lucy backed away, this time wishing for a boulder or rock just to hide behind. On the open field, she told herself to keep the leaf still, so that she could focus, and as it trembled, right in front of her, out of the very air, stepped a woman side-sat on a horse!

Lucy gasped.

The woman held such beauty it was glorious, and Lucy took in all her movements as she glided along the ground.

She was so elegant and towered in height. Her creamy milk skin glowed, whilst her piercing, vibrant yet remote purple eyes regarded Lucy with their own inner light.

Her avalanching hair was the colour of rich Cornish clotted cream, with long silver strands woven into it: it fell in waves that downpoured over her shoulders, then abundantly past her back.

Lucy noted her dirt-speckled clothes, and wished for a dress like the long, floaty gown made up of panels, and how each panel represented a colour of the rainbow: it swept breezily far on to the ground and trailed in tails behind her.

Lucy tore herself away from the

lady and lowered the leaf, just slightly, as what she had first thought to be a horse, was in fact a Unicorn, but not like Prince Tumble, or the one she had ridden upon, for this one was taller and his complete appearance made him look like a mighty warhorse.

'Charger... no,' the robed woman said, along to the Unicorn.

Charger's ears whickered. Lucy couldn't quite believe how he was all black: his mane, tail, eyes, hooves, body, and the long, twisting horn on his forehead were all black.

The Unicorn moved its noble-looking head. Its long twisty mane trailed to the floor, and the black Unicorn spoke in a hushed whisper.

The lady placed a hand upon Charger's neck and announced. 'I am one of the two Guardians. I am known as, Aradene.'

'What... Guardian?'

'Come, it is not safe to speak here. We shall talk more later.'

'Where's Megan, why did she do this to me?' Lucy bawled, at once.

'I do not know.'

'You... don't know?' her lower lip trembled slightly.

'No, I sensed both of you entering here, but then one light puffed out. You shouldn't look so startled! It may have been merely when Abraxus captured Megan, so that is why I can't sense her no more.

'I knew you to be in grave danger and so came as fast as I was able too.'

'Do you think she's... has he...?' the last part of the question didn't need to be voiced.

'I do hope not, Lucy. It takes a being of great darkness and evil to commit such a horrific act, either on one of human or one deemed of Magic. I hope not.'

'But,' she said in lost despair,

'where's Princess Blossom, Prince Tumble... *anyone?*'

Aradene did not dodge the question. 'Abraxus' power has reached such depths and already he has trapped the Lands of Ocean, Unicorn, Dragon and Fairy. These are the ones that I know of, but there might be more. Soon, all will feel the pull of his claws.'

'Trapped, how?'

The Guardian stood, looked down and knew some answers would have to be provided; whilst others could be fended off and wait.

'Stilled, trapped in time. It is like they are all frozen. This is what I think has befallen your sister,' but Aradene didn't manage to finish whatever she had intended to say, for she looked round in all directions, glanced to the black Unicorn, then suggested, 'We must really press on. We can talk more soon, come.'

Charger trotted round. *He's not*

very happy, Lucy thought.

Aradene, in one movement, glided up on to him!

Lucy peered after her, a hand came down with white nails and as Lucy welcomed the help up to mount Charger, she noticed that Aradene's palm was cold, as though made of ice.

Charger then swished his head back side to side. His mane floating up, then settling down, and so with Lucy clinging on to Aradene, feeling the leaf and doll head in her pockets, she smelt deeply expecting to smell the familiar aroma of his other Unicorns, but none came, she inwardly gasped: Charger didn't smell of vanilla!

And as she craned her head out, she was incredibly disappointed to see that his fluting, twisting horn didn't sparkle of Fairy dust.

She placed a hand on to his velvet body, which felt like the cushions her mum would always fluff and plump up at home.

Then he tore off at lightning speed across the ground.

Lucy held on tight.

His tail lined out like a banner, and as Aradene's hair fanned out above Lucy, Charger streamed past trees that seemed to skim by, bushes and other once wondrous sights that become a blur, and Lucy was even sure that she had just seen a lion, stealthily lopping in wait!

Chapter Eight

Waterfall's Secrets

Megan had been dumped astradle.

All she knew was that *everything* was as black as ink. The nape of her neck was on something rather crusty-hard, and yet in a curious way, also damply wet.

Megan's head was rattling from side-to-side.

A queer gurgling noise hurried on somewhere closeby. The sounds were like torpedo hitting its mark-target.

Droplets of water caressed Megan's clammy face.

She looked dazed.

Megan slowly opened her eyes.

She awoke on a floor. She was on the far side of miniature cave, which smelt musty, in front of which was a surging, incredible waterfall!

Megan felt badly frightened.

Lucy? she thought.

Megan felt grave.

The water sounded like cannonball fire blasting off.

Megan centred herself to her Magic and held on; the better to be prepared.

Megan tried to upraise herself, though the most curious thing was, was that she was unable to budge.

Megan couldn't move her body!

She lay there, trapped in her mind. Megan couldn't move a muscle. She would have yelled, shouted screams, anything, but she couldn't even make a sound. Not even a squeal.

Megan felt panic-stricken.

Megan's mind raced. *What's happening? Where am I? What is that racket?*

Megan looked horrified.

A tidal-wave of thoughts assaulted

Megan as she lay immobile on the ground, feeling bedraggled.

Megan's eyes pricked with tears.

She was shaking and shivering, and shivering and shaking.

Megan felt as if a stick of dynamite had detonated in her head.

'Lucy! LUCY!' she rasped out, in a throaty voice.

Megan felt moisture and droplets splash on to her troubled face.

This really was unbearable for Megan.

She scouted round.

Megan's eyes strained to penetrate the deep gloom.

Megan looked wildly about.

The uncharted abyss was like a bleak shack with shabby net curtains.

'Oh bother.' Megan said, dismally.

Megan saw that amid the leafy foliage, a brigade of bushes had pink parading hyacinths dotted on the vines. Nearer too her, a gooey substance was on the ground, that looked all suspiciously like frogs-spawn.

A slight spasm tore through her.

Megan was not enjoying this interlude.

This was definitely tricky. And not just mildly so.

She tried to move herself round in a roll.

Megan sussed out that horrifically, again, she still couldn't move below her neck!

Megan felt as cold as ice.

'Piffle,' she mumbled.

Megan's spirits were plummeting.

Megan had to use every single ounce of her will to move. 'Mmmm. Mmm. Eeeeem,' she gurgled, and tried valiantly to shift herself. She constricted her neck, trying to force her head to swivel, then attempted to swing her arms up, in one shock jolt.

She saw over the way that dewspittled, ordinary rocks offered her safe substance to lean on.

This would require more of her to move.

Megan dug deep into the centre of herself.

Megan's eyes widened.

'Is anyone... *there?'* she called.

There was no response.

Megan gasped slightly from the silence.

Only the surges of water replied.

'Hhmm.' Megan said, pensively.

Megan's heart pounded drummingly.

Megan panned around.

She used all her will to break the air-shroud over her.

Megan galumphed about. A little duck-footed and unsteadily on her feet at first, like a young deer all arms-and-legs going in different directions. She could not co-ordinate herself. After a moment (or two), Megan righted herself.

Megan started to steady herself upon the rock but as she lent, she went backward, and slipped in a wobbly motion.

She tootled down on her backside.

'Ish.' Megan felt nauseated.

Megan landed like a trolley on its side.

She gazed up to the black cosmos stratosphere of the cave.

Megan felt frustrated.

'Huh... huh... huh... huh.' Megan was breathing hard.

Megan trawled over to her other side.

She centred herself. Feeling the familiar and welcoming Magic, she then in her heart and mind snatched at the warm fuzziness of it.

Megan eyeballed boringly into the choppy gushes of the waterfall.

Like a lighted missile, she shot up.

Megan stared numbly at the

gushing frothiness of her watery imprisonment.

The sheets of water carried on in an ever-flowing torrent.

Megan was thinking, all the time thinking. *What is going on? How did I get here? Where is here? Why am I here?*

Megan didn't feel she could bear any more.

The heart-stopping moment caused Megan too want to cry.

She looked around properly, and knew she had been landed at the deep bottom of a cave's pit, which had an open side wall that the waterfall washed down in vertical gushes.

Megan was situated just tucked back from the raging torrent.

Megan was sealed behind a waterfall.

She really was *trapped!*

Megan felt frazzled.

She scanned around again.

Megan felt hemmed-in.

Fear crept into Megan's eyes.

Feeling as if she'd already been cooped-up for donkey's years, she looked about her sphere of surroundings.

Tears welled in Megan's eyes.

Megan's peripheral vision critiqued the foliage comprised of bouquets of greenery, all congregated with plenty of pink flowers that clung to vines.

Megan's back ached.

Her left arm stung slightly from lying on it for so long, as if open pin badges had been stuck into her.

'Harraumph.' Megan said.

Startingly nothing made sense.

Megan calculated that the top of the waterfall, from where she could see, was that of a neck-height of a giraffe.

Like silver mercury the water gushed ever on.

Megan's non-idyllic scene was awful.

She looked left-to-right, navigating, or attempting to, her way round.

An intense feeling overcame Megan.

Is there a creature in here with me? thought Megan, alarmingly.

Megan's moonlit skin was looking like marble.

Her hue complimented some parts of the cave where the shadows were not touching the rounded walls; white swirls gleamed like spilt milk.

Megan put her hand to her head from how extraordinary this all was.

Hordes of thoughts continued to flit out of sight, but Megan was still trying her best to not shine her mind's torch-beam upon them.

Breathing hard, she took a moment's indecision.

Megan wanted to fly away like a dove.

Just then, a faint rustle slithered off, obscured.

Megan stood motionless.

Chapter Nine

The Prowling Panther

Megan was stood frozen to the spot.

Her eyes widened at the pooling water left by whatever had moved on.

Megan used every ounce of her strength not to scream.

Silver globs of the liquid mercury shimmered on the cavern's ground.

Megan half-expected the shrubs to sprout into something different.

Megan shrugged.

'Hmm.' she mumbled, keeping a fixed eye - just in case whatever it was decided to pay another unwelcoming visit.

Instinctively, Megan took a step back.

She postponed her walk-about for a

few seconds. She panted slightly.

Megan bit her lip.

She tentatively stepped forward.

Megan's heart felt like it was about to explode.

As Megan shambled forward heroically, she brushed by cucumber-green foliage.

Megan felt panic mushrooming in her.

Her lukewarm resolve was there, but now smaller; but still there, nonetheless.

Megan attempted to still not focus on the cavernous blackness like an aircraft hanger.

The monumental feeling of panic carried on sweeping through her.

Megan's lack of progress did much to dampen her spirits.

With a weary, tired movement, Megan moved onward.

Suddenly, Megan felt her arm was weighty from laying on it.

She froze again.

Megan felt rising panic.

At that exact moment, Megan's moral energy was soggy at best.

Megan let out her breath.

For about six minutes Megan stood dithering, that then ripened into a seventh minute.

Megan was simply stumped.

She sighed deeply.

Megan picked up momentum.

She resumed her walk.

All the while, Megan felt like icicles were sprouted on her skin.

A bolt-like noise of a *swioosh* in the watery current made Megan stop short.

Megan wanted to do an abrupt about-face.

Invariably, Megan being Megan, she knew that this would only prolong matters.

Megan sighed again. And bit her tongue lightly against her teeth.

She persisted on.

Megan nodded.

She felt renewed in an inflated way; if only to somehow get out of there.

Out of the corner of her eyes, Megan suddenly saw a specter had came back!

Megan's panic felt like a boiling pan on the stove.

She considered for a brief moment where to go.

Megan felt frightened and stunned.

She was on the brink of screaking in a loud scream.

Megan wanted to *shoo* the thing away.

Her lip quavered.

Megan greatly felt in trouble, but only she could get herself out such a terrible setting.

The pang of panic became more thickly clumpy.

Megan felt a sinking feeling like a liner out on the ocean in trouble.

Now, her '*Arrrrr*' voice rang with a note of horror. She turned her face. Megan screamed from spying the horrendously frightful black-wraith looked like a panther, patrolling and inching prowlingly toward her!

Megan heard her high-sounding heartbeat in her ears.

She gasped.

The yellow shining, reflective eyes inched in closer.

Megan threw her hands up.

As she was moving about, like playing hopscotch, Megan collapsed into the gushing torrents of crystal-blue and pink-tinged water, which was like an unstoppable juggernaut.

Megan cried out in a strained voice.

The thing stood looking at the bizarre sight, and waited.

'Ugh... Ooaugh-oua... ugh-ugh... ugh.' Megan was coughing up a tempest.

Megan righted herself; air-drying

her hands and flapping at her clothes.

Megan looked around with caution.

Of the thing, only her own company was there.

Megan longed for more than ever to get out from behind the waterfall.

Megan attempted to think good thoughts. *Just... can't... do it...* she thought maddeningly.

A chill crept down Megan's neck.

She took her time with schlepping over to where the bushes and boscage where she'd pegged to earlier.

Megan sliced into the shrubbery and chopped and picked apart the bushes.

Megan's fingers dripped with globlets of water.

In her misery, a mixture of fear and apprehension gripped and overcame Megan.

'Argumph.'

Megan cried out like a twanged chord on a violin.

She tried to tether herself to cope with the fear.

A convoy of miserable thoughts tormented her again.

Megan attempted with all her might to squash the horribly horrid thoughts of what might be in the bushes, lurking in the copse.

Where she walked to, a large granite colour stood largely in her way; she couldn't make out what was behind the slab. She felt about the bedrock, feeling for the end of the stone and to tell if this could be moved, as there might just be a hole behind it she could tiptoe into it, which, she hoped, may hide a way out.

Megan tried to apply all her weight against the juggernaut-feeling stone. 'It... just... won't... budge,' she mumbled to herself.

Megan retried.

Oh cricket, Megan thought

maddeningly.

As she pushed with all she had, unbeknownst to Megan, as she used her deep Magic, her porcine face became transfigured with traces of pink lines.

Megan looked curiously Elfin.

She was rooted into herself.

'Darn it.'

Megan paused.

Megan leveled a personal attack at herself: *can I do this?* 'Can I?' she said softly.

Megan's heartbeat thumped eleven-to-the-dozen.

One-by-one, harshly sodden thoughts carried on in her. *Can I really do this? Must I?*

Megan felt totally dispirited.

She sensed a danger-mark that if she gave up, even for a moment, she might not ever leave this waterfall.

Megan felt nearly washed-out.

She blocked out the phosphorescent

gloom from above - concealing goodness knows what.

Megan pressed on.

The atmosphere felt close.

Megan felt a pang in her heart of fear mixed with homesickness, for her bedroom.

Megan was feeling a growing hastiness to get out.

Having seen Ocean Land, from her last visit to The Enchanted Kingdom, Megan didn't quite know if she barreled into this waterfall, for escape, if it would drop into a sheer deluge port of water into the sea!

Megan did not want to scupper her chances.

The best bet was to dive into the bushes and see where they took her.

This did not particularly bolster Megan.

I-don't-really-want-to-go-in-there, she thought, in a rush.

Megan stopped short.

Megan began to feel very scared.

She walked on, still a bit splay-footed.

Megan dawdled about.

The thoughts from earlier still haunted Megan.

Can I do this?

Megan grunted.

I have to go in there...

Megan's eyes dissected the leaves.

Can I do it?

Megan kept an arm's-length from the bushes.

She looked about, left-to-right.

Megan nodded to herself.

I-I hav-ve to, she thought.

Megan ever-so-slightly inserted her fingers into the foliage.

She tentatively felt the under-carriage of the leaves.

Megan bit her lip.

'Hmm. They do *seem* normal,' she muttered categorically.

Megan nodded.

What ought I do? Megan posed, to herself.

Megan's resolve was disintegrating.

She felt absolutely scared out of her life.

I have *to go in there*, Megan thought.

Megan readied herself.

I just have to.

Megan felt bolstered and knew in a radiated way that she could do this.

Ten... nine... eight...

Megan careered into the leafy palms.

Seven... six...

Megan's walk went into a different gear.

Five...

Megan steeled herself.

Four...

Her feet quickened. She discerned vines snap past, and winding green bush-bark were fused in one another.

Megan's heart did not falter.

Her scope saw all the infinitesimal details of the leaves.

Three...

Megan bulldozed on to her expedition.

She'd never had such a badder day in her life. But, she would go on...

Megan felt full of flickering hope.

Two...

Megan's toes curled inside her pink canvas trainers.

One.

Megan felt ready, and she went through more of the bushy hinterland.

As she did so, Megan braced herself.

Chapter Ten

Sinister Trees

The tromping thunk of Charger's hooves and the blurs melded into one another. Dark lines eroded her vision and knowing that is was useless, to try and see what they were going past, she instead simply looked ahead, bowed her head and scrunched her eyes closed.

She realised that he was slowing down, until a trot rang on the slabs of broken stone, lining a path she hadn't seen before.

As Charger stopped, he swished his tail.

Aradene glided down like water.

Lucy swung her leg over and toppled in a heap: she would have damaged herself, if Aradene hadn't caught her ungainly fall.

Lucy snowballed down deeply.

Can't believe I just did that, she thought.

Righting herself, Lucy's face blotched cherry.

Charger stood majestically and trotted ahead slightly. 'I think it would be best if I were too go first... I do not know what awaits,' Aradene said to the black Unicorn and turning, she added, 'you, should wait here... I do not know if it safe for you.'

Lucy nodded, and actually took in the surroundings to where Charger had brought them.

Weeping willow trees stirred from being snipped at by flurries of the clamouring wind; the willows spread for lengths that Lucy could not quite see the end, or the beginning.

A light bulb came on in her head then, and she knew where she was: this where she had been before, with

Megan and Prince Tumble!

But, something looked different; the trees looked like flimsy fingers, waving to the crackling lightning as it stroked the sky.

They're here for The Brim-Tree, Lucy answered in her mind, he must be OK, because the leaf worked in her pocket, *he must, mustn't he?*

Charger didn't say, or do anything. He stood still with his mane and tail swirling, which matched her blond hair as it rose and fell.

She placed one gallant step forward and ignoring the cautionary tone in what Aradene had told her, Lucy traipsed onwards, past Charger, and followed the direction into the willows that Aradene had taken.

She had expected Charger to block her path, stamp a hoof, anything, but he didn't: he simply looked straight ahead, his black ears twitching before the growl of thunder was heard.

The willows leaves lifted. A grey drenching hue lay over everything.

Twigs snapped under her heels but sill she pressed on, turning back every so often to see if Charger had followed her. He hadn't.

At last she lost sight of him through the maze of trees, she couldn't remember the line the Prince Tumble had took, *and would The Brim-Tree even be there?* she thought, as she recalled the sight of the air shimmering and as it settled, there was the dying Brim-Tree, glorifying about Megan.

The leaf!

The voice in her head resounded; obeying she extracted it and as the topmost half of the leaf, along with the stalk remained black, the top alighted, and elbowed her into a purposeful direction: arcs bounced and penetrated the trees.

Because I'm holding the black

stalk, is it going into me? and then knocking the thought away she drove on, rushing under fluting willow branches as she went.

The faint smell of smoke still wafted on her clothes, making Lucy hope that the fate that befell the other scalded trees didn't happen to these inner ones.

Taking a deep breath she heard a faint howl and rustling not far off, and trudging ahead, she suddenly burst into the clearing, where she once been before.

The outlined figure turned and nearly screamed, 'Don't look!'

But, Lucy being Lucy, did indeed look and as Aradene glided over to the shaking child, The Brim-Tree remains presented itself: for it had been cleaved in two.

Lucy gaped.

Chapter Eleven

The Penny Drops

In a swirl of cloth, Aradene attempted to cradle Lucy away from such a sight; instead, Lucy gaped and slowly poured it in.

As the clearing was the same; in the middle was The Brim-Tree: half of it still soared into the sky but pitifully it was rotted, and the other half that looked like it had been snapped like a twig, laid on the ground on top of the tree's knotting roots.

In the wind, the sliced half of the tree on the ground shuddered and rocked; its own immense size preventing it from being blown away like a flower. Both halves were putrefied; Lucy was in such shock that she was led over to the side of the clearing, where a cluster of boulders offered her to sit.

Charger, she absentmindedly realised, was now stood within the clearing. Aradene sat opposite and simply looked to Lucy, and with the dead Brim-Tree loomed up, she awaited her to speak first.

Lucy sniveled.

She glanced to the black presence. Charger stared straight ahead reverentially at The Brim-Tree. It seemed to Lucy that he was almost willing the warm, wizened voice to speak: but none such wise-sounding voice came.

Lucy pulled her knees up and as the leaf twisted in her hands, she stowed it securely in her pocket, whilst Aradene crossed her left leg and folded her hands together.

The weather matched her hopelessness mood. 'What… what happened?'

A sigh from Aradene blended with the wind until it was lost, and then she began answers she knew must come, but some would only be said, until a time when Lucy was ready to hear them. 'Abraxus, has completely immersed himself in old Magic, which he has warped to his will. He is indeed very evil now.

'At first, I think we all assumed he only desired to destruct our Kingdom, but now, I fear, his intentions are more grievous that we had thought. I think his ultimate desire is too rule over all this, and us as his enslaved minions.'

'But where's The Brim-Tree... can't it help?'

'The Brim-Tree will only interfere if help, from no other source, cannot be found.'

'Is it really gone?'

Aradene turned her head slightly, causing her hair to spill down her face, then slowly answered, 'What will be, will be.'

A well of doomed emotions was coming to the surface, Lucy, not wanting to face them, pushed them down into a small ball and tucked them far away. And tactlessly, for some reason, she felt compelled to remark, 'You're very beautiful.'

'If, child, you reach your full bloom of adulthood, you will also dazzle others. Although, I think you already suspect that.'

'Oh, thank you,' purred Lucy babyishly, with affected modesty. Knowing that one day, just like Millicent had, she would be on the cover of *Vogue Bambini*, then be upgraded to gracing the cover of *Vogue Italia*, which would out-trump Millie and be something to sneer at her over.

Then feeling thoroughly shocked, as though she had just been slapped round the face with a wet trout fish, Lucy pointed a finger at Aradene. 'Y-you...' she stammered. 'You're my Sister's supply teacher!'

The serene-looking lady nodded her head to one side. 'Well observed, Dragon Keeper. I could see that you recognised me; it is true that I simplified my appearance. Mrs. Hepsibah Penny was how The Fairy Key knew me as, which I felt sounded particularly bookish.'

'But, why, I don't understand,' pressed Lucy, as a lamenting wind borne down on her questions.

'Just before Megan came upon Princess Blossom in her trapped form, The Brim-Tree sent me into your world.'

'Why?' repeated Lucy, with a puzzled air.

'I was only Megan's counterfeited teacher for nine days, and was to find and safeguard the statute of Princess

Blossom. The Brim-Tree had learned of her location, as he sensed a child coming. Though he did not know of the identity, just that it was a child, who would then unlock her trappings.

'Of Nugget, we did not know of his whereabouts, although he wisely used the leaf, as I'm sure you recall. If any developments had occurred, I was too report straight back to The Brim-Tree.'

'But then why didn't you just take Princess Blossom back here, if you finally knew where she was?' Lucy was tracing a finger down the grainy-feeling boulder.

'Even if I had brought The Fairy Key back, we did not know if Nugget would still be lost in your wilderness.

'Also, the Princess of Fairies would not have transformed back to her true self. Presenting Princess Blossom in her solid, statue form, would have only caused further alarm and distress to her loved ones. Thus,' she went on, 'I was too oversee her; indeed, I had only managed to track her locale as your world is so different, but when I saw The Fairy Key, who - one day, I hope, will come to understand the full title and power of what she is, and what sacrifices may come - actually spot Princess Blossom, I came back to The Kingdom, but the exact moment that I entered, I was captured.'

Toying with an idea, Lucy asked. 'Who's more powerful: me, or Megan?'

'Hmm, whilst you are not both equal,' Aradene batted away the question with her hand, then coughed delicately. 'You each have a dual purpose that your title bequeaths.

'You, being The Dragon Keeper, are powerful enough to keep Abraxus trapped in a locked stasis, or rather were. Whilst The Fairy Key is the one that saved Princess Blossom and started these chain of events,' Aradene explained. 'She is the one who knew her courage and Magic, faced a Dragon and looked out for your safety. Twas Megan who fought the infestation of Abraxus' evil, and it was she whom showed her true mettle. She alone harnessed both herself, and Magic.

'Megan is our champion; her life is a great and true example of the works of life.

'In short, you both have a different magical potency, but neither of you has fully developed these.'

'Oh,' prattled Lucy, not really liking the answer, then changed the subject. 'What other Lands are there? Will I see them? Could Megan be in one of them?'

'Again, I do not know where The Fairy Key currently is.

'Now, let's see child: you know of Fairy Land?'

Lucy nodded.

'But have not been there?

Again, Lucy nodded.

'You briefly saw Ocean Land and Gump Land, although, you have not actually been to either?'

Lucy shook her head.

'You know of Dragon Land, but again, have not been there.

Once more, Lucy shook her head, flinging her long ponytail back over her left shoulder.

'But, you have been to Unicorn Land and here once before, where The Brim-Tree resided.'

Lucy nodded animatedly. 'Yes, this clearing and willow trees.'

Aradene leisurely scratched her thumbnail. 'There are many, many other different Lands that make up this patchwork of a Kingdom. Each one is great in expanse of an Enchantmile, thus, it is impossible to know of all the inhabitants,' she desrcibed, her eyes glinting. 'Such large creatures live within these Lands, which it has to be big enough to house each race of creature, and each Land is territorial and an independent state, with Princess and Prince taking sovereign over the said inhabitants.'

Lucy blinked.

'Outside affairs take precedence,' Aradene continued, 'such as, before, when Abraxus went wicked and you both came here. All knew that something had changed forever, for when Abrauxs cast Princess Blossom into your world, it was the defining act.'

Finishing, Aradene placed her hands on top of one another, and looked quite unforgiving.

Chapter Twelve

The Guardian Goes

Lucy's mind's eye whacked back, and she recalled how her sister had pranced about showing off with that Fairy statue. 'And, Nugget,' she added quietly, then quizzed, 'but why didn't we see you last time?'

'As Abraxus drained The Brim-Tree he imprisoned us behind a foul waterfall, such as which we could not escape from, for we had also been commanded to stay.'

'But, why?'

'Well, The Brim-Tree did not seek to exile both of us. Rather we followed through with a preparation for two reasons: firstly, if The Brim-Tree had truly fallen to Abraxus, and Abraxus' plan came off, then The

Brim-Tree needed us too guard you and see you safe to your world. Also, secondly, with us being purposely in Abraxus' clutches, we could asses his planed route of attack, or any other plans.

'For ourselves, back up plans were created contingently,' Aradene went on, explaining what had happened, 'but, such course of actions were not required; we knew he had failed that time, as on our journey back to the clearing, we spotted Bront returning to his Land, who from above told us of the victory.'

Lucy asked something she realised had been pricking at her memory, since she had last been to The Enchanted Kingdom, 'How did Princess Blossom know about me and Megan?' she marshaled her thoughts, wanting to be as clear as cut-crystal. 'But Dragons and the Unicorns didn't? And yet The Brim-Tree knew what were? I mean, it doesn't make sense.'

Aradene was twirling strands of hair through her fingers; she stopped, blinked, and said, 'Child, such an upfront inquisitive nature, which should respectfully earn an honest answer.

'Princess Blossom, indeed all of Fairy Land, knows of your kind as they are connected to you and all like you. For when you all fall into sleep, the Fairies are the ones that come and dance within your dreaming unlimited dreams, and as they entre, they attempt to pour goodness in. How else do you think your human kind knows of us all?'

Lucy shrugged.

'The Fairies, many of your years ago, are the ones whom weaved our images into your dreams, so as that you have fantastical beings to wonder at, all within your imaginations. And to address the latter of your well timed question, that is because The Brim-Tree knows everything.'

Lucy made a clicking sound with her tongue.

'But, what about nightmares then?'

'Ah,' Aradene said, in a tone showing she hoped this wouldn't have came up, 'they were first caused by ones who played at being mischievous, but are now too far gone to be helped.'

Lucy was about to ask her to explain more, but Aradene broke her train of thought, as she suddenly, in one fluid movement, jumped up.

Charger swung his mighty head to their direction and as he clopped over, he pointed his forefoot.

Aradene let out a shriek that sounded like it came from far below the ground, through her and ripped out asunder: the shrill scream rang in Lucy's ears and she watched horror-struck, as Aradene put her hands to her head and in one jump, not unlike a splinted bird made free, she sprang like a coil right into the air.

As she soared in an explosion out of the clearing a bolt of black smoke trailed her ascent.

Both witnesses below saw her disappear behind a black, swollen cloud, and then Lucy and Charger saw her no more.

As Lucy was traumatized she looked high into the skyline, then back too the two halves of The Brim-Tree.

'I must be a herald and go off to inform - ' Charger finally spoke, deeply, looking about himself, but was then interrupted talking.

' - What about me? You can't leave me here! Can't I come!'

'No,' Charger said sternly in a tone that tolerated no argument, and in the next second, the black-horned

Unicorn simply wasn't there: dead scabbing leaves stirred in his wake.

She tried to see him, but his lightning speed made it impossible. She looked around, not quite believing that only seconds ago she wasn't alone.

As the leaves fell in bundles on the floor, more in front of her rustled, rasps came from the standing tree and she knew that she would have to get out there, *but where?* she thought.

She went to call out for both Aradene and Charger, but knew it was useless; she turfed up at some leaves, plummeted down on to a smaller boulder and pushed her now fully askew hair out of her face.

Looking around the circular clearing, she had no idea whatsoever, as too what direction to even go into.

The sinister-looking willows soared up, awaiting her welcome: they all swayed, as though in a dance only they knew.

In her blurred vision, she thought all the trees had somehow moved, so she couldn't even decide which way she had entered and found Aradene's graceful-looking back.

She shivered and drew the leaf out; the light from before didn't shine!

It crisped in her hand; nearly all of it was black so she replaced it back into her pocket, which chomped up in sticking hurtful notched points as she did so.

Sniveling and sniffling a bit, Lucy strode on.

Chapter Thirteen

Words Bound In Gumpish

Lucy resolved to walk in any direction that her sore feet took her.

So she got up from the now uncomfortable boulder, rubbed her hands together and moved past the lain half of the tree; she had to sprightly step over the fallen empty branches.

Lucy looked back and glumly wadded into the barrier of willows.

She hugged her arms to her, and ambled over the rises and dips of the earth, careful not to trip over the warrens of roots.

Her walking stretched until she couldn't walk no more, and yet with her mind as steel, she did just that; carried on plodding.

She had not an idea of the time, or how long she had been going through the willows. A grey haze lay like a gorged blanket. The wind licked her face and she spread her hair out of her eyes and mouth.

Thoughts, mad and wild had to be pushed down under a boiling pot of emotions, she looked to her white hands and as she lumbered her next step, a sudden giant-like *thwack* came from the depths of the earth.

Rumbling muffled thuds banged up through the soil: Lucy scurried down the decline of a small hill, whilst the willows offered no advice.

The thuds became such a clatter that she knew them to be close!

Roots sprayed up, and she looked to her right, as she was sure she had heard the tearing of a willow tree, being shorn from the ground.

The noise deafened her senses, until all she could do was to throw her arms in front of herself and in quick lunges, run in any direction with all her failing strength.

Twigs snapped, no birds sang and out through the clearing's edge, Lucy emerged.

Wheezing, she glanced back to make sure she had landed safe and sound, and there was the willows edge, streaming on and on, in opposite directions, but then it was if a scythe had severed away the divide, showing the barrier to entre, or exit, where The Brim-Tree sometimes lived.

Lucy felt like she was being pranged by distilled currents of the windy air.

As her hair thrashed over her face, she threw her gaze to the thuds echoing now in her head.

A field stretched like a carpet, and over the rolling dead-looking field, opposite to Lucy, was the other end of the crumbling burnt forest from before!

I thought I'd seen the last of that, she thought, then as the rumbles grew, the lining of the forest, of ringed black trees was pushed slightly apart - even in their burnt state they leaned back to their original stance - and as crashes sounded, this heralded walking enormous trees, which Lucy had to crane her head up to see clearly!

Lucy looked to her right, then down to the left, and still, out stomped these walking tree creatures.

Over the wind, incoherent mummers filled the air and were then became lost.

'*The Gumps,*' Lucy whispered to herself, as she backed behind a willow tree that looked most welcoming, when compared to the monstrous trees now stamping in front of her.

Their movements caused creaks and

taut, rope-like smacks to rise, much as though sails of an ancient fighting ship was readying for war.

The thunderous sounds was the walking of the creatures; she remembered seeing a few of these from far off above, when she was last here a handful of days past, in a happy-ending adventure.

Clumps of branches made up their arms, legs and heads, which grated out sproutingly from which was a tree body.

Leaves made up their hair, and the faces were formed out of bark and colossal, twisted knobbed gnarled branches stuck out of their bodies.

The Gumps moved in very slow motions and when they did take a step and lifted a foot up, leaves trailed down from the base of their feet and when they placed it back on to the ground, roots coiled out from its sole too burrow deep into the ground, only then to be dragged out, when a foot was lugged up.

Leaves rained on Lucy's head.

She shook and at first thought they had came from the willows around her, but instinct made her peer up and through the interlacing branches of her hiding willow, and having an unimpeded view, she looked high and saw that one of these things had stopped, and was looking directly down to her!

The Gump yipped out and waggling its arm, it pointed to the others, gesturing slowly to below, 'Ti si hatw?

'Doof ti si, wonk tnod I.'

'Emoc, enola ti evael gnilpmug!'

'Ha... tub'

'YwolliW ssecnirP dna nekaO ecnirP ot teg oot deen ew!' commanded the Gump, decisively.

Lucy, tired and more than fed up, bear-facedly came out and yelled in a castigatory tone, *'What?'*

The smaller Gump, she had just screamed her abuse at, merely cleaved its arm and joined its kin, as they scurried through their barky cousins standing high above the willows smooth line.

As they clomped past, they splotched out the murkiness and the shaded light filtered through their hair of leaves.

Lucy waited for them all to entre the willows; a couple of times these creatures came close to stomping on her, it was only for their respectful protection of not disturbing the trees, that she managed to remain physically unhurt.

Time wound on yet didn't tick, and as the last Gump galumphed its mark through the willows, Lucy scuttled out, running with energy she didn't know was there, over the field she hotfooted and as she ran, she knew the only cover was the once flaming trees, now charred, but to entre that domain might mean she could have fell down in the blacken clover, cried, and wept so much she would not have gotten up again.

And so Lucy dashed left, down the field, following the slight decline as it rolled on for an innumerable breadth.

Chapter Fourteen

Frozen Fires

Lucy's legs gave way.

With a startled heap in a muffled scream of fury, she fell sideways to the rocky ground that, quite oddly, was blanketed in pink sweetie strands.

'What is that stuff? Oh... it's! Urgh,' Lucy mumbled, frowning.

As she lay there, paralyzed and glaring, her side sticky with candyfloss, she cried out and blinked, because she had past the burnt forest and had left behind the willows and Gumps, but now, towering over the lip of the rise she rested on, were mountains jammed with a parliament of crowding assorted Dragons!

Despair fled as she realised she

hadn't somehow walked in a circle, but these were different mountains: for she noticed no snow spurred them.

As her hair whipped over the crown of the hill, she crawled and glanced down, pulling back as she did so, as over the hill a valley spread on for a length she couldn't see to, and there, as the mountains augmented, so did some of the Dragons.

'Dragon Land?' she whispered, she didn't know of its precise location, but somehow the sight in front of her suggested that she was right. *I've walked right into the heart of Dragon Land,* Lucy concluded.

It seemed that they were all somehow stilled, and here, Aradene's voice reverberated around her head, "Trapped in time, frozen."

Hundreds upon hundreds of Dragons were on the bushel outcrops of the mountains: all were arced upwards with their wings expanded, and some reposed, freezing their front claws open, still.

All had fire spurting out of their jaws with smoggy smoke hammering and wafting up from their nostrils; it caused Lucy too shudder to see the Dragons fire and smoke not moving, only lifeless, trapped in time.

Their movements had been stopped short: their eyes were open, and fire and smoke didn't *roar* upwards as indubitably intended.

Lucy made her way down the hill, staring at all the Dragons. One right in front of her was bright red and as she ambled down the rise, the true Dragons height reached up.

Brown dead grass welcomed her feet and as she stood on the hill's flat expanse, a gasp escaped her, as she hadn't realised she had came so close and could actually touch, if she so dared, for she had passed the clawed feet that housed the large Dragon. It was that tall, that even when lolling her head from below, Lucy was unable to see its Dragon head properly. Its wings were outstretched and showed the mottles of black over them: these blocked out the sights beyond, and its forked, spiked tail was held poker-straight.

Scales still flashed, and matched in colour of the streams of the trapped fire, bursting above, far into the writhing squirms of the clouds.

It seemed that in its final moments, of being frozen, all of them, including this crimson one, had attempted to ward off an aerial attack.

Lucy, glumy, saw that cliffs ran to her left, bowing out and running out to the side, and chunks lay at the cliffs bottom, *as though something mighty had been bashed into the side of it*, she thought.

She went to walk round the Dragon, and as she stalked under its tail, currents of wind shrieked.

She stood still and decided that as the Dragon was so big, she doubted she'd be able to walk around it and take in its splendor.

As the gusts howled their fury, sparkles were also carried on the wind.

What is it? she pondered. Glittery wind shone off the Dragon's scales, the puffs of glitters were then carried high over the hill and there, Lucy lost sight of it, being ensnared to the mountains beyond her periphery.

She lopped past other Dragons that plagued the ground, interweaving between legs and others, whose spiked tails lay curving and still, like fallen logs, upon the ground.

A much smaller, *a younger Dragon*, guessed Lucy, like its kin, was upright with small lined streams of fire coming out from its snarl: its tail was being lifted on the wind, then set down once it had fun playing with it.

Lucy heard the thud that its rising and falling tail made; she then decided to move away from this younger black Dragon, as it seemed far to eerie.

As she picked her way through the outskirts of Dragon Land, a sudden spasm again gripped her stomach: she fell to the floor, attempting to put her hands in front of her to soften the impact, but instinct made her hold where the pain was coming from, as though to wench out the stabbing feelings now racking her.

Hot tears ran down Lucy's face and as her vision returned, she ever so slowly lifted herself up. Her weak hands scrabbled at the edge of her jumper: the ebb of the pain still flowing though her, and as she proceeded to lift her jumper up, she wiped her face with her other hand

and glanced down, and stared in utter shock.

Under her skin, ran lines of pocketed veins, black and thread-like blue!

She knelt up and moved out of the shadow being cast from a Dragon's wing, staring in ghastly surprise at what was taking place under her skin.

The veins crept out, slowly running in lines, tracing a pattern.

Lucy rasped a cough.

She knew whatever dangers she had faced something was very different now, such as that she had never dealt with before.

As the lines under her skin spread their malevolent mark, her inner Magic sprang out, something deep inside her shot out like a viper and she knew, there and then, that the bonds of Magic that had lain over Abraxus, in his statue form, were still there, although, they were defiantly not weak, just tainted in twisting, as though, she realised, instead of her holding him, it was he, who was leaking his darkness into her!

In flash of desperation, her weakened arm dragged out the leaf, she waved it into the air, causing black arcs and beams of red to fly and bounce off the all the still Dragons bodies; it even reached the forested mountains in the far distance.

Her other hand brushed at herself, resisting, as though the threat was climbing up her like bombs of marching ants, and as the aerial Dragons reared above, still and silent, frozen ever unhelpfully, she crept down into a small ball.

And as Lucy's eyes dropped, shadowy spider webs writhed into her vision.

Chapter Fifteen

The Key Of Pandragon

Megan did not perish.

She walked. And walked. And then Megan walked some more.

She had hiked in a colliding rush for an age through the bushes, and yet, walking amid the fern-like bracken felt like it was only in a blink of an eye. A thickly-grassy side-trail led to where she was now.

Megan sucked in fresh air.

The sweet air made her not feel thirsty.

Megan had legged it.

So quick that she didn't notice she'd looked liked a dwelling creature who resided in a forest.

Her hands were toweling off the

last bits of spinnery from her clothes; she looked about properly.

'Whew!' Megan rendered the air.

Marveling, she stopped suddenly as if she couldn't believe her eyes.

Megan had happened upon a fantastical magnificent castle.

However did I get here? she thought.

Pink cloisters were hugging the castles framework, which to Megan, looked like lattice cut-out pastry shapes, that her dear dad sometimes fancifully adorned as decorations on his scrummy cakes.

Megan caught her breath.

The eye-catching stately castle looked truly incredible!

Megan's curiosity was aroused.

Megan stood.

The exceptional castle was studded with fields blanketing all dotting around, lying like patchwork quilts thrown out by a giant. Slap-bang in the centre was the castle. A flattened rise was dominated by a crenellated monument of rose and bronze-buffed stone.

Megan gawped.

Thirty towers stood like silent sentinels surrounded and stretched it, hugging into the castle. A turreted gate stood guard before the towers. Each tower looked like the yumtious icing from a Chelsea bun. It was all really very extraordinary.

Megan, gaping, looked even more at the alluring-looking castle.

It had a stuccoed-breasted front. The fortification did not so much dominate the territory, as this land was in the hundreds of miles bigger than any she'd seen.

'Ooh... aah,' went Megan.

It was like a Fairy tale castle Megan had always, *always*, dreamed of once living within. The fortress certainly matched a resemblance to those she drew, and one sketch in particular sported an equal likeness, which was styled over her Mathematics school exercise book, betwixt boring times-tables; the castle's drawing coursed over two pages.

Megan's eyes shined.

Looking at the outstanding castle, Megan scrutinated the keep that had spires and turrets. Like the one Princess Blossom described in Fairy Land - only this one was human-sized and hundreds of feet in width and length, the spires becoming lost amidst the mingling rainbows hanging in the now darkening sky.

Megan's eyes looked to the clouds, which weren't quite perfectly white.

This isn't quite right... is this like before..? Megan thought.

But the landscape (there) wasn't as when she had bolted out the cave into Unicorn Land, when she was last in The Enchanted Kingdom, so Megan thought all must be well.

As her sight came down, she saw twisting chimney-breasts poked out of towers and garrets into the glorious sky. The castle's topmost rampart had a spear impaled and a pronged pink flag was attached to the pole, bordered in cream scroll-work; the banner on the mast denounced:

Pandragon's Key

Megan had no idea where she was.
Pan-d-dragon's Key... Pandragon's Key, Megan thought, trying out the castle's name.

No-one had came out.

Megan stood on one foot then the other.

She walked forward stepping in thriving, lavish grass. Pink poppy-shaped flowers were teeming within the greenery.

Megan walked by the dingle

bushes, and came up to the fortress-like castle.

Still, nobody came out to her.

Megan walked on.

She was now in a courtyard, which had tiles and slabs fitted against each other on the grounds of the outer castle.

Megan decided to explore the exterior of Pandragon's Key.

Two wings lay in hushed lullaby ruins like from a forgotten era. Battle-works and ramparts were rested in medleys. Two yawning outer-walls stood still, ever watchful. A pink stellar gate was in the middle of the walls: the gate was wrought iron in splashed pink paint; all manners of different pinks.

A much welcome breeze rifled through Megan's russet-coloured ringlet tresses; she pushed back a swathe of hair with her left hand.

Megan looked at the turquoise-blue

and grey sky and the stripy rainbows. Glorious sunshine still beamed down from the three suns.

The sight around Megan was truly wonderful.

This Land truly seemed to be steeped in Magic.

Megan's head turned right, and she saw a gunmetal-grey gauntlet, hung on a hook outside of the gated open wall.

A more fantastical castle had Megan never seen.

The structures seemed to have been farmed by an expert sculptor and stonemason.

Even the spires and crenellations were engineered in precious glitzy gems of topaz and silvers.

This wasn't all a mere illusion.

A lone stone cream-coloured bench, with a pink bolt of mutli-pinked fabrics draped over it, looked invitingly to Megan.

Megan poured in the sunshine.

She sat down for a moment.

Megan smiled.

This central sidestepped section of the castle was slightly smaller. The structures herded round in an accompaniment of assembled passageways.

'Humm-mmm.' Megan sighed.

She was sat, taking a breather, on a length of rasberry-pink material.

Megan scratched her forehead.

She got up, looked around and still not a creature came and said a hello, or the worse: brandishing an axe in an ambush.

Megan walked under the whitey-pink stoned archway.

A tapestry somehow was tacked to the wall, but she couldn't behold any visible poking nails.

Megan's hands traveled over the ripples of cloth.

On the wall which occupied the

woven cloth, Megan witnessed this was metres-upon-metres long and wide. The stitched picture gave the viewer an appraised scene of magical creatures. In amid them all, Megan caught an identified character study here and there, but she couldn't be *sure* as sure.

Smiling, Megan was ogling at the crocheted embroidery.

She came to move on, giving the most arresting wall-hanging another look.

As Megan compassed around a corner of the castle wall, pink stone and white ceramic-like foundation pillars rested underneath a main gallery, which skedaddled round the next level of the castle.

Megan was riveted.

A black-and-pink railing lipped on the open square gallery's upper-floor, and on iron bars were maybe thousands of pink carnations.

Megan honed in on the flowers.

The aroma was like capering through a glen full of fauna.

Megan sniffed some more.

Chapter Sixteen

Unicorns And Dragons

Megan smiled wider.

She approached the back-wall of the castle that escorted into a lowered planked bridge; pink flowers were grained on either side and flowered down into the empty moat.

The quad did not feel of gloom.

Retracing her steps, Megan went now under a narrow passage which was opposing the entrance to the bridge.

This place felt of Magic and power.

Hundreds more spires and archways stood erect. Though an occasional one lent against its stoney second.

Megan's heart palpitated.

Down on this level, gates hung

open in the keep's outer walls.

The walls themselves bore stipples of acrylic pinky rouges, and looked like they'd been cosmeticed by a flustered hand.

Megan set off.

A mural in pink chalk was drawn over white walls. The scenes were of similar magical creatures, and slotted in were pyrotechnical pink fireworks, rupturing in fizzling chalky lines for the walls distances.

Megan advanced down the corridor.

The hunks of cobbles and flag-stoned floor made for a slightly nippy feel.

A drafty air stroked into Megan's curling hair.

She socked some of her curly curlicuing hair out of her face.

White friezes of Unicorns and cream frescoes of Dragons were decorated on the ceiling

Megan scratched her nose.

At the other end of the corridor, a bannister following a spiraling staircase was punctuated with hosts of rioting carnations and roses that were so full, Megan looked at the rustling petals.

The receding banks were lost to her sight as the stairs and its handrail went into the netherworld.

Megan took a measured breath.

Lengthy columns of more stairs, spiraling or running ladder-straight were all in diagonal, interfolding, confounded ways.

Megan looked over her shoulder.

The dormant castle offered no-one as a companion.

The span of the corridor was deserted - apart from herself.

Is there only me here? Megan thought.

She focused on a spot of pink petals, looking aside from the toss-up-one's-cookies causing stairs.

Megan concentrated on her breathing

She convened along the lower bannister, and smiled at the sparkle from the petaled bracts.

Megan oriented herself.

The stairs were excessively enticing, but she judged it would be rather easy to become lost within the labyrinth of stairs.

Megan devoted some more time back to pictures of the chalk Unicorns and Dragons.

The silence was totally and completely comfortable.

Megan's cool eyes stared at the elegant and subtle forms of the Dragons and Unicorns.

Megan didn't shut her eyes; instead, she kept looking.

Megan was eagle-eying a smashing Dragon, which, even though was in proportion much more larger than the Unicorn, its drawn-self did not still surmount the wall - nor did any of the other Dragons outdo each other, or the Unicorns for that matter, those bespattered on any other of the walls.

It was if the walls themselves knew how big to be to accommodate their magical, almost-animated presentments.

Megan boogied round the curve, her eyes were following a Dragon's wingspan, and she thought Lucy may be just around the bend.

Megan was dumbfounded.

Thoughts of The Dragon Keeper were gone for now, because, as a bonus, the castle showed its corridor now united into pink brickwork.

This had a spotlight with an inner pink lighting lensing down from a pink, crystallized quartz chandelier.

Megan was flabbergasted.

She walked under the chinks of the

rainbow-prisimed lights, and cruised into a different face of the castle.

Megan gandered into an arched courtyard.

Central pink panelling was on the walls.

Megan loitered briefly.

Restarting, like a wind-up mechanical solider, Megan tromped by the entryway at the back of the courtyard.

Megan snooped into the pinken-lighted archway.

A white-walled lobby had a pink door set into the pink-panelled wall. Frills and embellishments on handsomely gold-gilded, wooden chests, that were sat at intervals down the avenue, looked inviting to her.

Adjacent to her, by the end of the archway, near-enough sliced into the wall, a screen blinded was what behind itself.

Megan slightly bulldozed one half

of the screen to one side.

She was hankering to know what was on the other side to know if Lucy was hiding there. Instead, Megan perceived fields lying all around hills, a peak of which was dwarfed by one-side of the buffeted stone, crenellated castle.

Nine towers stood around the main back-part of the castle, and a spired pink courtyard was directly in front of Megan.

She turned back, letting the pink-gauzy screen flute back into its folds.

Megan did a u-turn and came back to the corridor.

This really was like a palace!

Hundreds of rooms were siphoned off corridors. Of the mystery rooms, each had their horizontal, wooden-planked doors shut.

Megan stopped at moments in silenced awe.

She walked down the foyer.

A detachment of more corridors spun out of a circular chamber.

Megan knuckled her forehead.

She by-passed the doors; not really wanting to open one in case the Boogeyman catapulted out.

Megan looked tight-lipped.

She avoided the tempting, gold-gilded handles.

Walking down the long, long corridor (wisely leaving the doors closed for fear of a Goliath bucking out, trying to snatch her as quick as a slingshot), Megan came to a circular stairwell at the end of the hall.

It all looked like a vast museum!

By golly! Megan thought.

Where she had stopped, quite near to the stairs, a handful of the doors were open; each framework drenched different pink lights into the chamber. It was only when Megan bellied up to the doors that the lights showed themselves.

This part of the chamber looked like it was doused in so many different colours of pink lights.

Megan felt safe.

One door, ajar, looked most attractive.

Megan felt slightly magnetized.

Still feeling in a safe space, she walked on toward the door, and under the top of the frame.

Chapter Seventeen

A Buccaneer

Megan blinked.

She was standing in a room.

The ring-like auditorium was massive in size. No windows revealed themselves.

She confirmed the door was still unlatched.

Megan nodded.

Her head swung back to the items on the floor: a golden goblet the size of her dad's drinking flagon was posed next to something, lying butt-flat against the floor.

Megan tried to heighten herself.

She was on her tiptoes, but her balance went left-then-right like an egg capsizing around.

Megan walked slowly over, and bent her neck to see a plank of wood was next to the goblet cup. Both ends of the wooden-planked sign looked old. Really old. Megan could almost see this on the hull of a barnacled-bottomed-covered sturdy prow.

'Arrrh... Me... Hearties.' Megan said, laughing to herself.

The plank of wreckage wood was not cut neatly at either end; both ends seemed as if a dog had chawed on one then gnawed on the other.

Megan looked to the black paint still bright as if blocked on there only yesterday: Smuggler's Arms

She then looked up to the ceiling, quite certain that another candelabra would be up there. Though none was.

'Where's the light coming from?' Megan said, browsing about.

Still no light source shone.

'Mmm.' Megan maundered.

She backed out the room; the door

stayed open and delivered her back on to the chamber's corridor.

Megan looked about.

The next door down, on the same side, the right side, was also open. A similar squirting light dripped into the corridor. Megan would not have been surprised to see a rushing Lucy as she made her way under the arched doorway.

Though, alas, there was no sight nor sound of her sister. All that welcomed her was a pink-wooden easel in the square-boxed, room's centre. Not a sheaf of paper was held in the easel's ledge.

Megan couldn't see any visible art equipment.

She sometimes would see older children in higher forms use easels, rather like this one in the school's Art studio. Though the miniature wooden, pose-able human-like doll figures unnerved her so, what with their lack of faces.

On the left-hand side of the room, a glass cabinet of the finest variety held itself ram-rod straight like a saluting Sargent.

Even the closet's middle looked see-through. The accumulative effect was one of the extravagant.

Megan looked up, just to try and see where the light was coming from in this room. But, her look-see showed no lamp; dimming or otherwise at full-blast.

No rainbows either, Megan thought.

She'd wondered if sparkly, expanding rainbows might have been up in the air with the treacle-brown timbre rafters.

Megan looked rather fretting. She was trying to not brood on Lucy's whereabouts.

She turned and walked out the closeted chamber.

A cavity alcove set within the pink-streaming wall had a stone settee waiting for someone who needed a rest.

Megan was just down the way from the room, up further on the right-side of this wall of the castle's maze-like layers.

She sat against four of the eleven pink piled cushions.

Megan had explored quite a lot and now most certainly needed a sit down.

Chapter Eighteen

Round-And-Round The Bends

'Hyyum.' Megan breathed.

She looked left, then right and then back to the centre of where she was.

Should be moving on, thought Megan.

She also knew she could merrily stay there for an age. But, she had her sister to find, and to try and locate someone who owned such an extraordinarily stupendous castle.

Megan's palms bunted against her thighs as she stood up slowly.

She moved right, a portion of the way she'd came from.

Megan vamoossed up the long passage.

The pink lights from the open doors

were much behind her back now. She turned right in the vestibule; two white-coloured symmetrical cloisters were positioned on the left, where Megan now leveled up to the threshold of the staircase.

Megan looked up the round-and-round spiral stairwell.

She put her right foot on the step.

Megan bit the inside of her top lip.

With an awful lot of reluctance she commenced up the stairs, one-at-a-time.

Up she went. Round-and-round.

Round-and-round.

Megan felt like she was in a speeding dodgems car.

She stopped her walking.

Megan leaned her head against the pink metalwork of the stairs bars.

She'd neared a landing area where Megan was then able to hitch-off from the stairs.

Megan was nonplussed. Rather

fishily, in a curiously queer way, she wasn't feeling too hot so as that she didn't want to melt into the stairs.

'How baffling.' Megan said, quite true.

Her head came to the access level of the landing, and wreathing around the stairs, her feet finally took off from the step and Megan was docked on to the landing.

'Oh!' Megan mouthed.

This floor was marvelously all-out pink.

Megan's mind boggled.

She could see herself living here, when in The Enchanted Kingdom.

'Wouldn't that be something.' Megan said, exhilaratingly.

Megan smiled.

As she went round the pink corridor, looking as if it went on in all directions for one-hundred football grounds, Megan thought she heard a cough.

Megan stopped for a trifle moment. No-one snared her.

'Must be nothing,' Megan said aloud.

Chapter Nineteen

Where Be Lucy?

Megan thought she heard a sound like wings of a moth doing the conga.

With a Herculean effort Megan did not scream.

Slowly but surely she looked to her right shoulder-height.

A warren of corridors fed-off the passageway. Ceilings and walls contended one another at jointy, impossible-looking angles.

Then interrupting Megan's vision was a wizened Elf!

'Psst! Peek-a-boo! I see you!'

Megan almost leapt out of her skin.

'Why, hello there Megan Button! Fancy seeing you here! At last! I am Mr. Bumblebeaux. Chief Librarian here at Pandragon's Key. '

'Huh!' Megan said, addled.

Megan blinked at such a grand name and title.

Mr. Bumblebeaux had a hard-lined face, and looked slightly to be of stiff-necked.

But his eyes looked kind.

Megan lugged at the hem of her top.

He flew a bit more, closing the space, so he adjoined her.

Megan looked scared out of her life.

'I'm... Me-egan.'

'I know.'

He gave Megan a conspiratorial nod of his bespectacled head, and flew in a miscalculated way, which lent him a hippety mobility.

Megan looked pale.

'Are there others here with us?'

Mr. Bumblebeaux pushed his spectacles up the ridge his nose with his Elfish left forefinger.

'Others? Oh yes, and much more than only Elves here.' he replied sportingly.

'A... Lucy?'

'A what?'

'My Sister - '

' - She - '

' - Is she OK?'

Mr Bumblebeaux looked at Megan.

She was still a tad worried over Lucy.

Preoccupied thoughts percolated through Megan.

Is she fine? What has happened to her? Is she here... somewhere?

'Yes. The Dragon Keeper is well. So I am told. You will see your Lucy very soon,' her relief must have shown itself on her face, because Megan looked a bit more relaxed, and felt much better knowing about her now. 'For now, though, this is your time.' Mr Bumblebeaux mimed to walk on.

Megan did so.

Heavy-looking, gold-enameled double-doors suddenly parted open!

Mr. Bumblebeaux used his hands to demonstrate toward them.

Megan's footsteps were not as brisk.

She moved to her right, and all of a sudden the Elf went into the room!

Megan's shoulders moved up-and-down.

She went on.

A sideboard was on the far side of the room. Upon the cupboard, dainty thimbles, gold bells and wheat-yellow whistles were exhibited. Megan moved over to the furniture table-top; the gold treasure trove of trinkets gleamed in such a brilliance it almost hurt to look at them.

Megan came away from the cinnamon-coloured sideboard.

She saw now what she hadn't when walking into the room: the walls, and everything within it, bar the bauble packed cupboard, was that all else, the walls included and the carpet, were of a pink bon-bon colour.

Mr. Bumblebeaux nodded to chairs.

'Do feel free to park yourself.'

'Anyw - '

' - Wherever you like, Megan.'

The material of her deep-backed chair felt butter-soft, and as Megan thumped down, she noticed her chair, like many of the others, was satin-covered in a lovely shade of multifaceted pinks.

'I tell you what,' Mr. Bumblebeaux said, after a while, putting one knee over his other as he sat on the lipped edge of the mahogany reading table. 'Why don't we move on?'

'Move on?' queried Megan.

'Well, yes. I'd imagine you'd like to discover more of this castle, no?'

Megan smiled.

Mr. Bumblebeaux took her on a little chaperoned tour of the keep.

As they exited the room, and the doors closed quietly behind their departure, Mr. Bumblebeaux was neck-height with Megan. 'Soon I shall bring you to the great Library.'

'That sounds wonderful.' Megan said, truthfully.

'I suspected you'd like The Library. Countless books, why, more so because all font of knowledge has been collated from all worlds,' Mr. Bumblebeaux was explaining, his voice rising and looking incredibly excited. 'To catalog, house and protect herein these walls.'

'Aaaruh,' Megan said, nodding, wondering how big this Library must be.

They were journeying down a pink and silver corridor that had no doors latched within the walls.

'This castle is *huge.*'

'I do agree. I've before now attempted to compile a static floor-plan. Though this undertaking is quite problematic.'

'Why?'

'Because,' he explained to Megan. 'Sometimes, rooms grow as each one is needed.'

'O-o-h!'

'This forty-two leveled layered castle is most often like this. But, on occasion, one can fly into different areas round a corner.'

'But do you not get lost?' Megan quizzed.

'Not so much. Even if when coming out a room, and in a wholly differing place, that very same place you've been expelled in feeds back to the right place you want.'

'That's...'

'Magic?'

'Yes!'

Megan was bowled over.

Leagues away from Lucy's mishaps in

the south-easterly regions of The Enchanted Kingdom...

Mr. Bumblebeaux fluttered on.

Megan waved her head from side-to-side.

She turned a sharp-left then was in a corridor, not much unlike in colour-theme to the last, however, this passage inverted slightly, giving the look of it decreasing in size as the corridor streamed on for uncountable lengths.

Mr. Bumblebeaux said after a while, in a companionable voice, 'As is here, your world is of beautiful words. Poetical and harsh. All glittering words. I do like the romanticism, grace and serenity in your literature.'

Megan remembered what book she had last devoured with her keen eyes.

'You know, your life-work is beginning.' Mr. Bumblebeaux said, in a divine tone, not just to himself.

Megan stopped. She felt frazzled. 'Huh? My life's work?'

'Yes.'

Megan blinked.

She didn't know what else to say.

My life's work? Whatever does Mr. Bumblebeaux mean? Megan thought, feeling rather alarmed.

As she continued around the castle, having moved into a different zone, she walked over the threshold and into a hall.

A great golden cloud was in the room with her and Mr. Bumblebeaux.

Megan looked upward, and noticed how the cloud was so large it even buffeted against the ceiling's rafters.

Silver stars were spangled in the air.

Megan's face lit up.

Rainbow lightning drifted down and abounded all over the room; every time Megan padded on into a bolt of the lights, it would *zap* out, leaving nothingness in the air, and then reappear a moment later.

Megan giggled.

Megan saw Mr. Bumblebeaux had moved on, so she caught up with him.

As he shepherded her around, he was murmuring something about '...heart of the tragedy.'

Megan's heart panged.

'Did something very sad happen?' Megan asked, with care.

Mr. Bumblebeaux sighed sightly.

'In a way, supposedly it did. One was here who scribbled down those tragedy, mystery and comedic plays.'

'Oh, OK.'

'Thankfully we have the completed works. But of the notable hand who writ such gems...'

'Look at that cloud.' Megan suddenly said, awed.

'Indeed.' Mr. Bumblebeaux agreed, who seemed too posses a better mood.

'And to where the golden cloud leads to!'

Megan glanced at him.

'L-leads... to?' she questioned.

'For another time, maybe. Come come. Toot toot!' Mr. Bumblebeaux fluttered on.

In the gallery, which had corridor arteries leaking off it, he stopped and asked Megan, 'Which way shall we go?'

Megan also came stilled.

'That one.' she made up her mind at last on the second to left entranceway. They both went out the lobby and entered the arched, vaulting-ceiling corridor.

'That's the ticket.' Mr. Bumblebeaux said, in a broadcasting tone.

Chapter Twenty

Witchypoo And Shuttlecock

Megan was walking down the corridor.

This one had an effect like when at a sea-life aquarium, and scurrying down the glass-round gangway with scary sharks swimming around.

The corridor also had a slight phosphorescent pink light.

Megan felt queasy.

Mr. Bumblebeaux's eyes saw her and he went into a room whose doors were already open for visitors.

'Open sesame?' Megan half-joked.

'Ha! No. The room knew you were near.'

Megan's dopey feet shambled on.

Her illumined outline became less

so as she patrolled into another reading room.

Megan sat in a chair.

On its plush pink armrests were a blue book and a red book. *Witchypoo* was balanced on one-side. She looked to the right armrest and saw a red hardback, titled: Ignatius Shuttlecock

Everything was glorious!

Every other chair had a low-squat, occasional table between each of it. The chairs were not of any right design; some were tall, some were neat, some were big enough to seat three, and nine more looked only for one sitter.

Megan probed over the left armrest; her hair shed on to *Witchypoo*. The trestle table by her was treated with warding beautifully cloth-bound books, in-betwixt albums that were open to show scraps of written parchment under the films.

Megan caught a slight uncertainty

there from reading the random words:

…never answers... indisputably... relinquished... grated... aimless... airless... phrases... personal deity of self... ear-marked... justice... The Bare-Footed Fairy... imprudently...

'A bare-footed Fairy?'
'Sounds funny, I know.'
'It does...'
'In these parts though, The Story Of The Bare-Footed Fairy is legendary. You can read its tome of The Bare-Footed Fairy when you next do a visitation.'
'Thank you. I'd really like that!'
Megan got up.
The bookcase, running for many shelves, hosting so much of the many hardback and paperback books, was, in compassion to Megan's own hardback and paperback bookcase, quite colossal.

Her bookshelves included a copy of Megan's favourite book: a now water-damaged, paperback copy of *Anne of Avonlea* that had once been submerged in a lavatory.

Megan embarked on a nose around the titanic-sized, over-flowing bookcases.

'Curious title,' Megan mumbled to herself.

She critiqued what she had hit upon: a heavy-set volume was stood erected like a taut forefinger.

Megan followed the gold-gilt edging pattern with her right thumb. She divested the weighty tome, and holding the hardback boards betwixt her hands, she skimmed through the book's pages: a lot of rules, guidelines and numbered graphs appeared to her. Some of the ink writings and accompanying diagrams were clear, whilst others showed the test of time and were opaque - at best.

'Gobbledegook,' Mr. Bumblebeaux remarked, noting the title her hands held.

'Trolls.' Megan muttered, in a tone of quality for non-understanding.

She respectfully lifted the book back to its resting place, and before forging ahead along the bookcase and shelves, Megan looked at the title at the top of the spine:

Troll Tournament Handbook and Rigorous Rules

With the book's author's name at the opposite end of its spine:

Tudley Taxing

'Gosh.' There was a pleasurable note of distinction in Megan's voice, admiring at the bookshelves:

Bead. Histories, Chronicles

Poetical Verse

Tumultuous Times in Bygone Days

Sonnets, Crispin de la Shake-Selby

Megan had the impression these books were olde-worldy.

This incident was intoxicating.

Her panorama, at every turn, came at spying gorgeously sheer grandeur.

Megan immensely enjoyed the interval.

She sniffed, smiling. Pink and creamy-white magnolias were in crystal vases and the flowers whiffed of candy.

Pink lace carpet had dyed tinges to show a swirling riot of all manner of pinks.

'This castle is amazing,' Megan said, with awe in her voice, as clear as a *ding-donging* bell.

'And what's more Megan. This. Is. All. Yours.'

'Pardon?'

'Yours.'

'I don't understand, Mr. Bumblebeaux.'

'The Fairy Key...'

'That's supposed to be... or no... it is me.'

Mr. Bumblebeaux smiled comfortingly.

'The Key of the castle will stand and *must* do. Not only as a symbol but also the very Land it is situated on.'

'The Land?' Megan asked.

'Yes.'

'Why, what Land is this?' she quizzed, expecting to hear from Mr. Bumblebeaux that the Land she had found her person in, was to be called Fairy Land.

Mr. Bumblebeaux eyed Megan.

He breathed in deeply as if to announce something vital of utmost importance.

Mr. Bumblebeaux's eyes glinted.

Megan leaned her elbows on the back of the pink chair in anticipation.

Mr. Bumblebeaux steepled his fingers. 'Megan. This is The Fairy Key Land.'

Chapter Twenty-One

All Souls Librarium

'*B-but... but that would mean this Land belongs too...*' Megan couldn't finish, for she had been so dumbfounded.

'You.'

Megan looked overwhelmed.

'Ta-dah!' Mr. Bumblebeaux said, smiling.

'*This Land* is *mine?*' Megan asked in great surprise.

Megan's eyes looked as big as golf balls.

'Yes, it always has been, dear Megan. For you are prestigiously The Fairy Key.'

Megan's head was spinning.

'Hick.' Megan hiccuped.

'I am being quite serious, you do know?' Mr. Bumblebeaux reiterated.

Megan clenched her fists passionately.

'Huumh.' A gasp of stunned jubilation came from Megan.

'You are incomparable.' Mr. Bumblebeaux praised.

Megan's lips twitched.

'You are an individual,' Mr. Bumblebeaux went on, 'your individuality stands you in good steed.'

Megan's gaze locked with Mr. Bumblebeaux's, 'W-what do you mean?'

'You're a person of important, Megan Button. The Fairy Key. Of course, many in your world, both little people and elder, are also, but you are of extra-noteworthy importance. Yes, you believe in us so strongly and with such fondest, pure feelings. But you are on the path to start fully believing in yourself, now.'

Megan blinked.

'Isn't this a *marvel!*' Mr. Bumblebeaux enthused.

Megan was confounded.

'This Land will be here for you, forever. It is yours, and no-one or no creature can take that away,' he affirmed. 'It has been here waiting. In part mobilizing all knowledge for you, arming itself in readiness for your arrival.' Mr. Bumblebeaux dedicated, in an authoritative tone.

Megan's mind boggled not for the first time.

Oh good grief, she thought.

Upheavals in her chest came after one another so her speech was bit off in her gnashing mouth.

Megan didn't understand what was going on. *Um...* she thought... *I...* 'Err,' she stammered.

Megan was tongue-tied.

Mr. Bumblebeaux seemed to

understand.

Megan suddenly didn't know what to say.

'I see this is quite a lot to take in!'

Megan looked as if thrown into a tizzy.

'There is a place here that I think would unlax you.'

'Unlax?' Megan asked, her mind's eye not getting the word.

'Somewhere exciting, and yet where you may feel more at ease. Then be able to take in the rest of your Pandragon's Key.'

Megan still could not clench the plumbing of the depths of what she was being told.

Megan stared at him in astonishment.

'O-okies.'

Megan checked her pink Alice-band was in place; it was, just so, though more to do with being tangled into her ringleted spiraling curls.

'Shall I take you and then you can see for yourself?'

Megan nodded her whammy-feeling head.

Poor Megan's brain was so addled she wasn't able to think properly.

'Off we go then!' Mr. Bumblebeaux looked rather excitable.

Megan's face looked nonplussed, puzzling.

'Come along.' Mr. Bumblebeaux chaperoned her on a tour of the building.

Megan moved at a fair rate.

She nodded this-way-and-that, when he explained a painting or room that stood vacantly open for them.

As Megan cruised down a halled corridor and Mr. Bumblebeaux flew aside her, going down in an atrium, all of a sudden, a kaleidoscope of pink lights spouted right in their way.

Mr. Bumblebeaux smiled to Megan. 'Watch.'

Megan's eyes looked back to the pink lights that were now soaping her face in a pinky glow.

The drapery of the pink-lighted-veil suddenly snuffed out.

A semi-rotunda was on the other side.

Megan was moving along the way.

The steady *flippity-flipp-flippity-flipp* of Mr. Bumblebeaux's wings were to her right.

A channel corridor was the main one as it was in the middle and slightly tallest in size.

Megan follwed Mr. Bumblebeaux's gliding wings as went into the corridor.

Upon entering the other end, which came surprisingly quickly, two, nine-hundred foot-high doors in pink stone were stood open.

Megan ogled.

Each humungous door looked as if they'd need a mob of Cyclops' just to get it open, even a little.

Megan was escorted past the warded-like, warden doors.

Megan's eyes went up.

And up and up.

Megan stopped motionless.

A fabric billboard in multifaceted pinks had golden threads stitched into it. The evident name of the room where she was, read:

All Souls Librarium

Megan's gaze went beyond the massive placard hanging in the air, which had no wires suspending it.

Megan blew her cheeks out.

'Oh... gracious!'

Scores of bookshelves were filled with books.

Megan was rendered completely astounded.

This was a sublime place. An impossible place.

Unbridled shock shot through Megan.

The orbit-sized hall was absolutely sensational and far exceeded

anything she'd ever anticipated. Its size was like the inter-galactic Milky Way.

Megan stared open-mouthed.

The memorable bookshelves to her right and left showcased 'Anthologies.'

Mr. Bumblebeaux flapped by her, and was smiling. 'Hopefully, one day you will get the gist that all the infinitesimal books, collected works of paper with ink scrawled on them had blossomed and led you, in part, to here.'

Megan gasped.

'I... is... what?' Megan gabbled.

Mr. Bumblebeaux smiled more.

'It's all OK, Megan.'

The labyrinthine vault had even more thousands of corridors

connecting off from the main one where they talked.

'This is your Library.'

Megan's eyes nearly popped out of their sockets.

'Th-his... this-s?'

'All Souls Librarium.'

'All Souls...'

'Librarium.'

'Why would *this* be for me?'

'Why not?'

Megan felt stumped.

She was going to answer Mr. Bumblebeaux, but Megan heard mumbling coming from somewhere to her left. There was a sound as if a crab was moving about, bumping into unseen and hidden articles.

'Where's that blasted...' said whoever it was, unleashing a blister of words on books and the, '... Mismanagement of the The Cryptic Area,' and what, 'The barreling, unkempt state the Junior left The

Emphatically Secluded Mystical Section in...'

Megan looked to Mr. Bumblebeaux.

'Maybe we should leave?'

'Leave?'

'Yes.'

'No, no-no.' he said, adamantly.

'That's just a temporary Curator, and anyway, this is yours. So you call the shots.'

'Aaa...' Megan said.

'I don't mean to overwhelm you again. So let's be moving on in here, and they've most likely taken their book cart too The North Wing, to The Mysteriously Classified Zone.'

'R-right.'

Megan dilly-dallied.

'It really is alright, ' he smiled, nodding. 'Trust yourself.'

Megan set off, and Mr. Bumblebeaux shadowed her down the promenade of the corridor. Reading tables with pink-painted light-shades were at every nine paces. Assemblages of comfy-looking chairs were freckled around each sturdy, study table. The lights of the table turned on as they went past, then snuffed-out as Megan and Mr. Bumblebeaux saddled down the lane of tables in the library. Each lighted lamp-shade also seemed to blend with the slight white glow, that was everywhere in All Souls Librarium.

'We're nearing the vicinity of The South Wing, which has categories in The Magic Marvelous Sector. But for now I think we'll bypass those.' Mr. Bumblebeaux nodded, to himself.

The deep precinct he piloted Megan had pink temple-like columns. Mr. Bumblebeaux saw the advancing columns. 'Ah. Dorick's and Ikonic's Order Mark.'

Megan had a questioning expression on her face. 'Pardon?'

'Oh. You wouldn't know of these?'

Megan looked blank.

'I do keep forgetting this is your first actual visit!'

Megan smiled.

Mr. Bumblebeaux smiled back.

Megan scratched the back of her head.

'Dorick designed and had made these columns,' he explained, as they walked past the pink-stoned column. 'A Dorick column could bear most weight, and they are often used for the lowest level of multi-story buildings, reserving the more slender Ikonic columns for the upper levels.'

Megan nodded at this unexpected magical history lesson.

Mr. Bumblebeaux carried on, pleased for once to find a welcome ear. 'Would you look at this! This is a perfect example of an Ikonic column.'

Mr. Bumblebeaux took Megan to the right, to see the pink-stoned column that did look to be slightly more small-wasited.

The Dorick columns shaft was wider at the bottom and fluted. The smooth grooved column was rounded off at the top with capitals.

'Are they both around now?' Megan asked.

'Who?'

'The.. builders?'

'Oh no, dear. They made these around The Pink Golden Age. At least that's what I think such an episode was labeled in your world. Though we did manage to salvage these, and other contributions by both Dorick and Ikonic themselves.'

'I see.'

'I've always so liked this bigger Ikonic column.' Mr. Bumblebeaux put a hand on the column, then he flew *way* to the top and stood on the scroll-shaped ornaments on the capital, of the top.

Megan waved back.

Mr. Bumblebeaux now flew in his haywired way by her left side. Parts of Megan's hair flew up as he *zoinked* down the column, nearly jouncing into the masonry several times.

'They must each of have been very clever.'

'Rather!' Mr. Bumblebeaux attested. 'The Library has some of the original preparatory and completed artwork and manuscripts. They're most likely all in RRR.'

RRR? Megan thought.

Chapter Twenty-Two

RRR

Megan walked on down the wide corridor.

Of the standing columns they had been left behind moments ago.

Megan's forebrow creased. 'RRR?'

'Restrictive Relics Roundroom.'

'That sounds important!'

'Indeed.'

'Will I able to see it?'

'Whenever you like! It's yours! For you! Though I would advise that, because the room is - '

' - Round?'

'You've got it! It really is cylindrical and after a brief visit, one's head can make you go weak-kneed.'

'Oh. Right!'

'I, myself, have been slap-happy in that Room.'

'Does the feeling last long?'

'Not overly. Usually it passes as it comes. But on the rare visit the haze can last longer...'

'Why?'

'No idea!' Mr. Bumblebeaux said honestly.

'How...'

'Some of us here have theorized that it's owed to the lay of where the RRR is situated. Because these levels each either move about, or slice straight up, or bend in directions. But when in a Room, you couldn't tell.'

'But you'd feel it?'

'Exactly! You have the idea!'

Megan felt a warm glow.

'I do!' she said.

'Though must admit that, whilst your castle and Librarium moves itself, when you do come out of a Room, or level you were in, you may then be a different place to where you entered.'

'Isn't that scary?'

'Not really, Megan. Pandragon's Key provides safety. The castle and the Librarium always get you to the right place, even if, along the way, unforeseen twists-and-turns rear up to affright you.'

Megan didn't feel too deeply frightened. Yet.

Her eyes took in a silver chalice and gold coins shed on a squat, dark-varnished table. In with the treasure were slabs of bullion.

Megan looked down and felt the gold glow coming off the bars.

Gold ingots were also around, each embossed with stenciled imprinting initials: MB

'Why are these here?'

Mr. Bumblebeaux held his hands behind his back as he replied. 'These are all from The Extended Magic

Archive. Each item is awaiting to be moved back. The Senior Curator, Mr. Bluff-Gordon, oversaw the cleaning of these.'

Megan stopped at another table, the same in size to the one before it.

'Calibean. "Be not afraid; this place is full of noises."'

'Good quote, that.' Mr. Bumblebeaux said.

Pink Ash Wednesday Roses had been placed in a circle around the single-sheet of parchment, which the statement was squiggled on.

'How big is this Library, Mr. Bumblebeaux?'

'As big as the Key and Librarium needs to be.' he replied, in a veiled way.

'Do you need Membership?' Megan asked simply.

'A creature would have to book an appointment with Squire Rapheal Dartington, Logger Of Membership.'

'I'll have to ask his assistant!'

'No need for an All Souls Librarium Library License. For you!'

Megan grinned. 'Is everything safe in here, Mr. Bumblebeaux?'

'Sometimes we have the errant rascal trying to stuff a book up his smock for Magic Librarium Lessons... Dealing with such barefaced robbing... You see, nothing can be checked-out, but any items can be viewed on-site.

'Circumstantial events can multiply, and security measures here always offer no anxiousness discomfiture.'

Megan blinked a lot.

'The practicality,' Mr. Bumblebeaux went on, having taking pains to explain, '... anyway, I ramble on!'

The corners of Megan's mouth smiled.

More tables down the left-side of the wall were chock-a-block.

Megan slogged on.

Her eyes took in books, quill pens, pieces of paper, and on a table near to their walkings, Megan saw an incongruous look of pink netting stored in big bales. She had the insightful thought that if even one movement too close, and the whole reams of net would slip on to the floor.

'Anyone who has a love or even like of history would revel in that aisle down there.' Mr. Bumblebeaux said, with his wings giving him a look of a puppet whose strings were being pulled by a baby. 'The History Department is separated into two.'

'Two?'

'Indeed,' was the answer. 'This part of the residence of All Souls Librarium has Compassing Histories Of The Magic, which is the First History Department, and the Second History Department, is, The Ordinary Prevalent History Cycles Of The

Provinces.'

'They sound just great!'

Mr. Bumblebeaux smiled.

'There's such an extensive Compassing Histories Of The Magic, and those of the First History Department and the Second History Department, contain some rogue Magic Historians, who prefer to instead label All Souls Librarium as The Magic Library Of History. Such a lofty namesake!'

Megan smiled.

'The Magic Library Of History is quite incorrect,' Mr. Bumblebeaux lengthened on. 'The true name of the place is All Souls Librarium.'

'All Souls Librarium.'

'That's the ticket! The name of Pandragon's Key's Library is All Souls Librarium. Even if a militant Magic Historian, or two, don't much favour its name. Such bullish interference!'

Megan looked slightly over-awed.

To her right, his listener was mincing backward by two tables, also squat, and toad-like.

Megan hitched up to them.

Glass jars held some sort of gooey, swampy liquid. The kind as would be best found out on a moor.

In midst these was a lined piece of holey-looking scrap of paper.

A threatening line read: *Beware Wolfrick*

Chapter Twenty-Three

Snubbs By Name, Snubbs By Nature!

'That does not sound good.'

'Let's move on!' Mr. Bumblebeaux was wanting to scram Megan forward.

'Who's Wolf - '

' - Snubbs be gone!' Mr. Bumblebeaux said all of a sudden, out loud.

What is a... Snubbs? Megan thought curiously.

'Who? What?' she said, thrown from Mr. Bumblebeaux's outburst.

'Snubbs by name, Snubbs by nature! My infernal Under Junior Librarian,' Mr. Bumblebeaux explained.

Megan looked blank. Though did her best to be polite and smiled warmly.

Mr. Bumblebeaux blinked.

'Righto.' Megan replied, attempting to absorb all of the events.

'Oh, yes. I mean, Snubbs be my apprentice. Fine Elf. Though always flitting about with his head in the clouds.'

'Literally,' added Megan.

'Ha! Yes, yes. Very witty!' Mr. Bumblebeaux laughed, as he weeded at his white whiskers.

Megan heehawed heartily.

Mr. Bumblebeaux laughing along with her.

Grinning, Megan plowed on.

Later in the magical jaunt...

'Where is Snubbs?' Megan asked, wondering if he were to pop-up, out-of-the-blue.

'Snubbs has probably gotten his mind lost in the tons of sonnets, orchestral overtures and drafted preparatory writings. We're cataloging them all, and inter-collating all miscellaneous scraps of musings into the main jamble. Quite an undertaking, I'm sure you'd agree.' Mr. Bumblebeaux puffed up his tiny chest.

Megan nodded sagely.

Though she was, in truth, rather blinded by what she had just been witness to in speech-form. Sensing this was indeed Megan's predicament, Mr. Bumblebeaux jabbed a thumb into his temple, and bid Megan to sit down.

A plump armchair looked most inviting to Megan.

They each sat regarding one another.

Megan held her breath.

'One of the last human beings to be here was a good man,' Mr. Bumblebeaux said evenly, without changing expression. 'Rather addled by the end by severe double pneumonia, which I gather is still a bother to your world.'

Megan breathed.

'I-I think so... I sometimes catch a cold.'

Mr. Bumblebeaux nodded. 'Anyhoo, he was partial to go walk-about over your glades and thickets with a spear in hand. Snubbs believes he bought that from a bazaar and the spear originated from Imperial Rome. But me thinks Snubbs has quite a fanciful imagination.' Mr Bumblebeaux sucked in his teeth.

Megan goggled.

He continued, 'I have taken the liberty of collating and cataloging all the one with the spear's work, so if you ever wanted too, you'd have a complete, stored compendium to read as a resource, or indeed for light-reading.'

'M-my. Thank you.' she said, though at a loss too know to whom an identity of such a wordsmith might be.

'You are a born written orator. A lover of words, Megan. You self-taught yourself. So did The Fairy Key do this.'

Megan smiled self-consciously.

'Don't be afraid of your mind, Megan.'

'Hmm,' she nodded, scratching her head and slightly buffeting about the chair.

She didn't want to hurt Mr. Bumblebeaux's feelings of telling him she didn't believe this was all hers, and plus how much a lot of it was to take in, so with her face smiling and looking calm, Megan felt frazzled inside.

'Well, over time you will come to understand and develop your most cherished gift. You are The Fairy

Key. And as such this castle, name, and its innards is yours and yours alone.'

A bearing weight pressed down on Megan's chest.

'Um...' Megan bit the inside of her cheek.

'It is okay. There is *all* the time.'

Megan visibly relaxed.

Tables, chairs, sofas, some small as if baby height, others much miniscule obviously for Fairies had been put in a corridor, and she only noticed them when nearly walking into a sort of chair that looked as if it had once been a sofa, sawn in half. Or eaten in half.

Megan thought flittingly and wondered if Princess Blossom had been here.

Megan went for a mooch about.

She assumed the bigger chairs, the more ordinary-sized ones she was accustomed to seeing, were here for her in preparation for her visit - for which she was very thankful for.

Chapter Twenty-Four

The Fairy Key

Megan gave a meticulous eye to the table content.

Language Consignment:
Liishengyrfa

'What is that, exactly?' Megan enquired, ever inquisitive with her curiously curious mind.

'It is Fairy speech.'

'Fairy speak?' Megan asked staringly, eyeing Mr. Bumblebeaux for the first time.

'Yes. In Fairy Land our natural language is Liishengyrfa. You can learn this too, being here, and as you're the Fabled Fairy Key, of course.'

Megan gulped.

'So you're not speaking it now?'

'No.' Mr. Bumblebeaux again nudged his half-moon spectacles up the ridge of his crooked conk. 'At present, I am employing your native tongue.'

'Righto,' Megan said, slightly understandingly.

'You thought I was uttering Liishengyrfa, but in the Magic it transfigured into making itself into a speech mode you'd recognise?'

'Err. I think so.'

'Alas, no. Though perhaps I could, and maybe as The Fairy Key you'd understand the lexicon quite perfectly. We shall try this soon. If you so wish?'

'I'd like that. I should be glad to read about it. Thank you.'

'To be quite honest, I do so enjoy using your language, too.'

'Why?'

'Mmm... well... because all languages of ages gone, civilizations here in The Enchanted Kingdom and there, in your world of the scepter'd isle, are real and lived, and do indeed still live, and as such should be kept alive and fleshed out,' he narrated. 'Knowledge need not to have constrictive bounds, Megan,' Mr. Bumblebeaux pronounced. 'I'll jot you some varied words down.'

'Of Fairy speech?'

'Quite so. So as that way you can then take them back to your world and scan them at your ease. Or you can leave them here, contained. You have choices and options, Megan.

'You can stay here, spend a day, an eternity, or pick-and-choose. The castle shan't be offended,' Mr. Bumblebeaux added as an afterthought, chuckling.

'Time doesn't work like in my

world here, does it?' It's like the rest of The Enchanted Kingdom.'

'Quite correct.' Mr. Bumblebeaux gave Megan a look to suggest she was slowly getting the hang of this.

'This castle. Its secrets. It's true self will reveal more and more as you grow. It shall mirror you, Megan, and in each turn show you something. Of course, you could go and spend an eon of your worlds time here, devour everything with words, though,' Mr. Bumblebeaux steepled his fingers in thinking. 'Though... I believe it much more better to take your time. There is no rush.' Mr. Bumblebeaux had caught sight of the gleam in Megan's eyes, caused by the wondrous thoughts forming that must be here.

Megan pressed the palm of her right hand against her forehead.

'Erm...' she muttered.

'Isn't this place just something!' Mr. Bumblebeaux harmonized lyrical.

'All the books,' Megan whispered sincerely, 'it's breathtaking. I can read all of these?' she asked, still timidly, not still believing this was truly hers, and if daring to accept it were, would mean it all evaporated in an instant.

'Yes,' Mr. Bumblebeaux confirmed. 'You can read each and every single book, document, parchment... well, everything. It belongs to you and the castle of Pandragon's Key. For you are Foretold as The Fairy Key, decreed and anointed by The Brim-Tree.'

'I... am,' Megan said, half-questioning.

'*You* are the Foretold Fairy Key.' Mr. Bumblebeaux regaled.

'Beg you pardon?' asked Megan, startled beyond belief.

'What is it that is the pardon for?'

'Erm... I just thought: even you know of The Fairy Key? I mean... me?'

She had been that concerned before with helping Princess Blossom return home to The Enchanted Kingdom and Fairy Land, she'd never really thought too question how Princess Blossom, Nugget, well everyone, seemed to know of her.

Mr. Bumblebeaux eyed Megan.

'You, or rather scrap that, you as The Fairy Key, have been foreshadowed as a harbinger for a long time here.

'Not only in Fairy Land, so all manner of Fairy folk know of you,' Mr. Bumblebeaux explained. 'But all of The Enchanted Kingdom know of The Fairy Key.'

Megan's face looked like a white-sheeted ghost.

'Oh.'

'What-t's a harbbb?' Megan's tongue felt thick.

'Harbinger?'

Megan nodded.

'A sort of bringer. Though for you, yours is because it *is* you.'

'I...'

Mr. Bumblebeaux looked bowlegged as he flew about Megan's head, her coiling hair spiraling in strands, giving her a look of Medusa with her snaky mane. 'You chose to help the powerless.'

Megan sat forward in her sludge-green seat. 'W-who?'

Mr. Bumblebeaux grinned. 'My Princess Blossom. You did not think of your own person, I should imagine?' Mr. Bumblebeaux smiled. 'You listened to Blossom's story and her sadness, and then wanted too help.'

'I-I.' Megan's voice shook.

'Without your help, Princess Blosom could not have made it back here. Even your immediate safety didn't occur too you nor phase you. You chose to empower yourself, and, in doing just so, empowered the powerless.'

Mr. Bumblebeaux bowed.

Megan remembered a flash of memory when Nugget and Prince Elfin had bowed to her, and she again felt rather flustered.

'What you achieve inwardly will change the outside world, ' said Mr. Bumblebeaux, looking thoughtful. 'Be that here, in The Enchanted Kingdom, or in your planetal world. You touch others simply by existing,' he finished, philosophically.

'T-t-h-hat's...'

'I know. Take heart: you will understand, one day.'

Megan made another sound like a frog going *ribbit.*

Mr. Bumblebeaux took in poor Megan's overwhelmed face, and added, 'Though more details you can learn over time, on the visits when you arrive here once more, in The

Kingdom.'

Mr. Bumblebeaux pushed his spectacles up the ramparts of his nose.

Megan bit the inside of her right cheek.

*

Hundreds of batched papers in the mini-reading room were packed in various sizes, according to their manuscript dimensions. Megan pulled at the topmost sheet and saw that, in fact, these were drafts because she was, at that moment, staring at a page that held lines scribbled and gouged out.

Playbills, pamphlets, charts, graphs, glyphs and strange texts were in one section, headed with: *Profiles Of Lunar Settings*

Megan's mind's eye was so full of solar-systems, planetary alignments and interstellar descriptions, that she had to shake her head to erase and start over; though she knew they'd all be stored away in her memory, rather than be cleaned away for good.

They'd traveled down a remote grey-stoned corridor, and then journeying out in the high-walled foyer, realised that they'd been down the adjoining pink-stoned corridor that had the cramped vary-sized sofas.

'This is different!' Megan said in a spirited tone.

'I think Pandragon's Key, and the All Souls Librarium within, is re-arranging itself.' Mr. Bumblebeaux assessed, perceptibly.

Megan's left arm ached for some reason.

She waggled it about like a cricket bat.

Mr. Bumblebeaux had followed a way and they found themselves back to a place they'd not trod nor flown before.

A door was banging open, as its other was left looking closed. Mr. Bumblebeaux flew on in, and Megan walked past the half-closed door. It was a bit of a tight-fit to get through the frame, specially making it so she had to bend over.

Once through, though, the room was a sight!

Megan, engrossed, read along the titles of the slips of parchment sticking out with handwritten titles on each book, relating to the book it was resting out of.

Leather-bound books, girth immense, and others were teeny-weeny little palm-sized volumes. Titles with their front-covers showing out, read:

A Magic History of The Enchanted Kingdom

The Battle of Abraxus and the History of All Connected up to Key, by noted Parnish Pollum

Lands in a Compendium, by distinguished Enchantedtopographer, Helenius Hoodlam

A Miscellany Of The Magic Of Time, Uni Wanverisv

Proudfoot's Prolific Ponderings On Magic Power

Mrs. Garbles Syllabus

Swinging her neck back, Megan saw, in the room, which was big enough to comfortably sit a stadium, that over on the other side was a stone fireplace. Its hearth looked long-cold and was in ornate stone, tens of feet long and wide, and clinging up the ceiling where the counterpointing effigy figures crept up and then on to the wall with the fireplace, spreading out to the storeroom's two-half-square walls, on that side of the reading repository.

One of many tables was situated directly in her path. It was walnut, very heavy, impossibly long, and around its black-leaden corners were all manner of chairs: spindly ones, clumpy ones, some with their ornate fabric gleaming from an unseen inner power which made Megan, even not quite near to its location upon the flagstone tiles, could feel the toasty warmth, that was emanating an audible sound. Corner tables, chairs, some were pristine, others less so but equally charming with stuffing or springs *boinging* out of their worn riptides.

A party of high-necked, wing-backed chairs stood upright. Megan sat, and rested a heel on the accompanying periwinkle-pink, squishy foot-stall.

Megan's hands delved over the manuscripts on the high-standing table nearest to her, and she traced her right forefinger over the near-faint letters, some hampered-up and more used sparingly on single sheaves of rolled-out paper. A manner of something sweet, not unlike an onion slightly permeated the air.

But as Megan carried on her examined viewings, the percolating aroma evaporated.

Leaving only a stale smell, and then nothingness.

Chapter Twenty-Five

Marmaduke's Maritime Miscellaneous Misadventures

'These were wonderful examples of illustrations of Medieval castles from your world.'

Megan looked to the frayed binding cache, signed with an inscription on a top-sheet:

Rockby RX

She had no notion of who RX was. *Does Rockby mean the cook who first baked a rockcake?* Megan thought. *Or is RX the person who first found a Tyrannosaurs Rex bones?*

Her mind came back as Mr. Bumblebeaux was speaking to her about, '...Pandragon's Key has been an independent institution.'

Megan smiled along.

The domain had changed into a slightly large room, after having passed plinths with missing busts, rowed opposite one another down a long corridor.

This room had been put back from the main thoroughfare, and if walking down, as Megan did, they'd be no doorframes to see. That was until one suddenly came into view as if summoned!

The table Megan had moved on to had small comic drawings, about which also dwelt pink chrysanthemums, gold pendants and silver lockets.

The quality was of such a standard Megan thought, *Mum would wear those*.

One smaller table was deserted. But a next one, more oblong, had mottled manuscript piles.

The igniting floral scent was still in the air as she moved on.

Next to what looked like a cubbyhole, which was just back from the main room, a table had a gigantic board-backed catagloue, with gold leaf on the front cover denouncing: InterMagic Gallery. 102

Opals were attached on the cover, and matching gems had been decorated about the gold-fastened clasped book.

Megan sidestepped into the alcove behind the table.

Her fingers sifted over wire-bound descriptive logs.

'Oh, Mr. Bumblebeaux! This is all so exciting!' Megan said in joy.

'I'm muchly heartened you feel so! And you may well be more, to know we have the current used label,' Mr. Bumblebeaux indicated, 'then move on to a more fullest catalogue description, like those bigger indexes, and you even have the very earliest entries!'

Megan obtained approval by looking at Mr. Bumblebeaux, who nodded. 'Of course! Read away! This is yours, after all!'

Megan ran a careful hand over the volume; her fingers took in the embossed covers, which on the front, had a pink motif of a pyramid.

Check-marks stuck out the top of the book, and peeling the volume open, notations were in the margins and extensive footnotes had been scribbled at the very bottom of the text; sometimes the actual lettering was so very teeny, Megan fancied she'd need a sphered glass just to read it.

Megan couldn't distinguish the words.

Mr. Bumblebeaux produced a piece of paper out of his right waistcoat pocket.

'I'll just put these jottings from Miss Floorburk into the book.'

'Who?' asked Megan.

'The Accumulator Of Magic Cataloging Stores.'

'That sounds like a very important job.'

'It is. The Junior under my tutelage cares for it, as I do with The Junior, and all everyone else, as overseer. Though there is a sub-division I am supervising of Non-Magic Cataloging Stores, which was created because we found our Magic items were growing so much, the Nons just couldn't be kept in a storeroom of their own.'

'Because the Magic Catalogues were becoming so big?'

'That's it exactly!'

Megan's right cheek twitched occasionally.

A thought was still niggling in the back of her mind.

Megan felt the base of her back turn

cold.

'Is... Lucy... still OK?'

A pressure forced itself behind Megan's eyes.

'Lucy, that is to say The Dragon Keeper, will be fine. Trust me. Trust in The Enchanted Kingdom.'

'I do,' Megan said robustly.

Mr. Bumblebeaux smiled as she nodded fervently, then turned aside from the alcove and tables, and his jingly-jangly legs kept on going left then right as he flew on.

Shortly thereafter...

Megan cruised on leisurely.

The route Mr. Bumblebeaux took was not disastrous, as she once may possibly have feared.

Megan was feeling safe.

The corridor housed mini-tables, on which each had a spoonful of porridge-looking mixture that was somehow suspended in the air, with the glop spreading in a fan on the table's surface.

Megan walked by one such ornate table in gold trim, and looked to the ladleful of pottidge.

Mr. Bumblebeaux's eyes were set in half-lids.

'Tastes rather nice, though can get cemented in the mouth quite a lot!'

Megan fixed the Elf with bright eyes.

Unsteadily, Mr. Bumblebeaux went on.

Out of the corner of her eye, she saw the flitting felt-green knee-trousers, dusty-looking black boots and gold-tasseled waistcoat over a white, high-necked shirt and his feathery legs were in a fawn-coloured hose.

Mr. Bumblebeaux smiled at her.

At one end of the corridor, gates barred any entrance.

Megan wanted to overtake Mr. Bumblebeaux, and look at those iron-railing gates more closely; not that she had any notion of pushing them open. Simply only to see them up-close.

'You should go there on another visit.' Mr. Bumblebeaux advised.

'Not quite now... though?'

'Well. If you did, then you may miss the fun that's here, and should you go up to those gates, and maybe a nose beyond, then when you come back to this spot...'

'The corridor might have moved itself?'

'See! You're getting the hang of this lark already!'

Megan blushed.

Mr. Bumblebeaux looked as if he may burst into a tune any moment.

Megan smiled shyly.

'Off we go!'

'W-where?'

'A room.' he said, leading the way.

'Of course!' Megan almost wanted to slap her hand on her head.

'Here, try this one,' Mr. Bumblebeaux said, after they'd wove on for a little while.

Megan was feeling a sense of becomingly much safer.

The room itself she trod into was crammed and yet in parts, particularly up in the ceilings, the room seemed to be baggy and humped in non-straight lines.

Megan turned away from the ceiling.

The tightness in Megan's head gradually lifted.

Fragile-looking charts were hung on tapestries in the air. The table nearest her looked as if someone had emptied out the bottom of their pencil-case on it.

'Feel free to go for a walk-about.' Mr. Bumblebeaux injected.

Megan did.

Pencil shavings were dotted around on the tables. *Is there not a bin in here?* Megan thought.

Increasingly, the prosperous tables with their booty of pencil snippets thinned-out as she went by the bookshelves, which were assailed with volumes and folios.

Megan couldn't help feeling as if she was intruding.

She went back to some of the tables hunched together in a crew.

The society of bureau-edges held writing surfaces with etched-in scarred workings. Megan thought that they also were under the whole tables and smaller desks, save made invisible by the hoard of papers.

Megan poured over the papers with their blank-sides flat down.

Bent down she espied margins, some left empty and then Megan sighted others with teensy writing, which gave way to their pages of scraps of ink and pencil, or ink splodges on the plain sheefs of cream-white paper.

'Such disarray!' Mr. Bumblebeaux proclaimed.

Megan angled her head over her heels.

'Of course nothing can be touched or cleaned-up,' he explained, moving in the general direction of nowhere, 'because the room likes how it is presented. Even if shambolic!'

A sensation of power prickled in these hallowed halls.

Megan quickly withdrew her fingers.

This place, the room, and all of Pandragon's Key, had the knack for the absolute out-and-out mysterious.

Megan felt slightly shaken.

Mr. Bumblebeaux smiled as he saw her move on to the other side of the room, which had a wall lined with bookcases.

Megan walked up to the irresistible bookshelves.

Betwixt the bookcases was a ladder which could be moved around on a wheeling contraption; so as the ladder had the ability to be pushed left or go right, or back and then forth, then once used, be snuck back in-between the bookshelves.

Megan scratched an itch on her left cheek.

Books by her held gilt-golden lettering on their spines.

Megan scrutinized a book she'd taken out from the shelf: a pink pyramid symbol was emblazoned on to a shining, glossy pink fabric, wing-backed tall chair.

She could establish the edition was old. Stupendously old.

The book was abnormally light, Megan thought, considering it looked like it weighed an astronomical size.

The other tomes around on the bookshelves didn't lack such a grand air either; scores were of gold-gilt edging, or hundreds more cloth-bound.

Megan turned the age-old pages that creaked slightly when flipped over. Torn-out pages had a slashed appearance, which look very sad. The other paper halves could not be seen.

Megan sifted through the wordlist, then glossary, and came into a heading section of illustrations: she saw a clear glass tube, with a pink rose inside was on the first page of the layered illustrated works.

The encyclopedia demanded the final curtain fall.

Megan saw how this book was unlike its others, because they had bookmarks sticking out their pages, with tiny writing hosting a subjected title.

The bookish situation was rather

wonderful for Megan.

'Some books, eh.' Mr. Bumblebeaux said.

Megan nodded in agreement.

'A lot can be learnt from any of these.' Mr. Bumblebeaux philosophized.

Megan gathered her senses.

The colours in the book were starting to have a lullaby effect.

Megan touched here and there.

Each luminous colour was a work in itself.

The pages blurred as lines blended together. As she picked up the next page with her left forefinger, she saw something jarring in the subject bar at the top of the chapter:

The Fairy Key

Megan squashed down a cry of shock.

She closed the book with a thud.

'The illuminating illustrations are

most stellar, hymm?' Mr. Bumblebeaux said, putting a small volume of work back on to a shelf, which for some reason, had been left on the red-and-gold hearth-rug on the floor.

Megan smiled back.

She put the book back unregretfully to its home.

The source of the dusty smell faded as the gap in the shelf went on in book standing order.

Megan walked over to by where Mr. Bumblebeaux was hurriedly packing up books into a brown cardboard box. 'Would you like a hand?' she asked helpfully.

Mr. Bumblebeaux smiled.

'If you could please put that one in here, ' he nodded to the book's place, whilst his arms strained to hold one hardback book. 'That would be a great help, t-thank you.'

Megan added the book to the piles

within the boxed crate, and saw Mr. Bumblebeaux firming tape down along the open edge. He flew over to a table, picked up a label and a little-finger-sized pencil, and wrote a word on the non-sticky mailing sheet.

'Won't that come off?' Megan watched.

'Oh no. Magic will hold this in place. Look...'

Mr. Bumblebeaux pressed the cargo-label on the box's lid, and each end rolled down from the middle like an unwinding slug. That then wouldn't come off, even as he demonstrated to Megan. 'It has to be asked to come off, then in a jiffy it does so.'

Megan's microscopic eyes went tray-sized.

'Do we need to take the box anywhere?'

'How kind of you! Though one of the Juniors of this Wing will oversee the delivery transportation.' Mr.

Bumblebeaux explained, with a smile.

Leaving the box by the first bookcase, he flew to a table. Megan walked idly by and looking back, then on, and then looking back again, saw the accompanying lettering on sheets of paper transfigure into star symbols.

Megan was hooked.

Spindly traces of handwriting were scattered over the parchment.

Megan lassoed for an answer but just couldn't think of one.

Looking at words and symbols re-arranging themselves fluidly, she thought, *Magic*.

It felt just right to look, and wasn't at all scary.

Megan's perspective was closer as she knelled down.

Set back from this table, smaller trestle tables were under the papers which piled on to their surfaces. Shadows played under the sheets, and as the words kept on moving about the pages like hyper millepedes, she carefully and respectfully hefted a few up by their corners and placed them in the same state on an empty table-top to her right.

Books had been hiding under the sheets.

Megan's shaky fingers hesitated above the books:

Marmaduke's Maritime Miscellaneous Misadventures

The Unsighted Crone by Hansan & Gertrudel

The Dragons Specified Dragarum History, Felicity Lettice

Mary Celeste

Neptune, by Norris Newt

Magic Geographical Survey, Melinda the Mermaid

Chapter Twenty-Six

The Pink Four-Poster

The air constricted as if an Amazonian anaconda was coiled and tightening in on itself.

Megan recovered herself.

The deserted room was apparent with books; books on top on each other, books in lined formations on the pink-cobble-stoned floor, books on diagonally-placed catawumpus shelving so over walls, big ZZZZZ's were keeping the books from tipping and falling down like tin soldiers.

Mr. Bumblebeaux was busily doing something behind her, to Megan's right. She looked over.

Mr. Bumblebeaux, in a rustling *frou-frou* sound, was piling up the cerise-pink drapes of a four-poster bed!

It was so beautiful.

The bed had been lost in the book-crazed confusion of the room, and now Megan could dissect the boundary of the bed from the books around it, as if summoned from a person who could, or would not, fall asleep.

It was so unexpected a bed!

Megan left the short range of the table on which sat *Marmaduke* and the other books.

Megan stepped forward.

As she moved over, the room itself with the four-walls stepped back. An airy space was now about the bed. Spacious gaps gave way to the books.

Megan dared only so far go with ignoring to not think on the possibility of what Magic was in here.

The bed had engorged out, and like a rubber dingy being blown-up, the bed-frame had grown as well.

'Oh goodness,' Megan said, in a small, respectful voice.

The drapes of the bed flew into many colours of pinks, each stitching themselves as if seamstresses were working on them. But no hands were seen!

The threads of ribbon and stitches of material fused and even though the bed before was beautiful, how it had amended itself gave Megan a hearty sight!

Are Fairies here but I can't see them? Nothing dared fit with Megan as to how the bed had done this - so she cast each possible thought out. It was simply Magic.

The pink drapes folding themselves back on the wooden posts bled down into a russet quilt cover, this was giving way to pink and-gold stitched threaded embroidery, trimmed with pink clouds of foofaraw tulle.

Megan wagered that whoever this

bed belonged to was completely lucky.

Megan had no idea what to do with her hands.

'Have a feel, if you want!' Mr. Bumblebeaux said, standing on the massive wooden bed-head, which had magical creatures carved into it.

Megan loved the touch of the bedlinen.

'So *soft*.'

'And old. Much like me!'

Megan smiled back.

'That was once an Egyptian thread-count, if I remember rightly.'

'Oh right.' Megan said, failing to know if that were good or bad.

She loved the touch and feel of the softness of the fine cloth. Gold and silver stars were running on the quilt. Amid these dots, were pink stitched triangles.

'Myself, I am very much inclined towards the stars. Such beautifully created...'

'Stars?' added Megan, smiling.

'Y-yes. No matter!' Mr Bumblebeaux said, lost to himself there for a moment.

'The pyramids are just as nice.'

'Mmm... you think so?'

Megan smiled and nodded.

She felt as if she were being tested on something. The fact she had mentioned the triangular symbols in passing seeming to be the crux.

Mr. Bumblebeaux, Megan thought, looked at her approvingly in the same way he looked at his student Juniors when teaching.

'Let's go and look at a few books.'

Megan nodded slowly.

She looked back to the bed; just to see if it remained there.

'The bed usually stays in the same state you first saw it,' Mr. Bumblebeaux explained, as they moved about the winding rows of books columns.

'Does someone sleep in the bed?' Megan asked.

'What was that, dear?'

Mr. Bumblebeaux had gone out of the range of hearing.

'Does somebody use the bed to sleep in?' Megan repeated, more louder.

'Oh good gracious, no!'

Megan caught her breath.

Have I asked the right thing or the wrong thing? Megan was just not certain which.

Mr. Bumblebeaux smiled.

'The bed is for rest; a sit down and a read. The bed is not to be slept in. Well, unless it agrees to it.'

Megan stared back. 'Agrees?'

'Why yes. The bed can be fussy. You did very well before!'

Megan felt all discomboobulated.

'W-what does the bed do if it doesn't like someone, or want to be touched?'

'Why, it'll either toss you off, or the bed will fold in on the occupant.'

'Fold in?'

Mr. Bumblebeaux looked back, nodded, then his elbows disturbed a pile of books. 'Y-yes... thank you,' he said, as Megan helped him steady the books threatening to burst out of order. 'Where was I? Oh yes! The bed! Well, if the bed folds in on you, then it'll dispel you somewhere else.'

'Where?' Megan's mind was whirling.

'Oh, nothing like a dungeon!'

Megan laughed.

Mr. Bumblebeaux smiled.

'No no. Some other part of Pandragon's Key.'

'So you'd sit on the bed, and either be thrown off, or eaten and find yourself - '

' - not in the same room, that's for sure!'

Nothing had changed for Megan; she still loved the bed, even more so now for some reason.

Megan's spirits thrived.

The room Mr. Bumblebeaux had flown into had high ceilings, that ran into heights lost to Megan's sight.

Fastened books were of clasps, inlaid with coloured jeweled precious stones.

'Charming, mm?'

Megan nodded to Mr. Bumblebeaux.

A fireplace and grate stood empty of any impending roaring fire.

Ink stains were on a piece of old-looking parchment that read

The Palimpsest Who

Captions, and copious textual depictions of descriptive Mermaids and Dragons were by the parchment of the *Palimpsest*.

'Move on! Have a nose! Mr. Bumblebeaux said hurriedly.

Megan beamed.

On tables, periodicals of examples from centuries long since gone, were in a chronological state. 'All these rows of books, indeed all the historical volumes and associated papers, run in numerical order.'

Megan was a tad perplexed.

'Oh no! I do hope you are not unnerved?'

Megan shook her head. 'It's just a lot to take in!'

Particles of Fairy dust nursed the air as Megan moved her head about.

Some of the dust fell on scrolling penmanship that was on manuscripts; some crumpled, some starch-straight.

Megan shook from head-to-toe.

Ripped binding showed on a few books, whilst others more looked as good as new from the day of being bound and published.

Megan felt as if all the titles were staring at her accusingly.

'These will all still be here, Megan. For you,' he assured, with firm certainty.

Megan's cheeks rosy reddened hotly.

'I... thank you.' She said slightly tightly.

Megan found she couldn't think straight.

'How about I show you now smaller parts of All Souls Librarium?'

Megan's mind still pitched and careened from her bewilderments at what she had seen.

'I should think that the mere fact this all exists can be a lot?'

Megan nodded, gratefully.

'Well, let's have no more struggle!' Mr. Bumblebeaux said.

Megan felt comfortable; at ease, serene. In truth, she had always felt that - even with feeling daunted by all she'd saw.

Megan's eyed followed Mr. Bumblebeaux's sweeping hands.

'This part of Pandraon's Key we're ascending goes up and down, and left-then-right.'

'H-how easy is it to - '

' - lose one's way?'

Megan nodded.

'Quite easily so!'

Megan's eyelids twitched.

'Many an instance I've sent a Junior here for some such errand, and they became lost, or the castle moves them about if so feels like it.' Mr. Bumblebeaux shrugged.

He took his place outside a smaller corridor, out of which Megan heard an arisen babbling sound.

'Books.'

'Books?'

'Books talking to one another.' Mr. Bumblebeaux accounted.

'Books here *talk?*'

'How else would they learn?'

A feeling of mulled senses washed into Megan.

'Not all books, of course.'

Megan nodded. 'O-of course.'

'Some are just books; paper, binding, and inanimate objects. Though others, the more senior citizen ones, or what would be deemed ancient, like to converse with each other.'

Megan had never dealt with a talking book before.

'Let's see what's hidden behind this door, shall we?'

Megan's neck moved side-to-side.

A timbre-paneled door with a black iron door handle opened. Inside, fenced with small gates, in spaces, the room looked overgrown with treasures: books.

Chapter Twenty-Seven

Roller-Coaster Road

Megan crossed her arms as she went a walk-about.

Mr. Bumblebeaux flew startlingly level to her shoulder-height.

Megan fleetingly caught sight of one hard-backed book bearing the name *Cornelius*

The gated community of books were ringed in such a way that a pathway cut through each of the thigh-high fences.

Megan groaned as she padded on, not wanting any of the fences over in a spilt way; lest they disturb the books.

Megan's face was smooth in concentration.

'Don't understand the title,' she said drily, standing next to a gold-tasseled book, inside the enclosure of the fence.

Megan found she could only sustain reading these for a brief moment.

Poetical lines washed over Megan's understanding, opaque.

'There will be time, don't worry!' Mr. Bumblebeaux assured.

Megan gradually looked from the piled poetry over the pieces of papers, and then scurried on, dismissing the poems for now, and this time staring raptly.

Megan examined the rickety tables in the part of the room, down from the door entrance-way.

A danger sort of look a book had. It was lava-red, big, had a gold manacled chain strapped around it and was topmost on a pile. She went on, glossing over this novel and on to other books.

Megan wasn't quite certain about the fences. Then an idea came to her.

Megan gazed at the book, thoughtfully.

A wooden stool was by the fence.

'Feel free to have a look.' Mr. Bumblebeaux said at once, in a reassuring sort of way.

Megan looked on with an expression of interest.

She sat on the stool, not fully, and made sure that the three legs didn't tip over.

Megan squatted down.

There was only inches of space to spare in this one fence.

Megan was avidly staring at a book the colour of a cream éclair.

'Try touching the fence... see what happens,' Mr. Bumblebeaux said, mystifyingly.

Megan's face turned; she was staring at the very back of a fence, enclosed within were books.

Megan fancied she saw a cooper tankard poking out of two books butted together!

Megan listened to the silence around her.

Some of the fences at the back of the room were about as tall as Megan, who was a well-grown little girl for her age.

Megan stretched her fingers out to the books.

Her slightly quailing fingers neared the wire which looked as if plucked from a chicken-shed on a gardener's allotment. At the touch of her skin from her oncoming hand, the spaghetti-like fence ties unraveled, then rippled back!

Megan beavered about, reading.

A scrap of paper had symbols which were all disorderly and untidy. Great big words that looked something like Chinese were written over, under, and sided by smaller text of squared numbers. The words read:

astrological numbers, arithmetic, trigonometry, context linked numeral system, positional numbers, numbers and values positioned in context decimals infers as the function to notate the 59 non-zero - and functionality of any sign value notations, the measurement of space in Time and Magic, highly composite number of Nine has its radix point in the prime factorization of Magic Three

Sheltering underneath the paper was a dried soft tablet, digits had been impressed from reeds on to the tablet's top surface. They looked like some sort of funny-looking words and sums.

The contents of which Megan had never ever seen before now.

Without her knowing, Mr.

Bumblebeaux backed away.

The fence-book room where Megan spent so much time, and looked as if a three-ringed circus could fit cozily in, already now had a familiarity to it.

Megan withdrew her head out from over the wire fence. In spite of the fence moving itself, and allowing her gain entry in, she had had enough; for now.

Megan looked up at him.

Mr. Bumblebeaux smiled as if he understood.

Megan released the book of *Peregrine Wannammaker's Magic Merywether Words*

Beyond the fences, far across the other side of the room, a door swung open on its own axis.

Megan smiled slightly.

Mr. Bumblebeaux directed to Megan to go, if she so wanted.

Megan got up from the seat, and put the stool back in the place she had taken it from. She tried to make sure the legs were in the same position; there was no dirt on the floor to have now seen clean-spots, though Megan had been alert to which way the legs were situated, and did want too disrespect the room by leaving the stool in any other way than all present and right.

The door had not been properly closed.

Megan had looked back, and over her left shoulder, saw the one door remained closed, and the other that had opened on its own, and of which she had walked through, and Mr. Bumblebeaux flown, this door kept itself open only by a crack.

The door did not bang shut.

Megan did not shiver with fright.

Mr. Bumblebeaux's flyaway white hair moved about as he rushed on.

Megan strided over a well-trodden path.

Empty brackets bared no lanterns.

Walls and the ceiling were gold blushed.

The ground in this part of All Souls Librarium, inside Pandragon's Key, was of like a road. Pink cobblestone-flag-stoned paving, made Megan go about slightly over the uneven bumps, like a Will-Not-Go-Down Rubber Ducky in a full bubbly bathtub.

Mr. Bumblebeaux's visible flight was straight-on.

Whether on purpose or not from Megan walking slowly on it, the ground, most frighteningly, heaved like a massive turtle was upping its shell-back.

Megan went from right-to-left, then left-to-right. Forth-and-back, and back-and-forth.

Megan was not quite enjoying this!

Out the corner of his eye, the out-of-focus slurry shapes made Mr. Bumblebeaux look down.

'Just hold on!'

'O-on... t-t-to... wh-h-at-t?' Megan yelled.

'Hang on!'

'Aaarguh!' she was yelling in echoes, desperately.

Megan was brave.

She let the floor give its way and carry along her with it as she flopped about.

Mr. Bumblebeaux let down a hand.

Megan went to reach out.

Though, just at that exact moment, the ground went as it was before. If not mistaken, Megan thought she caught sound of the ground actually *sighing*.

With an unpleasant spring to her heart, Megan fell flat on her face, stiff as a surf board.

Megan took a deep breath.

'Well!' said Mr. Bumblebeaux.

Megan was quite sure she had not at all really liked that. The ride was like when on a scary roller-coaster at a funfair park.

She sat down on the ground.

Megan shook and nodded her head to clear out the dumpy dicky birds.

'Better?' asked Mr. Bumblebeaux.

'Much. Thank you.' Megan replied, taking her head out from leaning on her crossed forearms.

'I don't think that was a fine joke being played.'

Megan smiled.

Mr. Bumblebeaux nodded, incredibly glad she understood.

'Must be moving about, and I suppose didn't so much recognise me. So this part of Pandragon's Key moved itself, for some reason.'

Megan took a steadying breath. 'Pandragon's Key stopped when it realised I was now here?'

'Hm, surely sounds about right. Unless Key was told you were in some other section of All Souls

Librarium, though that thought would mean somebody had purposefully wanted too sabotage your visit,' said Mr. Bumblebeaux, talking now out loud, to himself.

'Why would anyone wish to do that?' Megan asked, getting up and now standing rod-straight.

'Probably isn't!' he figured, 'but that won't happen again, so fear not! Pandragon's Key would not harm you.'

Megan chortled. 'It wasn't boring though!'

Mr. Bumblebeaux faced Megan.

Megan laughed like anything.

With one hand on her head, she just-about stopped exploding in laughter as Mr. Bumblebeaux laughed with her, and she looked into his watery-brown eyes. 'Let's move forward with our perfectly wonderful time, shall we?' he asked.

Megan nodded.

Chapter Twenty-Eight

Irenie

Frail hand-written sheets, and books that looked very worse for wear had been piled on over-piled tables. Megan wouldn't have been at all surprised to hear some of the poor books snuffle and sniffle, and pull out a red and white spotted handkerchiefs, from each being sorry at their own state.

Megan thought the books looked extra cuddle-some.

The bruised books on the over-piled artifact table had also another slightly larger book, which on its front cover had a picture of a spiky tree.

Nearest to the crew of books, a monumental number of silver bracelets, a tiara and mobs of necklaces were displayed on a reading table.

The silver light was not pale. It shined of gleaming rays.

Megan took the pieces of paper in one hand.

Over her shoulder, Mr. Bumblebeaux saw Megan's fingers next clamouring over the books. She held one in her right hand *Irenie's Idioms*

Ah-ha. Good choice, Mr. Bumblebeaux thought.

A pinky-plum coloured winged armchair offered a seat, so Megan sat. She went to browse through *Irenie's* book.

Megan hesitated.

'Are you still enjoying your stay?' Mr. Bumblebeaux asked her, though interrupted himself for he was flying upside down, ' 'ere, Megan?'

Megan nodded excitedly.

Mr. Bumblebeaux's hands rose

slightly.

Megan still felt quite contented in All Souls Librarium.

'I just really like being here,' she found wit to say.

'Good job, all told! Seeing as though this is yours,' he smiled. Mr. Bumblebeux had not joined Megan, but was flying by bookshelves.

At least fifty books were on the floor, Megan noticed, as she looked about, riffling past the Edition page of the palm-sized *Irenie's Idioms*.

'You could have met Irenie,' Mr. Bumblebeaux chuntered on. 'Though she's now in Fairy Land.'

Megan looked up.

Mr. Bumblebeaux was righting himself midair. 'Fairy Land?' she asked.

'Irenie? Yes yes,' he replied, checking that none of his pockets had came undone and the deep-capacity, full-looking pockets not unhumped themselves.

'What is she doing in Fairy Land? Megan asked, not too sure if she should be minding her own business, and so if she were being a teensy bit nosey.

'From what I can recall,' Mr. Bumblebeaux responded, clearly not finding her nosey at all. 'Irenie sent me a field report after she'd journeyed and arrived near to Fairy Land's castle walls, at River Hamets, by route of Joocker, who's a Fairy student of mine, and rather stubborn at times.

'Anyway, Irenie's textual document which stated her referenced mission: a projected statement to collate, compare and collect local non-standard speech words from Fairy Land, was going outstandingly well. There are already more slang words to be accounted into her *Idioms* work,' waffled Mr. Bumblebeaux. 'Oh, and you are not unparliamentary. I doubt you could ever be impolite.'

Megan drew breath.

Pipe music had suddenly started like a record being played on a turntable. Megan half-thought there must be a sound-speaker at some such place by her, connected to the walls which were coated in glitter. She looked around. 'Are there Faeries about?'

'Bound to be,' Mr. Bumblebeaux replied, 'especially here.'

All of a sudden Megan looked round more; thinking there might be a band of Fairies playing little instruments.

Megan's face broke into a wide smile.

There were no clarinet-banding Fairies, though the astonishing music was sounding so cozie.

Megan had a breakthrough.

'Is I-Irenie's work like... Liis...' she couldn't get the word to form in her garbled-looking mouth.

'Liishengyrfa?' Mr. Bumblebeaux asked, guessing.

Megan nodded, smiling.

'Let's break the word down.'

Megan grinned more.

'Liish,' Mr. Bumblebeaux said.

'Lissh,' Megan parroted.

'Eng,' Mr. Bumblebeaux went on, with kind patience.

'Eng,' Megan echoed.

'Yrfa,' Mr. Bumblebeaux nodded.

'Yr... fa... Yrfa,' repeated Megan.

'Now, string the letters and those words together, and what do you have?' Mr. Bumblebeaux asked, his eyes shining.

'L... hang on... Liishengyrfa!' Megan pronounced, she knew she got it.

Megan caught the intense expression in Mr. Bumblebeaux's eyes. He was looking over at her from standing on a bookshelf; half ran with books, and now the other half was home to an Elf. 'You are particularly observant.'

Megan's shoulders bunched up.

'I-just-wonde - '

' - Well, your intellection was dead-cert.'

Megan shifted in her seat.

'You thought well, Megan.' Mr. Bumblebeaux's voice was deeply warm.

'T-thank you,' mumbled Megan absentmindedly, looking more closely than was necessary at the book's back cover of *Irenie's Idioms*.

Megan went red from her forehead down to her neck.

Mr. Bumblebeaux caught sight of her and smiled to himself. *What a loving little heart you have, Megan Button*, Mr. Bumblebeaux thought.

To Megan's enormous surprise, Irenie's Idioms was listing such bizarre words. She only knew them to be of Fairy because underlined chapter headings alerted <u>Fairy Land</u>, then underneath, in neat footnotes, gave which regional areas of toadstools used the lyrical-looking words.

How strange, Megan thought.

Mr. Bumblebeaux came to the seat. He stood on the points of his toes on the chair's arm.

Megan nearly jumped.

Lo and behold, she said, 'Mr. Bumblebeaux!'

'I didn't mean to give you a fright!' He laughed along.

Mr. Bumblebeaux's wings moved around a lot, making him look like he was on a see-saw at a playground.

'I'll leave you to it,' Mr. Bumblebeaux said smilingly, fluttering off.

Chapter Twenty-Nine

Spindlestein

And it was there that as Megan came by, Mr. Bumblebeaux was putting one of the books right on a shelf.

'You always do put things right, don't you Mr. Bumblebeaux?'

'I do try. As does the Megan I am coming to know, if am not mistaken?'

Megan smiled.

'Take a look at those items over there,' Mr. Bumblebeaux point-blank nodded to a table. 'I think little people in your world find such amusement from fun with playing with any of them.'

Megan swung round.

Bats and balls were by red frisbees and kites which looked scarecrowish; the washy colours of the silk were faded.

She liked the look of the kites, though the bats, balls and frisbees weren't so attractive because she found she couldn't catch as well as other children, which was why she also dreaded Games class, as well of being bullied, of course, when the Sports teacher and teaching assistant weren't in ear-shot. If Megan had her way (which she tried to make happen), she would be left well-alone by the clementine-orange coloured sack of beanbags, and blue unending hula-hoops.

Looking past the toys, Megan gazed at elaborate shelving, yet they compared curiously with the rigid sturdy grey bookcase that ran thirty feet high into the air, because its framework looked like something of a knightly period piece, and the shelves were much more ornate in gold.

Megan, having a breakthrough,

realised what this Library was. 'It *is* Magic,' she said.

She progressed down the shelves.

Megan did not look disappointed.

A prettiest of big books was on a small black plinth, up on a raised dais, much like a device her dad used when baking and cooking, taking formulas from his instructing cookery books, or inventing as he went along, writing shorthand (only he knew) in notebooks. Though his books and cookery-book gadget stand tended to be dusted in pasty flour, baking powder, and yolked into near-oblivion.

None of the books bore any signs of being held recently (of which she could see).

Megan looked hard at the glass-fronted cabinets.

A writer's name had three fore initials followed by a fuller surname:

G. H. M. Spindlestein

With a hand behind her back, Megan walked over on to the crates. She asked Mr. Bumblebeaux out of habit, 'Who's Spindlestein, please?'

'Spindlestein?'

'The name's on the front of that pink and white book... in the book cabinet?'

'Ah! Him!' Mr. Bumblebeaux remembered, slam-banging a hand to his forehead, and then picking up a cloth, passed the coca-brown coloured material over a silver drinking goblet. The chalice looked quite suitable for Megan. As he buffed-up the goblet, he added, 'I haven't seen Spindlestein round these parts for a while. Wonder where he is...'

'I-I don't know, Mr. Bumblebeaux.' Megan replied, sitting down on the edged brink of a weighty table holding no books.

'Well no, I suppose you wouldn't! How significantly invalid of me!' Mr. Bumblebeaux laughed.

Megan smiled.

'You'd like Spindlestein. Such a swashbuckler. He always has seafaring tales to tell. And other such yarns,' he said, and Megan felt very certain she would indeed like this Spindlestein.

Mr. Bumblebeaux glanced over to the long, undingyish book storage lockers.

He had not entered this cavernous room for many a while. Taking one step further in the air, Mr. Bumblebeaux looked to the book that had been such an object of curiosity the The Fairy Key had mentioned, and his thoughts then turned to The Dragon Keeper.

Mr. Bumblebeaux shook himself.

Trying to shake off the slight look of anxious worry from his face before he flew around in a flourish, smiling.

Megan looked to the sounds of the muffled voice drifting from afar down the curve of the broad, pink-beamed-ceiling corridor.

Megan heard the disguised mumblings getting a bit louder.

After a sharp turn, she walked in a slow locomotion farther down the pewter-grey corridor to the black door, where she stopped in her tracks, watched and listened.

The near-to-voice stunned Megan.

'Cannot stand he brings *her* here,' the voice was saying, 'What if they find out? Thank you very much, indeed! That does it! The nerve! The Elffool doesn't forward-think properly enough... the claptrap meddler... his devotion to The Fairy...' whoever's flat voice it was, it rose as it had gone on, getting out of hand, with a definite edge, and more odder still, the voice sounded proudly chuffed in its crafty plotting.

Megan shuddered.

Something about the voice caused some of Megan's hair on her head to stand up.

Megan shivered from feeling cold in spite the walls of Pandragon's Key thrumming with warming Magic.

Mr. Bumblebeaux flew down.

'Wonder who's in there?' whispered Megan, standing up.

He turned his head toward the closed door, latched by means of a small, barricading house-brick being in a hole that looked like a letterbox, but which instead when the handle was turned, was used as a release catch. Mr. Bumblebeaux flew closer to the door.

Megan took a deep breath.

Pressing her ear against the door, this was close enough.

Mr. Bumblebeaux gasped.

He suddenly tried to straighten himself, 'Off we go! No need to loiter here!'

Megan half-smiled.

Mr. Bumblebeaux nodded vigorously.

Megan was trying to clear her ears out. Her fingers tightened on the wall for a more better grasp; otherwise she was nearing falling over like a coat-stand bearing far too many raincoats and bags.

'We should be off,' Mr. Bumblebeaux said.

Megan very nearly leapt up.

'Why?' Megan softly asked, reasonably.

The obstacle of the door was still having mumblings on its other side. But muttering with Mr. Bumblebeaux made her miss some of the stranger's scheming words, though she heard the venting voice now sounding more wildly pleased than ever, 'The dingbat. He does not have the brains I posses... The idiot... mind, on the other Elfhand, come to think of it, I have waited sensibly, so a few more wasted waiting's won't matter... I would give my right wing for it; if I had one. No, 'tis not entirely circumstantial. I alone fulfill the requirement for the job of - '

' - Come on, Megan.'

She looked up. Mr. Bumblebeaux was smiling, humming to himself.

Megan exchanged a smile with Mr. Bumblebeaux.

'Megan,' he began firmly, making a grab for her arm.

She looked away from him, back to the grumbling door.

Megan didn't answer.

She pressed her ear more closer still to the barred door.

Mr. Bumblebeaux tugged at her right elbow.

Megan shrugged a little.

'OK-K,' she answered, scrambling to her feet.

She knew it to be rather rude to listen into others discussions, though something about that nasally flat, not nice voice made Megan feel like she'd caught a cold.

Mr. Bumblebeaux waved her on.

Megan walked away.

And she had the oddly uncanny feeling the voice was talking about her.

Chapter Thirty

To Cough Glitter And Sneeze Sequins

Megan's eyes looked puzzled.

'Do try to turn your mind away from what you heard.'

Megan gazed up at Mr. Bumblebeaux.

There was a thread in the sentence that Megan felt she needed to yank on.

Mr. Bumblebeaux cast her a thoughtful look.

'Honestly,' he went on, 'there's some niggling squabbling here, concerning Magic inter-departments. Only pomposity. But all will be well.'

Megan smiled.

But she couldn't quite see Mr.

Bumblebeaux's face because he was now zipping so far up.

Mr. Bumblebeaux didn't say another word on the subject. The real reason Mr. Bumblebeaux had judged it a time to hurry Megan away from the closed door, she could not think of. She promised herself she wouldn't ask more; Mr. Bumblebeaux had very clearly not wanted to join in with her guessing-game of Who Owns The Voice?

Megan felt very confused.

Mr. Bumblebeaux looked now sideways at her, finally he said, cheerfully, 'Care for another turn?'

Megan hadn't even realised Mr. Bumblebeaux was so close.

He looked rather troubled, though happy.

Mr. Bumblebeaux smiled.

Megan smiled back.

'Come again?' Mr. Bumblebeaux said.

'I said I'm glad I didn't turn the pink

brick in the door,' said Megan in such a undefeated tone at the shuddery, that Mr. Bumblebeaux laughed one burst-out laugh. 'Look around!' said he.

Megan, still feeling slightly frustrated, stared around the bare room as if expecting to spy something quite exceptionally extraordinary in there with them.

'Oh, it's gone.'

'What's gone?' Megan asked, disappointingly.

'You'll see...'

'Is it playing hide-and-seek?'

Mr. Bumblebeaux cocked his head to one side. 'In a way, yes.'

'OK.'

Megan still could no see anything in there, with them. She paused, looked out beyond the jaggy doorway then walked out.

'When ready, it'll show itself too you.'

'When who's ready? Me?'

'Or it. My, you are very clever and thoughtful!'

Megan's cheeks blushed a crimson rosiness.

Far down the bricked and walled corridor, Megan turned right.

She saw at once the light, owing to the slivers of gold light being cast out from under the gaps in a closed door, to her left.

Megan kept her ears open for any more voices overhead, underfoot and anywhere else in-between.

'That looks n-nice.' Megan said, a little nervously, from the light.

Mr. Bumblebeaux replied, grinning, 'It does indeed.'

A thought popped up for Megan. 'It's still alright that we're here?'

'We are not intruders here. *You* are not a trespasser.'

Megan still couldn't believe what she was being told.

Mr. Bumblebeaux's sticking-out

eyebrows shot up. 'What I say is the truth.'

Megan took in the hushed quietness.

Megan sighed.

Moseying on down the small, crammed corridor, she still felt overwhelmed.

'Please don't feel overcome. I understand the prospect is a tad daunting and - '

' - Scarey,' Megan finished.

'Exactly,' Mr. Bumblebeaux said.

Megan traced the hem of her top.

'Though take heart that this is yours, and there is time, as discussed,' he thoughtfully reiterated. 'All the time, for you and you alone.'

Megan didn't dare believe this was the truth. All This. For her.

Megan still did not tire greatly.

Her footsteps rang and echoed on the cobblestones of the floor, 'Will P-

Pandragon's Key-y go?'

Mr. Bumblebeaux puffed up his chest.

'Never,' he replied. 'Pandragon's Key, The Fairy Key Land and All Souls Librarium will always be here for you. Even if in your world, it's the next day you visit here, or the following week.'

'Because time works so differently?'

Mr. Bumblebeaux looked at Megan, and her hanging question. 'Your attentiveness does you credit, Megan.'

Megan's mouth tightened.

'Thank you,' she blushed.

The corridor lay still as Mr. Bumblebeaux flew from side-to-side like a ping-pong ball.

'What you say is correct,' he said, making his wings flap a little more smoother, 'time's so very different here. Although you wouldn't age here, physically, you could spend hundreds of your years here and then go back, and you'd return in the same second.

'As for The Fairy Key Land, and all composed within, I am merely the custodian here. Resolutely in place for you,' Mr. Bumblebeaux said, with a fierce pride.

Megan rearranged herself.

Megan touched her right cheekbone.

Somewhere up on one of the higher levels, Pandragon's Key and All Souls Librarium was moving itself to goodness knows where, and in which parts an unsuspecting quiet Magic creature would be now hurled screamingly to. The vomiting moans of the rooms, contents, walls, floorboards, Wings, grounds, staircases, and foundations and ceilings were very creaky as they let loose.

'Are there ghosts here?' Megan asked, standing still.

Mr. Bumblebeaux steamed his spectacles with his breath, wiped them on his waistcoat then reapplied them back on. 'No. There be no phantoms or ghouls here.'

Megan trekked on.

'Look.'

'At what?'

'At that behind you.' Mr. Bumblebeaux held his arm out to stop her.

Megan turned around in a Sargent Major's Officer move.

The air shimmied and moved on to itself in folds, like a batter being whipped in a bowl with a spatula.

Megan stared about her.

Something totally extraordinary was there.

This surprised Megan.

Mr. Bumblebeaux had happily pointed out a flash of gold light. The gold lightning, incredibly, took on a build-up for an even bright golden light down the corridor's winding passage. The gliding light did not look normal.

Megan's face scrunched up as though someone had lit a camping torch right in her face.

The cloud was strange and mysterious, and that ferocious in intensity that Megan thought it might have blown the roof off.

Megan armoured her eyes.

'The light's OK.' Above, Mr Bumblebeaux was glad that Megan didn't have a look of terror upon her face.

Megan didn't seem at all upset.

She brought her hands down.

Megan's face split into a smile.

Neither of them stayed closed-mouthed. Megan's was dropped-open, and Mr. Bumblebeaux said, 'I forgot how beautiful this place is... I spend so much time with my head clobbered in ledgers.'

Megan recalled other lights she'd

seen when having fought Abraxus. None of those lights could contend with the one now revealing itself getting bigger and more rounder. Nor did she think any others ever could.

'W-what is it?' Megan asked Mr. Bumblebeaux, wondering aloud in amazement.

Mr Bumblebeaux spoke more, 'The light's just doing its workout, if you will. It'll be gone in a jiffy.'

Megan gasped.

Showers of streaming stars whizzed through the crackling air. The fizz-popping stars fell short of Megan.

She stared more than ever, as the gold light fumes were altogether more than anything that Megan had ever seen of lights. It even beat the one a little earlier she remembered watching with its spangling silvern stars.

Megan eyed the cloud.

It took quite a while for the extravaganza of the lightning to flutter off, leaving melting fluffy gold blobs that vanished quickly. All of a sudden, gold shooting stars sprayed out and they, too, also departed into whizzing thin-air.

Megan stared open-mouthed.

Nine times the amount of shooting stars mingled with air and then liquified in gold, silver and pink lights that then suddenly *puffed* out, right in the air between where Megan was stood and where the cloud had been, moments ago.

Megan stared.

She almost had to pick up jaw up from the floor.

Mr. Bumblebeaux heard Megan's intake of breath.

Megan thought it must have been a trick of the light because she could have sworn she heard the golden cloud chorus, in very murmurous, low-toned voices, 'The Fairy Key.'

Megan gave herself a little shake.

Blinded by the series of golden lightning lights, and then the blaze and noise of the stars.

Deafened, Megan blinked.

You are of Magic. Such Magic is in you, Mr. Bumblebeaux thought, *I wouldn't be taken aback at all to see you cough glitter and sneeze sequins.*

Megan walked on.

The room she had just entered was storing small luggage cases.

Astonished, Megan was gobsmacked.

'Feast your eyes, Megan.' Mr. Bumblebeaux said.

Gold was sputtered on the walls. The four walls looked like they each had been dipped in vats of liquidized melted gold, then whipped out, erected and constructed into walls.

Megan grinned.

The cases packed on the left side of the room were piled in willy-nilly ways.

Right by her, a towering suit of armour was stood stately on a plinth, a grand silver crest shield was by the august-looking armour's, clanking-when-moving feet.

Megan looked away from the silver brilliance. As her sight left the noble, six-foot suit of armour, she saw the baggage holds were thousands deep and thousandth long, all spinning out into four directions, lost to her sight.

'They're all bits of broken furniture from Fairy Land.' Mr. Bumblebeaux explained, picking up a small, dusty corked bottle and putting it by hills of fabric, which looked suspiciously like a pink cloak.

'Why would they all be here?' Megan asked, turning away from the sheer glaring illuminating gold light thrown from the walls.

'All these tokens from Fairy Land require improvement from an expert hand. I say Fairy Land, though now any Lands send in there goods for mending. Out-sourcing and agreeing too having delivered belongings brought in is such an ordeal, and as an off-shoot, means more work for The Magic Melioration Restoration Repairer, but, as the betterment skills are second-to-none...'

Mr. Bumblebeaux shrugged his bony shoulders, flew down and stood on the leg of a two-pronged stool - that was there as its third leg required repair.

Near to the stool, an old-looking, bronzing-brown-and-gold hollow crown was by a silver jeweled headdress, which had a pink crystal stone in the raised metal middle of its pointed cornet.

Lodged into spaces all on the floor all over the room, were:

Thousands of books with each having their spines split open.

A strap, wrist-length that looked

like it could be tightened on the arm and a mechanical-looking device could fling off a clay plate, blasting off into the air, a bit like a thrown shot-put.

A stuffed toy, much larger than Megan, which looked a little curious as although it had two arms, two legs a neck and a head, they are all in a different order. So the grey head was where a left leg might have been, the left leg in turn was on the right shoulder, the right arm was attached to the neck, a left arm was sticking out of the bulging stomach, and the right arm was flopping on to left shoulder. Hair was roughly shown in stitched, small broom bristle ends.

Megan's gaze roved on from such a bizarre sight and she saw:

Ginormous cracked-open gooey eggshells. The outer shell shards were individually coloured in white, cream, pinks, browns and greens and blacks, goo still dripped in slobber on the piles of eggshells. Each of the eggshells had some a sort of clawed line or notched notation on the outer side, giving it an uneven name or number.

Floppy hats.

A tattered-looking copy of *Neptune, by Norris Newt.*

Tiny bottles of misty vials that appeared to contain some kinds of lotions and potions, but which on a closer look, Megan could see they were instead petite perfume bottles with atomizers. Parts of the sprayers were missing or the bottles had dents in the glass, which were each the size of Megan's little fingers.

A trashed-looking bust of such a creature Megan had no idea as to what it was.

Small Fairy cloaks in blues, golds, reds and yellows.

A six-foot long figure of a rainbow,

arched in blown glass.

Speared on the the end of what looked like a giant silver lance was a black horn, that seemed as if modeled from a ram's horn and then enlarged and doused in black ash.

An old, small backpack which looked like it was made of dried mulched grass.

The remainder of the time spent in the room, she caught unavoidable sights of:

Small chipped drinking glasses.

A silver scroll-work framed large picture of what look a fish; the Magic creature had the head of a snapping crocodile, but the body of a sturgeon fish. This framed picture, of the red and blue spotted Magic creature, was in a nook by a clump of small wooden swords, the practice weapons standing up in squared iron bowls that showed one or two steel swords of same height.

Large sling-shots only possessing one half, or with the catapults rubbers lying over-used in the swishing and so made badly mishandled.

A small, stumpy teapot with pink and white stripes in fine bone China, missing half its spout.

An assortment of identical cream handbags, similar in size of Megan's ones that had came boxed with some of her dolls. Only these handbags weren't in such pristine condition: damaged with the outside instead of in, beat-up broken handles, crumbly ripped seams, open linings had holes, studs had long-ago fallen off, cream pipping split or bent in oddly-sticking-out ways, well-broken zippers, and fifty or sixty more had worn-out linings.

Amelia Earhart's Aviation Winged Exploration by the High Fairy, Nagy Nougat. The massive long and big wide book was laid open, the line on the third page (the first being the title page and room just underneath for Nagy Nougat's author's signature, the second page giving the book's print edition) starting with: *A long time ago, in a far-flung pleasant and green land, there...* Megan looked on to what looked like unfolding maps, planned penciled designs and hastily turned-up, ruffled-looking charts sticking out of its book's pages.

Turning away from the tremendously piled squashy handbag victims and *Nagy Nougat's* book, she spied they were quite near to small, cake-sized silver platters that had been stacked carefully on the gold floor (one or two rather tarnished).

Megan saw a couple of light brooms, one very small and one she thought her dad could make use of in the garden, or when having a sweep-up in the hall and conservatory of number Nine, Marlberry Mews.

Chapter Thirty-One

The Green-Eyed Monster

Megan's brow creased.

'I don't quite know... I-I don't get it,' she said, honestly, to no-one but herself.

Out of habit, Megan rested her knuckles on to the curve under her chin.

Writing materials, notations and a peppering of scratched-out letters were over and above one another.

Megan's smile fled at once.

Mr. Bumblebeaux was now with a lotion of balm from a small phial, taken from his side-pocket, wiping a silver medal and tidying up the frayed ribbon attached to the smaller silver clasp, used to pin on when wearing.

Megan shuddered.

Mr. Bumblebeaux looked down from the bookcase, smiled, and then looked a bit worried for some reason, then pottered on with his medal.

With her tongue between her teeth, Megan concluded these particular faded formulations were way beyond her. They may, after all, as well have gone zooming over head. Although this sheet was completely different, she was taken to thinking, *how like Chemistry*.

Megan suddenly felt pressed-in.

She got up from the lumpy chair, went for a walk-about and came back.

Megan fidgeted a little.

'Oh, what a load of codswallop!' Mr. Bumblebeeaux suddenly said.

Megan looked over to the ceiling. 'Is everything OK?'

At that moment, Mr. Bumblebeaux was breathing heavily and flew in his zany way down to Megan. 'Yes yes.

Quite alright,' he said loudly. 'Thank you Megan.'

To her surprise, he chortled.

Mr. Bumblebeaux looked at Megan with warmth and respect blazing in his spectacle-clad eyes.

Now she came to think on it... Mr. Bumblebeaux always smiled at her in that warming and respectful way.

'Such preposterous writings up in the corner.'

'Why?' Megan asked.

'A prankish Elf or another Magic person has graffitied a piece of paper.'

'W-what does it say?'

'Oh, nothing of much importance,' Mr. Bumblebeaux replied quietly, 'such ludicrous comments on how their tutorship is much better under their teacher's, and dispraising my teaching abilities.'

Megan, smiling, looked at Mr. Bumblebeaux, and her sight saw him grinning back.

'Do you know who wrote it?' she asked, and out of the corner of her eye saw piled on more bookshelves, yonder away, the eye-catching sight of novels and novellas standing straight like a soldiers succession, out on a saluting uniformed show.

'I have a right good enough notion of the culprit, yes. But, of course that's their opinion and well they can have it, too.

'Still, such glary disrespect won't be found of going unpunished. Even if enforced by myself.'

'Can't their teacher give them a detention?'

'Good point. Though this grumpy teacher doesn't always insist on detained times after a lesson. Especially for favourites.'

'That's not very nice that someone would do that to you,' Megan commented, sitting back in the chair and crossing her leg over her left pink, corduroy trouser-covered thigh.

'Thanks muchly. Very nice of you too say,' Mr. Bumblebeaux nodded, standing on the cream-coloured doily-covered table, to her left.

Megan looked like she wanted to, right there and then, give Mr. Bumblebeaux a humongous hug.

'Occasionally, in Liishengyrfa, I get labeled what you might know to be a fool,' he confided, 'or a crackpot old simpleton, because I want teaching too be held true to the foundations and cornerstones of their subject origins.'

'Oh right.' Megan blinked.

She took her time with her mind digesting that. 'I don't think you're a fool.'

Mr. Bumblebeaux smiled back. 'Thanks. I don't feel so much a fool. I feel like myself. But, teaching is only the cover.'

'For what?'

'Well, one or two want my position.'

'Here?' asked Megan.

'Indeed.'

'So they say that about your teaching because they want your - '

' - Title, yes.'

'Did no-one else apply, then?'

Mr. Bumblebeaux nodded. 'Oh yes, many did. Balloting, pressure applied for votes, but, what they all forgot was that it's Pandragon's Key's choice to chose its Chief Librarian at here, All Souls Librarium.'

'Which is you,' Megan pointed out.

'Which is me.'

'So why are they still, erm...'

'Jealous?'

Megan thought this sounded right. She nodded.

'Jealously can be such a bitter feeling.'

Megan placed a hand on top of one another. 'I've never really been jealous of anything.'

Mr. Bumblebeaux cast Megan a sideways glance under his shaggy eyebrows. 'Or anyone?' he asked.

Megan shook her head.

'I thought not,' Mr. Bumblebeaux guessed. 'You are not the sort to become angered through jealously, or I dare say for jealous sake. You see, blistering bitterness can alter someone, and when coupled with major pails of jealously, well...'

'I sometimes look at other children and wish I could be left alone, too,' Megan said, looking away from her revealing admission.

'Ah. But that is not jealously. I can see why you'd wonder if it were... but no. It's completely understandable why you'd watch other children who go about unscathed, and think why me?

'Though what I feel is topmost important for you, is that you kept ever on. Not giving in. No-one, be they of your human sort, or even an evil Dragon, could squelch you down and win. And, I suspect, those children who are savagely monstrous to you, when older, simply won't be so painfully popular, and those little people will not be nice as grown-ups, either.'

'T-there's... t-there's just no need for it and everything.'

Mr. Bumblebeaux nodded his head from what Megan just said. 'I quite agree,' he responded, compassionately.

'Will you be OK?' Megan asked, in thoughtfulness.

'As you are, and as you will be, I shall also likewise be all alright.

'These times make you stronger.'

Megan nodded along.

'For those under me after my Chief Librarian status, instead of accepting what happened, their envy grew. But it's not as if the best Elf or any other

Magic person was beaten to the post.'

'Because it was Pandragon's Key's choice?'

'Exactamundo.'

'I don't know why they just can't see how things are.'

'Agreed. However, as determined and devoted some are to jealously, jealous thoughts and concealed jealous actions, I view those as avoidable.'

Megan lent forward a little.

'I think you're a really great Chief Librarian,' she said firmly, nodding.

Mr. Bumblebeaux's chest puffed up a trifle. 'Thank you,' said he. 'We all think and feel differently. But coming from you, as I am your Chief Librarian, then how most brilliant to hear!'

Chapter Thirty-Two

The Magic Storeroom

A tinkly bell rang-out in bellows somewhere inside the bowels of the room as Megan stepped inside, and Mr. Bumblebeaux swooped on in, upside down.

Mahogany trestle tables, sideboards, lamp tables and spindly-looking occasional tables all rubbed against one another.

Tons of lists. Forms of books. Oodles of papers. All competed for space with thousands of narrow upright books, and thousands more bigger, all sorted according to the topics written within the dusty pages.

A lone cart that looked like a wheel-barrow her mum and dad used (only this one was in a purplish-cerise and flaky brownness), was storing barrels of plucked yellow and magenta-red bouquets of strange-looking herbs. Supplies of bright powder like ground cumin in topped corked tubes were standing on the pink-cobble-stoned floor, as was collapsible brass weighing scales. Hung from the bare patches of walls were strings of well-conditioned, miniscule mauve-coloured cabbages, and nectarine-orange turnips.

On four sofas, long-armed brown and gold telescopes had been lined as if once counted. Packages had been left on top of the table-smothered books of ostrich, peacock and flamingo feathers, or what looked like they were, but in closer reassessment by Megan, gave her sight to each being of slightly different fluttering colours.

Such a fascinating enough of a sight!

Strangely, Megan felt like she had crossed into a very strict area. The zone and its very dust inside the windowless room seemed to prickle.

'What is that noise?' Megan asked, looking around.

Fwwwwwwwwwwwpp.

Went something in the depths of the room, sounding like it was coming from the left-hand side of the walls, behind a table and in front of a full-looking bookcase. The two pinky concrete doors were still stood open.

'Wonder what it is?' mumbled Megan.

Fffww. Fffww.

Mr. Bumblebeaux moved closer to Megan.

'How bizarre,' he said, scratching his head.

For some reason, the back of Megan's neck itched.

There was suddenly a loud whanging noise.

Is that something trying to get in through the walls? Megan thought.

Whang. Whang. Whang. Whang.

On went the loud rapping noise.

Rap. Rap. Rap.

One noise sounded as if it originated from something unseen, while the other was as things were being banged over by the smasher.

Rap. Rap. Rap. Rap.

Then came more fighting items being pushed over, which sounded as though kneecaps were being used as a pair of maraca castanets.

Megan looked about as a small coat fell off the back of an ornate-looking chair.

The rapping gathered speed.

Rap. Rap. Rap. Rap. Rap. Rap.

The other sound was like an airbed being pumped up.

Phweuuhhh. Sh. Phweuuhhh. Sh.

The noise was mingling with the heard items being all hugger-mugger tipped over.

On carried the sound, this time like a puffing tent having itself blown-up by a wheezy rambler.

Fssshhhp. Fssshhhp. Fssshhhp.

Wide, smart eyes looked back at Megan. 'This started expanding itself out,' Mr. Bumblebeaux grunted, tying the end of a stringy loose cord on to a an empty hat's hook.

Megan wished she could blink.

An airplane was now docking up by the ceiling's rafters.

Megan was surprised.

How odd that it blew-up on its own!

'This is... not... very... pliable,' Mr. Bumblebeaux described, nodding, and double-tying the rope a bit more tighter.

Megan sank into a smooth-downed chair with a happy sigh.

She thought with so many questions assaulting her mind, she could have filled most of the empty pieces of scrap, blank paper she had seen throughout her journey.

Megan panned around.

The Zeppelin aircraft had knocked over a book. Megan went and picked up the heavy paperback, retrieving *A Non-ridiculous Zoological Starter's Handbook to Magic Creatures, by Rufus Rueful*

A sudden blasting clangour sound crashed outside.

Megan left *A Non-ridiculous Zoological Starter's Handbook to Magic Creatures, by Rufus Rueful*, next to a small, but very thick-paged hardback of *One Trillion Events On Nons Notations, Alasdiar Nore*

She eyed Mr. Bumblebeaux drop a citrus-green feather, and flap out under the massive threshold of the now half-open doors.

What is it? Is Lucy now back? thought Megan, feeling a little bit disappointingly dispirited.

Chapter Thirty-Three

The Throw-Away Stairs

Megan had broken into a rather begrudging trot.

Reluctantly, she walked out into the corridor.

The passageway, from where the sound blasted and banged, was shivering in movement then became fully still as it eased into place.

At the far end of the gold and brown corridor, stairs just then cracked into being butted into place; dust and a pelting shower of pink stoned debris fell down and then was lost into the floor. Ripples on the smooth floor made babbles of watery waves float, like when she used to try and skim a stone over a lake's surface (only Lucy, with much pained laughing at Megan, could achieve this).

The stairway slotted back in place from having been dragged from some other area of the castle, and the stilling vibrating look of the stairs appeared as if they had swung up and maybe down, then sided like a pendulum, and might even have flipped over.

The creamy stone flight of stairs looked most attractive!

'Jump on if you want,' Mr. Bumblebeaux said, flying up by the stone curved ceiling.

The stairs had stopped vibrating.

Megan placed a tentative step on the stairway.

Not quite sure if the staircase would suddenly *whoosh* into life and spirit her shriekingly away!

Megan quickly dashed up the flight of stone stairs.

Each formed step looked like glass, slightly sheer and pearly-white-and-cream.

Whispers abounded in the enveloping gloom and Megan hurried her feet.

As she climbed on up the stairs, she peered left and right over the stoned railing. Dotted once or twice she saw sliding-looking doors down candlelit corridors.

Megan came to sudden halt.

The top stair gave its way to a level of ground. As Megan crept up the last four steps, she suddenly, finally saw this leant on to a much wider and taller gallery corridor.

As soon as Megan's last foot left the step, the stairs all of a sudden creaked then swung right, causing a stony scrapping, which made the ground on that she was stood slightly shake.

With herself shaking, Megan looked up.

The hundreds of portraits staring back at her were of one or two grown-up people, though the rest were of forests, weasels, Dragons, funny-looking cows, Fairies, and shining silvers of Magic creatures, so bright Megan had to avoid looking at what was causing them to glow brightly.

The bits of walls here and there were gold, not flaking, and under the rows of portraits, seats and tables had been set up as if an observer could sit, and watch the silent painted noble-looking figures.

Megan glanced over her shoulder. She pushed spiraled bunches of hair aside and saw the yawning gap that had been left by the stairs, which she could still hear grinding on to some other location.

Megan was not tempted at all too prod a foot at the end of the ground where the stairs had been, moments ago. As her neck came back, she saw many other stairs moving this way and that, up on different levels above her, and way down beneath, on a lower floor.

As Megan walked by far below them, the frozen staring painted eyes gazed out.

The gold-gilt framed pictures were each hung simply by small silver pins, hooked on to gold shiny nails.

Megan hardly glanced at any of them.

It would not have much surprised her if one, or all, suddenly sprang to life and leapt out of their frames!

In parts, it was very hard to think there were any walls at all, the paintings were hung with sides so tightly pressed together and tops and bottoms of the frames so snuggly close.

'Do you know any of them?' Megan asked.

Her hands clenched the back of a

square chair in pink and white stripes running up and down, parallel. The golden tassels on each of the chairs looked heavy.

'My, all of them.' Mr. Bumblebeaux said, pointing to a Unicorn. 'That was my predecessor.'

'A what?' asked Megan, sitting down.

'The one who had the post before I,' explained Mr. Bumblebeaux, 'such a wonderfully rattling good Chief Librarian.'

'Where are they now?'

'Moved on.' Mr. Bumblebeaux said, re-straightening a portrait of a glen filled with trees, bushes and a pooling slash of water.

'To where?' Megan was curious.

'Back to Unicorn Land. Tumble - '

' - Prince *Tumble?*' Megan burst out.

'The one and only,' Mr. Bumblebeaux looked at Megan,

smiling.

'Prince Tumble was a Chief Librarian here?'

'Indeed so.'

Megan was flabbergasted.

'And always very fair, he was,' Mr. Bumblebeaux nodded, to himself.

Megan's eyes blinked.

'T-that's...' she just couldn't begin, she was that dumbfounded.

Mr. Bumblebeaux flew over, landing on the table sparse save for a reading copy of *The Hall Of A Million Faces: A History, by Hugho Milleaser*. Mr. Bumblebeaux's boots landed on the thick-looking book's front cover, then he nearly tripped and fell stumbling over the hardback spine. Megan kindly lent forward quickly and helped him too right himself, and she felt his wings beat against her guiding hands.

'Achcum,' Mr. Bumblebeaux coughed. 'I thank you.'

Megan smiled.

'Now where was I? Oh, Tumble! Yes. Before the Land of the Unicorns chose him as their Prince, Tumble Wuddlegoobly was Chief Librarian.'

'I just can't...'

Mr. Bumblebeaux smiled at Megan, who was sitting back now, but the gold tassel poked into the top of her back. Megan looked sideways at the identical tassels on the other chairs.

Might as well stay here, she thought.

Mr. Bumblebeaux looked about a bit shiftily. 'He hasn't always been so grave and serious, you do know?'

Megan shook her head.

This was getting wilder and wilder.

'Even when younger, as a Unicolt, Tumble could be prone to pranks.

'Such a natural born leader. He led. No surprise too me he was elected Prince, of course,' Mr. Bumblebeaux confided.

Both he and Megan were nearly bent forward, talking quietly and quickly, as if they were co-conspirators, planning to steal candy confection from a sweet shop.

'He used to give his Mother, Barbar, such a merry gallop.

'Mind, Joahn, his Father, used too nearly want to beat his horn against a wall when Tumble would get into one of his Magic capers. His sister Tifftiff was the same.'

Megan was still blinking.

'Tumble, when taking up the mantle of Princedom, really did settle it on completely,' Mr. Bumblebeaux said, from what he'd determined in his observations, 'in a manner, being Chief Librarian prepared him in some ways.'

'How?' Megan breathed.

'Responsibility. Making sure all under him were cared and catered for. Even then he didn't let the power go to his head, unlike some who would. He grew to be noble, even back then,' Mr. Bumblebeaux smiled at a memory. 'His earlier times when a Unicolt were just jest, fun, never harmless. I used too advise Joahn and Barbar that Tumble would grow out of them. And he did.'

Megan was gripped!

'So you knew Prince Tumble would be... Prince?' she asked, finding it altogether very odd too call Prince Tumble, Tumble.

'I knew of the potential in Tumble, indeed I did.'

'That's so weird to think of him before he was a Prince,' Megan said, reflecting on just how very weird it was.

'The role of the Prince of Unicorn Land has made Tumble appear... serious and fairly stern, but, scratch the surface and you'll find a fellow Magic individual who greatly cares for sentient beings.'

'What does sentient mean?' clarified Megan, nudging forward a little in her seat.

'To live. Live, animated. And with thought.'

'Thank you.'

'Most welcome,' nodded Mr. Bumblebeaux. 'Prince Tumble has a kindness and warmth his family and friends can, and do rely on.'

'And he's always been like that?' Megan wanted to know, finding it hard too think of Prince Tumble in any other way.

'Yes. His kindness and warmth have always stayed intact. Now he is Prince, those are still there, even if others wouldn't recognise this. But then, being a Prince effects one.'

'How?'

'Well, for example: Prince Tumble would have to set himself apart, be the leader, the only leader, and know he is followed. And then when he needs or has too, he then requires to seem at ease, and make others who are nervous less so around him.

'Like a Prince among many, but stood apart.'

'That sounds difficult.'

Mr. Bumblebeaux bent down, and pushed the edge of the spine of *Hugho Milleaser's* book back a bit, to give him more room too stand freely. 'In The Enchanted Kingdom, a Magic creature isn't created in greatness, rather this comes as that Magic being grows.

'I've known Tumble far longer than most in The Kingdom, and Tumble when younger surely didn't keep his feelings or thoughts in check. Though he learnt a lot under the Magic Archivist, Arcee Alphaa, or moreover had many of his formed thoughts confirmed. But then, by being so popular, he was called... different...

even before he was made a Prince.'

'Why?'

'We're back to jealously I am afraid.'

'Ah.' Megan said.

There was a loud 'Ooooh!' from Megan.

They had both gone down a stairway. Backing off from The Hall Of A Million Faces.

Trekking on past a long, twisty-turny corridor, she saw no obvious light splattering from the empty lanterns, which were hooked at intervals on both sides of the walls. And yet, very curiously, this didn't create such a gloom, rather the walls again had light that was pink-based, with gold and green flashes.

As she walked on, the spacious room slashed into a pink-flamingo coloured antechamber.

Straight in front of her, upon a chiseled stone, on top of a marble grey plinth read a carving: The Great III Hall

Shyly going on in though the open, massive and heavy-looking double doors, Megan then swanned into a gigantic vault of a room.

Megan's first thought was that this place was very important.

Her sight saw three long tables, each running down the length of the chambered and broadened room.

Megan had never thought of such an odd and extraordinarily sublime a room could exist.

This big golden chamber was filled *scranch-scranch-sounding* sparkly Magic.

Megan couldn't wait to get started walking properly about.

The crunches of the Magic fizzed in bitty-little exploding firework lightning bombs.

Greens, golds, silvers and pinks whizzed and whirred in gales.

Ambling through the Magic, like the *buzz-buzzes* of vile midges and gnats in high summer (only the Magic felt to Megan prickly-tickly and fizzed), she traveled past a table to her left, and a table to her right.

'We're now directly in The Great Third Hall.' Mr. Bumblebeaux explained, whizzing up by a magnificent tapestry of a red and gold Unicorn, and the wall-hanging opposite was in pink, with a Fairy perched upon an arm of a branch.

'The gallery up there is for Magic Minstrels to play their music and provide entertainment.'

'H-how would they?' asked Megan, overwhelmed, now taking in the golden gallery streaming in half-height banisters around near to the top of the room, but not quite touching by the ceiling.

Megan thought the gallery looked a pleasant sight.

'Plays. Jokes. Merry-making, that sort of lot,' shouted Mr.Bumblebeaux, flitting on up on the ceiling, worked in cream-coloured figures of Unicons, Dragons, Mermaids and Fairies and Elves, and again, similar to the other Magic creatures, hanging in The Hall Of A Million Faces, Megan hadn't the haziest idea of what they were. One such fantastical Magic creature in its creamy-stoned statue, looked like a large-mouthed lizard, with a very long tail, the same size of a Saint Bernard dog.

Rambling through the room, the tables were sturdy-looking, yet appeared to be many years old, if not centuries. Extremely clean, each one glittered and shone with silver goblets and plates, all empty and sitting at dotted spaces as if ready for a banqueting meal.

A scattering of small crystals, like dropped opals, gems and shiny stones, criss-crossed the tables right on down past her.

The straight-line walls of The Great III Hall were adorned with more impressive wonderful tapestries, trophies and coats of arms

This place definitely had room to swing a Dragon by its ankles with its wings fanned-out.

'Impressive, huh?' Mr. Bumblebeaux nodded.

Megan nodded back.

She would have to try and grasp that that sort of thing would be part of the course when in The Fairy Key Land, Pandragon's Key and All Souls Librarium.

Crouched within the goblets and plates, was little hills of sandy-golden twinkly Fairy dust.

Hordes of whisperings suddenly sprang up like fizzling campfires.

Megan carried on roaming around the room.

She attempted to brush off the mumblings.

A rustle and a crack all of a sudden erupted from somewhere up in the gallery.

Megan leapt backwards.

She couldn't ignore the mutterings any longer; she looked round for the rustlings to her right, the quiet whispers incoming in zooms to her left.

Megan waited. Then waited some more.

Nothing, or no-one stepped forward or revealed themselves in midair, which really would not have much greatly surprised Megan (apart from perhaps screaming to the ceiling).

Megan had the sudden feeling as if plunged into a dangerous, ice-cold river.

'Hu-uh... hu-uh,' gasped Megan.

Nervously, a part of her wanted to run in screams out the Hall, and another part wanted to stay-put, or maybe even dare go forward.

Megan roamed shakily onwards.

Nearest her, behind the long table to her right, she could properly now spy a raised portion. On which, in the centre, was a very large pinky-gold throne-like chair.

Megan felt like collapsing into the chair.

The whisperings and rustlings had stopped. For now.

Across from the raised chair, Mr. Bumblebeaux beamed, opening his arms wide as his wings made him zip to the left, then flap upside down (again). 'Such a sight to befall!'

Megan nodded, smiling. Smiling in part from The Great III Hall, and smiling caringly from darling Mr. Bumblebeaux.

He looked like nothing really could have pleased him more, there and then, to have cheerfully seen Megan,

The Fairy Key, standing and gawping in the Hall.

'The lavish glazing was introduced into the windows of The Great III Hall,' Mr. Bumblebeaux discussed, slightly panting, 'and this gave an added bonus of light from our three suns.'

Megan fully agreed that the light rays shining in mixed so well with the specks of Magic dusts.

'We don't tend to really make use of this space. But when we do, rushes are strewn down here.'

'What are rushes?'

'Mmm. A bit like strands of carpet. Or hay, that is what you have in your world? Hay?'

Megan nodded.

She sat on the flattened bench, which ran on up and down at least nine-hundred feet.

'Who made this all, Mr. Bumblebeaux?' her voice asked in

echoes.

'The architect, a good one, came up with the plans, as did Spindlestein.'

'Spindlestein again?'

'Indeed.'

'He gets around!' Megan laughed.

Mr. Bumblebeaux laughed back, 'More than you know,' he said most cryptically, his tone sounding dark with his face clouding over, then he looked more brighter. 'Both Spindlestein and Berkeley Baxley vied for the task of overseeing the Magic building, of all of The Fairy Key Land.'

Megan looked gobsmacked.

She just thought the Magic had created it.

'Oh, the Magic could have created it quite perfectly,' Mr. Bumblebeaux said eerily, as if reading her mind!

'But,' he carried on, 'The Brim-Tree's opinion was that this place ought to be given a hand that knows of The Fairy Key, or at least touched a foot in your world.'

'So Pandragon's Key and All Souls Librarium were helped by Spindlestein?'

'Of sorts, yes.'

Megan looked around The Great III Hall.

Plush gold leaf decorations, marvelous murals, silver-glassed mirrors and hundreds more marble ornamentations were also drenched in the streams, of the bouncing-back reflective lights.

To think that someone, maybe a Magic creature, could create such a wonder!

'Though Berkeley Baxley's projections were found to posses merit, and so the Berkeley Baxley Arch was added,' Mr. Bumblebeaux said. 'Would you like yo gaze at it?' asked the Elf.

Megan nodded, went to stand, but

sat back down again.

'Who is Berkeley Baxley? she asked, leaning against the edge of the table. Her back could feel the warming lights from what was on the table-top.

'Berkeley Baxley is a Pookiebooble.'

Megan wanted to smile. 'A... Pookiebooble?'

'You pronounced it right,' Mr. Bumblebeaux said, standing to her left on the table, and then moving, dangling his legs over the rim of the bench.

'Is a Pookiebooble from around here?'

Mr. Bumblebeaux shook his head, toweling out more Magic dust that had given him a look like he was wearing a golden hood. Megan quite liked her own. 'From Angquail Land,' Mr. Bumblebeaux said, shaking his hands, 'though that part of Angquail

Land used to be known as Pookiebooble Land.'

Megan blinked. 'Why did the Pookieboobles change it?'

'Long story that,' Mr. Bumblebeaux said, nodding, and flicking some lights off his waistcoat carefully that had clumped on his top, and which looked like dozens of golden wasps.

'Basically, the Angquails and Pookieboobles lived side-by-side as neighbouring Lands, but the Pookieboobles grew far too many Candyloss Plants, and well, the whole Land was nearly overrun... if not for the Angquails.'

Megan nodded along, fascinated and listening intently.

'The Angquails were aghast too see their Lands now fringed with Candyfloss Plants, and so a group of Angquail delegations went and asked the Pookieboobles to ever-so-kindly remove their Candyfloss Plants that grew so immense, the Angquails homes were being covered in, can you guess?'

'Candyfloss?' Megan hazard, smiling.

'Quite correct.'

Megan smiled, feeling happy she got the guess right.

'Poor Pookieboobles, they didn't intend for their Candyfloss Plants to creep into Angquail Land.'

'Why did they grow so much?'

'A well-placed question, Megan, and so much deserves an answer. The Pookieboobles had not factored in the intensity of the three suns.'

'How do you mean?' Megan asked, grasping the three suns, yet totally lost on how they caused so many Candyfloss Plants to grow so fast and so quick.

'The three suns are situated in the sky.'

Megan nodded, picturing in her

mind the three suns just outside: one cherry-red, one marmalade-orange and one canary-yellow, in the crystal-blue sky and fluffy white clouds.

'Yet, Angquail Land is wrapped on the northern ranges of The Enchanted Kingdom, and Pookiebooble Land is on the eastern front, so the Candyfloss Plants in Pookiebooble Land were slightly shaded by the mountains from the south.'

'And those mountains aren't by Angquail Land?'

'Exactly.'

'Therefore, when the Candyfloss Plants spread into Angquail Land, they had a whale of a time growing and not being shaded, so could luxuriate properly under the three suns.'

'Oh, I see... I understand. Thank you.'

'Most welcome,' Mr. Bumblebeaux said, grinning back.

'Is Dragon Land by Angquail Land?' asked Megan, observationally.

'How would you know of that?' Mr. Bumblebeaux asked, this time he was the one who looked incredibly flummoxed.

Megan stuck her hands inside her pockets, feeling a pink handkerchief and a couple of mint sweets. 'I remember Princess Blossom explaining that Dragon Land was by the north.'

'Then well remembered,' said Mr. Bumblebeaux, looking impressed. 'Dragon Land is indeed to the north of The Enchanted Kingdom.'

'And so is Angquail Land.'

'And so is Angquail Land.' parroted Mr. Bumblebeaux.

Megan smiled.

'Anyway, enough of my lapses in waffling! Let's go and have a look-see at the Arch!'

Chapter Thirty-Four

The Tower

From a Flying Dolphin's eye view of Pandragon's Key, it would show mainly the walls, towers and general keep of the castle. As well as the part-triangular and square castle, the circular and soaring towers had aerial gangplanks by attached walkways.

Pandragon's Key was such an impressive ruin, boasting pile of a castle, with great views to the north, east south and west; smaller towers stood on either side of the castle's back walls, and each slanted down in size that twinned the lower foundations of the castle, as it rolled on down in the slopes of The Fairy Key Land.

Far inside Megan, retracing her

steps, had padded back through The Great III Hall, and back into the other sections of All Souls Librarium.

The doors of the Hall had swung closed, barred from anyone now gaining entrance in.

Megan, in gleefulness, had difficulty with hiding her awed shock.

Even she, before now, who knew nothing on castles, really did think Pandragon's Key to be wonderful.

With a happy sigh, Megan had shinnied down the thinning path which had yawned open all of a sudden.

A small slash in the wall had no door. Rays of sunshine dappled into the lighted corridor.

This bloomed into the left side of the outer parts of Pandragon's Key. Megan looked back to the comfort of All Souls Librarium. She nodded. Then went into the unknown bits she'd not seen before.

She thought Pandragon's Key was still just as wonderful.

Megan, quite forgetting to ask who or what Spindlestein was, instead wanted to know why the Pookieboobles had their name given over to Angquail Land.

'The Angquails and Pookieboobles had lived fine. It was only this situation that caused the Angquails to be angered. And the Pookieboobles, who are a very giving sort, wanted too make everything all okies.'

'What did they do?'

Mr. Bumblebeaux looked at Megan, a bit sadly from what the Pookieboobles had gone through. 'The Angquails said the only way they could restore their good name, and the good faith, was too agree to Pookiebooble Land becoming Angquail Land.'

'For... forever?'

'Does that mean permanently?' Mr.

Bumblebeaux looked a bit confused.

'Err... yes. In my world.'

'Then yes, the Angquails wanted Pookiebooble Land to known as Angquail Land as a permanent fix.'

'That's awful.'

'Indeed. But, those Pookieboobles are not daft at all.'

'Why? How?' Megan was wanting too know.

'The Pookieboobles got one over on the Angquails, because, as the grouped delegations sifted through the proposition contract of cleaning up the Candyfloss Plants, and too agree to the replacement of the name in Land, the Angquails did not look at the bottom clause.'

Megan stopped, excited. 'What did it say?'

'It said that the Pookiebooble Land would also be known as Angquail Land, however, *only* until the Candyfloss Plants have been removed safely from Angquail Land by a few of the Angquails, though more by means of the Pookieboobles, and then when the Candyfloss Plants have been cleared out, then the name of the Land shall revert back to...'

'Pookiebooble Land?'

'You hit it on the nose.'

'Do the Angquails even know?'

'Not as far as I know. Anyhoo, don't feel sorry for them though, it was the fault of their own greed.'

Megan smiled.

Mr. Bumblebeaux grinned along.

The open air was as cool and nice as when she was walled within, moments ago.

Megan shook her head violently.

Dust rained down, collecting on her clothes and piling up on the ground. Megan laughed. She felt some of the Fairy dust on her cheeks, and noticed the strands on hair in front of her face were flecked in golds and silver, sparking in the suns beams even more than before.

Ahead, brambles of undergrowth was bursting in tangles up the inclining hills.

'There are many drawings which show the true beauty of Pandragon's Key, and the ingenuity of her architects,' Mr. Bumblebeaux said, leading the way and pointing to which way they were going. 'I plan to include a dedicated drawings section at a future date into RRR.'

Megan nodded; she understood what Mr. Bumblebeaux had meant.

She walked left, following a mini-maze of cut green-gold bushes that had been fashioned into small walls. The bushy labyrinth ran up to her knee-height.

The attractive, lived-in castle and outside white-blond walls was now a bit farther back.

A crunching path of small brown,

pink, grey and white stones was in a straight line, slashing through a green hedge with a curved hole sliced into the hedgerow.

Slap in front of her, Megan saw a very large sight.

Three lines of silver-white stone, one flat on the ground, two more raised in and with the tops leaning against each other, made a massive triangle-shape that was much bigger than Megan's house. The dizzying tiptop of the arc glinted in light from the three suns.

Megan, half-blinded, felt very dizzy.

'Yes, it is rather bright,' Mr. Bumblebeaux said, flapping around with his back to the stony structure.

On the ground, a little near to the triangle but not touching up on the grounded level of the archway, read a silver plague on a white plinth: Berkeley Baxley Arch

Over the line of the trees which appeared usual and not Gump-like, taller hedges were wrangled in first; giving the look like a step. First the hedge-heights, and then the dwarfing trees behind them. Altogether, the total appearance was like it was to keep something in, or keep something from getting in.

Megan's eyes traveled down, and she saw a rectangular tower poking slightly above the tallest trees, swaying from the breeze.

Megan looked up to the watchtower.

She felt completely dwarfed.

Mr. Bumblebeaux flew to the grass climbing up in tendrils on the tower's circular wrapping base. 'There are one thousand, four-hundred and eighty steps.'

Indeed, blacks numbers and words on an old-looking white sign on a rickety stick, swung in the gentle wind: 1480 steps

Megan's eyes popped.

Already, even from spying the step-count, made her feel exhausted.

There was a strong wall of massive masonry. Megan walked to side, going right. Following the wrap of the tower a ramp was strung that connected to a smaller tiered window, in the lower portions of the main complex of Pandragon's Key.

Breathtaking drawbridges drew on either side of the tower. The big patch of grass that homed the tower had a half-cut still lake running on either part, sliding around in watery licks where the tower wrapped.

Megan watched the double-entryway for a while but the doors didn't crash open.

A fluffing white cloud that was dotted in the sky passed over where they were.

The cloud looked like a massive

ball of wool moving along in the sky, merrily floating by on its way.

'This tower,' Mr. Bumblebeaux said, absentmindedly gazing at the happy-looking clouds, 'was chosen by Merlin.'

Megan stopped, awestruck. 'King Arthur? Knights Of The Roundtable? Excalibur? That Merlin?'

'So unusual hearing him spoke like that! Yes, that Merlin.'

'M-Merlin was here?'

'He should have been! Magbin Merlin used to be a Chief Librarian.'

Megan could not take in what she was hearing. 'Merlin... a Chief Librarian. W-was he the first?'

'Oh no. Let me think,' Mr. Bumblebeaux thought back, silent and flapping in many directions, 'Merlin was the third Chief Librarian.'

'W-what number are you, Mr. Bumblebeaux?'

'I'm the ninth to be inducted as

Chief Librarian.'

'Does that m-mean Pandragon's Key is Camelot?' asked Megan, feeling totally snowed-in.

'Camelot?'

Megan nodded, her head looking like a nodding toy dog stuck in the back of a car, with its movable head swiveling when the car was being driven.

'Then no. True, Merlin with The Brim-Tree's permission, did bring in some of the brickwork taken from Camelot.'

'All of it?'

'Not quite. A lot was left in your world so your people could have a monument too remember by.'

'C-Camelot is in our, I mean my world?'

'Camelot is known as Tintagel in your world. All ruins now, though.'

'Tintagel,' Megan said, trying the name out, never hearing of it before.

'In a region of my Land which uses Liishengyrfa, Tintagel translates as Camelot.' Mr. Bumblebeaux explained, looking at the tower, not concerned at all with chatting over what he thought was normal.

Megan, again, could not quite take in she was talking about Camelot, Merlin, her castle of Pandragon's Key, her library of All Souls Librarium, The Fairy Key Land and all of this being confirmed by an Elf, her Chief Librarian!

'I suppose, in a way, you could say Pandragon's Key was Camelot. Though only the brickwork of this tower. Then the complete lot of the castle, everything, became amended and made bigger, well, how it is now...'

Megan thought she spied the air next to her shimmer. 'I-is Merlin... a-around?'

'Oh, he's around,' Mr. Bumblebeaux

replied, smiling to himself.

A creak cracked. It sounded like boiling water exploding from a hob.

Megan turned, alarmed.

The watchtower's doors were gaped open.

'Go on in, if you like,' Mr. Bumblebeaux smiled, encouragingly, happy to point her in the right direction.

Megan dithered, stood on the spot.

Chapter Thirty-Five

55 The Hill

Inside, winding up the walls, they also had lavish gold leaf decorations, and mounted on the walls were marvelous murals, looking mirrors and marble ornamentations.

Mr. Bumblebeaux spoke slightly in a tour-guide's voice, 'As you note, this tower is very thick, strengthened at intervals by those smaller towers you saw ringed around here.'

Megan nodded along, having the alarming image of wondering if she should have brought a camera with her for snapshots.

'The castle was also built using lime mortar from your world, and not just those bits fused from Camelot,' Mr. Bumblebeaux nodded, pleased to include the reference, and also glad from spying Megan's nod, 'which was then injected with Magic, so would be more flexible, and even allow the walls to move in the event of Pandragon's Key moving itself completely around.'

'Which it does.'

'Ra-ther!'

Megan had gone ten steps up the spiral staircase and stopping momentarily, looked down; the doors were still stood open, sunlight streaming in pools on the stony ground, and two shadows showing where the doors were remaining wide-open.

One either side, opposite one another, were wound-up interlocking ironed-chains that when released, would clank and drop the raised drawbridges. These were fastened on the walls in big racks, and one such golden confined bundle was nearest to the bottom of the stairwell.

'This well-dearest tower,' Mr. Bumblebeaux waffled on, in his coach-driver's conducting voice, 'was one of the first to be erected. Sort of a testing tower... that's a little joke there.'

Megan nodded, smiling, and Mr. Bumblebeaux looked very pleased she got the gag.

'That not turning out to be an unmitigated fiasco, plans then progressed and vwala, there's now all of this here,' he spread his hands.

Megan had paced up five more steps, and all of a sudden, in a swish of Fairy dust, Mr. Bumblebeaux took the crook of her left elbow, pulled slightly, and Megan had the queer feeling of being pushed, forced, propelled and wiggled into many small spaces.

When she opened her eyes, dazed, and groggy, the strangest thing was that the spiral staircase was looping down below.

Megan was rooted now on the top step!

She had nearly fallen over.

Megan took the railing, steadying her feet. She wanted to move, but she couldn't yet lift a foot; they felt like they had pins-and-needles. And more worse, her movements looked like she was swimming through thick treacle.

'I do apologise. I should have warned you, so you could have equipped yourself with being ready,' Mr. Bumblebeaux looked abominably shamefaced.

Megan felt a bit queasy. She half-smiled.

The pins-and-needles had gone as quick as they had come.

'That's OK,' Megan said, jumping to her feet.

She worked her feet around and kneaded her wrists.

'Have you always been able to do that?' Megan asked, wondering if that was why he flew in such different ways to Princess Blossom, Prince Elfin and Nugget.

'Only me, yes. It's just something I've been able to do. A quirk of my Magic, if you will.' Mr. Bumblebeaux was stood on the top-part of a long, tall silver door. Enameled scrolls and vine-leaves with tiny-looking Unicorns, grisly-bears, Dragons and lizards were dotted on both sides of the door.

Megan shook herself, then opened the door a bit further than it had been left, then poked her head inside.

All was black. As black as a black night. As black as a night's sky.

Megan hung back.

Lights above sputtered as if flicked on by an unseen finger.

Mr. Bumblebeaux zoomed down the long corridor.

Megan rested a hand on the handle. And then followed.

A small rounding room was presented as Megan pushed back heavy-feeling, pink, crushed velvet-textured drapes.

Many layers of rugs and mats were on the piles on the floor, so many and much more that Megan could not quite tell if cobblestones were underneath. Fancy scrolls, swords, intricate-looking circle patterns and blocks of colours, all the colours of rainbow, and each shade between gave the floor a wild, eye-sore look if she tried to pick apart too much.

Antique-looking rickety tables had tokens of straightened bits of paper.

Megan went and had a look.

The curve to the room had set-aside a few covers of the mats and rugs, and revealed the grandest floor yet had pink tiles on the ground.

She walked up to a table that was

flush to her chest-height.

Megan stretched out a hand.

Yellowish papers had to contend space with thick envelopes, some open with their wrinkly flaps sticking out, and one and two more left sealed. No handwriting was on any of the envelopes. And none had any stamps on them.

But, looking back, tiny spiderly writing was scrabbled on one of the envelopes that was forefront on the pile, though which looked like it had swished itself forward. *Or fell off the pile because there's far too many?* Megan thought.

Megan made a grab for the missive before it plopped to the gold rug on the floor:

Tamy Truffle
55 The Hill
South Gatewood
Toadstool Way

Fairy Land

This small envelope was the only one which had a name on its surface, with the postal address (also in a tidy scrawl of cockroach-black scribbled coloured ink) described after the name of who it was addressed to. All the lines of the writing looked like they were handed by the same letter-sender.

Megan's heart rose.

A stamp was on the top right hand corner of the envelope, which was in gold-leaf, trimmed tightly, and finely ingrained with an image. It showed shoulder-shots of Princess Blossom and Prince Elfin. He behind his Princess, bandaging his arms adoringly around her. She clasping on to his forearms and both lovingly hugging one another, smiling happily out from the one postage stamp.

Megan's eyes glistened.

From what Megan could spy, the other unaddressed envelopes, she assumed, were for someone who was doing work there.

Megan smiled warmly from seeing both Princess Blossom and Prince Elfin.

She looked about. Then set back the envelope by pushing it a bit further from the piles - so as it wouldn't be again knocked over, and fall from being stuffed inside the filing collected batch.

Megan felt a growing feeling so happy as if a whoopee-cushion was blowing up inside her.

'Newly created, that is,' Mr. Bumblebeaux said. He looked very happy. 'And to think what they went through. It was all thanks to you though, who reunified them, by getting them back together, here.'

Megan looked away.

Mr. Bumblebeaux saw her face

redden.

He smiled. 'It wasn't nothing, Megan Button. You brought my Princess Blossom back. Thank you, Megan.'

She felt incredibly embarrassed.

'The stamp is new?' Megan asked, like an eager stamp-collector.

Mr. Bumblebeaux noticed her changing his line of subject, to pick and hone-in on his throwaway comment. He stroked his white-bearded chin, thoughtfully. 'Yes. Though I didn't know you were a philatelist,' he said, gazing over his spectacles, 'the stamp was put into production too commemorate and celebrate their returning to the throne in Fairy Land.'

Megan nodded, then walked on.

The outing in All Souls Librarium of Pandragon's Key was going resplendently marvelous.

Megan pulsed with excitement.

Fantastic!

Chapter Thirty-Six

The Dankly Dark Hole

Megan crept under the spired walkway.

They had both doubled back, and again Mr. Bumblebeaux yanked her and in a *whoosh* they glided down the one thousand, four-hundred and eighty steps. This time, though, as the stairs toppled out of sight, Megan, holding on for dear life, didn't scream an alarmed and excited screech, for she knew what to expect and so gathered herself, just before her right elbow had been jolted nearly out of its socket.

She'd never felt anything quite like that; the only comparison was when Megan had nose-dived through her bedroom doorway, when she first went into The Enchanted Kingdom with Princess Blossom, Nugget, and Lucy - who'd annoyingly tagged along.

Megan had found her way back passing the wide, sweeping spiral staircase inside the tower, which looked exactly the same as when she had last stepped up it.

She glanced over her shoulder, looking at the stairs, and the two sets of chains for the drawbridges. Megan wondered if some of the walls held concealed doors, if that were possible, and pretending to be usual-looking walls.

Megan had half a mind to knock and listen for whistling wind in drafty hidden corridors. But, Megan didn't want to put a toe out of line with darting along the walls, groping on them for unseeable corridors, rooms and noises. There was a lot to Magic,

Megan was finding out, that what meets the eye. She finally walked out.

As her back cleared, the two doors moaned into life and in crashes and creaks, shut closed.

Megan was very relived to find she had not been moved miles away into a different Land.

*

The quadrangle had lain unoccupied for a long time because Fairy dust lay in thick, untidy piles of bespeckles upon the pink-cobblestones. A bicycle could be ridden crazily about there was so much space, and even its thin inflated tires would let up ten-foot-high bombilations of fizzling Fairy dust from the ground.

Megan turned to stare at the scatters of pink carnations and yellow roses that crept up white-stoned pillars.

They were lined, grouping in

columns around a massive obelisk. This looked quite like the one column of the re-erected Cleopatra's Needle in London, that a then ear-muffed Megan remembered spying, which her dad had shuffled them to, on a weekend, when the Button's visited *The Nutcracker* stage show at The Royal Opera House.

After the performance, in the bustling foyer, her mum and dad had treated both Megan and Lucy each to a programme and a wooden nutcracker. Megan's remained looking as good as new (nestled by her dolls and other rag-dolls), with its lever still able to crush a walnut. Lucy's, however, became lipsticked and mascaraed, and its pulley bar broke off, when she attempted to crack off a doll's head by its poor neck.

Megan shook her head. The flourishes of Christmas memory of hanging stockings, mistletoe, army mice and a heroic nutcracker soldier fading in her mind, expanding back into her re-remembering banks.

Looking out, she saw the quadrant of the courtyard, to one side near to the back of Pandragon's Key, had pink ivy crawling along the ground, which was boarded to the assembly of long and tall standing-stones.

Megan was quite right to think the cloister assembly, she walked over to, was a simple enough covered corridor, because sticking her head in, this is what she found.

The copse of hedges and bushes was poured over a stone handrail on the left side of the ceiling-covered corridor.

Great slabs of light-brown stones made up the ground. No leaves or bushes were horded in scatters on the floor.

Miraculously, Megan's sight discerned a small doorway to her direct right, which was hidden within the bracken and nettles that were ensnaring a wall of Pandragon's Key.

Standing trees in the grove of the courtyard cast dark, deep shadows which also made the door's opening looked mostly-hidden.

As her eyes picked apart the leaves, Megan could see this leafy space was actually a hut.

Megan looked stumped.

It was so crowded with leaves and green and pinks of flowers that it was a surprise too find such a location at all.

Megan raised her brown-black eyebrows.

Mossy walls with dark green and bright pink fungus' creeping over the inner walls.

A battered-looking door was crooked on one side, sloped as if one joint at the top only held the door up.

Megan pushed it open.

It wouldn't shift. Heaving, and gripping the two sides with both hands, she managed to grapple the door to on to the wall, resting the tilted part where it was screwed-in, with the bottom half corner's sharp end leaning on to the ground.

The door felt so light like the wooden slats might fall down any moment.

Mr. Bumblebaux, flapping quite by Megan, saw her move forward and, it seemed to him, place a quite cautious foot past the door and into the darkly dank room.

Megan slightly shuffled in.

Smelly, moulding mildew whiffed out from behind the creaky door, as if the room hadn't been opened to any light in quite a while.

Megan squinted.

It was a very simple and basic affair - no more than a draft ridden and smoky room with just a hole in the roof.

Megan took her time to find out if the space was being inhabited.

Apparently, at that moment, the only inhabitants were The Fairy Key and an Elf.

Lines of tracks in the table-top dirt gave sight to small shapes as if someone (or something) had run a pencil's pointed end while mulling broodingly.

Megan, heading into the room, and ignoring the collected gang of rocks on a low table, saw another smaller, squatter table-top so matted with grime it could have originally been any colour under the three suns.

Several more feet in, and Megan nervously saw the room standing before them was over-grown with leaves and vines growing all over the outer-side, under the bushes, with tips reaching one another and grew in interlocking fingers, over tiny windows that were grimy and dirt-stained. The vines were so thick, they would have streamed to begin with, but now were covering the burdened wooden shuttering, making triple sure the room was closed in.

No-one could possibly use this room.

Megan gazed a little fearfully around the oddly proportioned room with short walls, broad ceiling and overlong rails running at half the walls height.

The room could have looked funny, but this place looked deadly frightening. Mr. Bumblebeaux did not blame Megan for backing away.

Megan concluded this room was abandoned long ago.

Contained no doors leading off the main room. Just as she turned, thinking this to be a spare room of some sorts, her eyes saw Mr. Bumblebeaux flitting by blackly yellowish nasty-looking goo, which was bleeding out of a black quill pen that was posed on an empty candle's tallow stand. The polluting guck was like congealed fatty lard on the table top.

Megan forced herself to carry on looking in.

A thin trickle of smoke issued from a pewter-grey and pink-stripped kettle, boiling above a small roaring coal fire that spat yellow and pink flints into the air.

The shouting smoke billowed up to just the small hole in the roof and then *puff puff puffed* out.

Megan frowned.

Anthologies. Encyclopedias. Each one once bound in gold gilding.

Gorged lacerations were cut into the scorched-looking books covers and spines.

By these dense-looking singed tomes, an ordered register of book titles and author names were lined on a sheet in five straight rows, close to which were structures of word usages on a separate sheet, and were phrased in theorized ways so that Megan was unable to absorb any of what she was examining.

'They have evidently been... borrowed,' Mr. Bumblebeaux said numbly, who nodded to the books, looking thoughtful and stroking his white-haired chin.

With a great sigh, he looked surprised to see them there. Megan looked surprised the books didn't sprout little arms and shoot-out tiny legs in succession, and go tearing about the dirty tables playing You Can't Catch Me.

Placed on the tables as if on purpose, for a showcased look for whoever or whatever possessed these, was writing equipment, and letters, which were once folded, but laid bare-open in slipshod stacks, unorganized.

'The books look worse than the others,' said Megan.

'Hmm,' Mr Bumblebeaux said, over at bays of ripped chairs.

Megan felt startled.

She kept one eye on Mr. Bumblebeaux, and divided her attention to the batches of awkward writings, snippets of sketches, procedures on old-fashioned notebooks and leather-bound journals and writing pads.

Still startled, Megan quivered.

The room felt it was something of the odd and ominous, which she did not like.

Megan stepped frowning.

A header on top of a browning-coloured sheet read *The Nine Solar Systems*, as well as hasty-looking words on: *Numerological Numbered Aligned Planets And Suns, Planetary Field Sources*

Megan finished the sheet.

There were more bizarre-looking freaky mathematical equations jagged on it, which were running in streams down the shaky-printed margins; the pen had been written with such force the sheet was more holes than piece of paper.

'Does feel.. sinister in here,' Mr. Bumblebeaux said in a slight hoarse whisper.

'It does feel... bad,' Megan said faintly, agreeing.

'We won't stay much longer.' Mr. Bumblebeaux was rifling through a stack of what looked like small cards, boxed in a narrow and tall filing cabinet.

Megan looked back to the dirty table.

She forced and ironed-out the parchment paper with the back of her hand.

Unrolling the paper, lines read: *The*

alignment to which the Foretelling by Fhilipsnokie   Mooglieschnoogleboo refers is nearing upon us

Megan was stunned.

She hadn't the faintest idea who this Fhilipsnokie

Mooglieschnoogleboo was, nor any littlest idea what the mysterious-sounding Foretelling could mean.

Megan wanted to bolt out.

'Perhaps it was ill-advised of me to allow you in here,' Mr. Bumblebeaux said, in a solemn tone, letting a sheet of paper titled with *Celestial Calculations* and numbered symbols drift out of his grip. 'Though I honestly had no idea this was the state and despair it's in.'

'It's not your fault,' Megan murmured, looking very concerned.

'Maybe not. Or maybe so,' Mr. Bumblebeaux looked upset at something, more than the condition of the room.

Megan had a sudden nasty feeling she was being watched.

Without her noticing, a black orbiting light suddenly crackled to her left.

Megan looked in horror at the light watching her, then gazed to Mr. Bumblebeaux, then looked back to her, then appeared more blacker if possible. Small and large bits of black Magic rained off from the light, making it look like a fast-spinning firework, trailing its slobbering in black showered sheets.

Megan felt eager to be gone.

They looked at each other.

'Watch out!' Mr. Bumblebeaux shouted, as the black fizzing light nipped past the top of her long-curly-haired head, then the wildly whizzy speeding globe splattered into the oncoming wall.

Megan didn't really much like the

room!

Chapter Thirty-Seven

Grassy Games

Megan scratched the left side of her nose.

Mr. Bumblebeaux watched the pinky-gold infused light all around her, which Megan was totally unaware of. Not for nothing, though, was Megan The Fairy Key.

In front of him, she gathered up the shrinking bunches of long vines, that gave her a clear walk-through and space for Mr. Bumblebeaux to flap.

Curiously, the creeping vines had at first strained against her touching, but the more she persisted with opening out the doorway, Megan, her face pale though very determined, found the curling vines followed her trembling finger orders of flailing back, giving her and Mr. Bumblebeaux room to exit, which was the only clear way out.

There was nothing else for it.

She would have to pick it up again.

'Ar...iccc...arh,' she trebled.

In a matter of mere moments, Megan rested the thin, mistreated door in exactly the same way she had discovered it.

'Humph,' Megan put the door in place.

Crashes of her pillates from her top swung about as her hand moved the floods of creepers, which gripped back into place when her hand left the door.

Megan shrunk back.

She watched in slight fright as the vines raveled inwards and rolled over each other.

Megan cringed.

'Lucky they moved, otherwise we

might have not gotten out!' she said, puling out her handkerchief and she wiped greeny-black muck from her fingers on to it, folding the gook up, making sure the slimy sludge was not going to touch the inside of her pocket.

With a gulp, Megan listened. No sound of the whizzing dark light came.

Nine paces ahead, Megan joined Mr. Bumblebeaux who was speeding around.

Her gaze fell on the astonishing sight of him seizing a small, rounded stone, mumbling to himself.

Megan stepped closer.

Mr. Bumblebeaux looked troubled. 'I thought this was lost. Obviously taken. I thought they did not crave this.'

His zooming around must have had a deeper purpose: Mr. Bumblebeaux clutched the stone as if his very Magic life depended upon it.

'W-what is it?' Megan asked, not wanting too interrupt much.

Mr. Bumblebeaux hid well enough the dread he was now feeling in his heart. 'Granted not much too look at, but still worth much,' he said, lifting the stone and letting the three suns rays bounce off the edges of the smooth surfaces.

They went together through the bands of hedges which had a slashed gap.

Megan walked up a bit more closer, 'Why would that have been taken?' she asked, remembering Mr. Bumblebeaux's mentioning that.

'This stone was thought lost.'

'I-I know. I heard you say. But why? You do seem really excited, and I'm pleased!' Megan smiled.

'Burning nor flaming suns could get rid of this stone,' Mr. Bumblebeaux said, more to himself, and flapped down and flew so close, he looked like he may very well nearly attempt to shove the stone up her nostril.

Megan didn't take a step back.

'This has such a beauty,' he went on, and she thought he looked a little dotty, as if he ought to be wearing eye-goggles, working in a laboratory on an invention and achieving an eureka moment.

'It does look very nice,' Megan commented.

Mr. Bumblebeaux looked more relaxed. He flew back slightly.

Megan gazed up at the suns, using her hand as a sun-vizor.

'This was my friend's,' Mr. Bumblebeaux added, appearing sad.

'Your friend?' Megan asked, looking now at the Elf, whose shoulders drooped in a flop as he flew upside down.

Mr. Bumblebeaux looked about him, as if surprised for a moment he wasn't alone. 'Yes, a friend. Archimedes.'

'Don't you see Archi... don't you see your friend anymore?'

'Sometimes,' Mr. Bumblebeaux sighed. He picked up a stray blade of grass that was blowing past in the breeze.

Megan regarded Mr. Bumblebeaux.

He let the grassy strand float out of his grip.

Mr. Bumblebeaux gave a little sigh. 'I'll go and put it back, that's what I'll do.'

'Where? Back there?' asked Megan nodding back, from below, letting her hand trail along the left-side of the hedgerow.

'Good grief no!' Mr. Bumblebeaux exploded in such a startled, almost angered way. He shook himself. 'Not back there,' he said, looking a tad more composed.

'Is the stone connected to the room?

Or who lives in the room?'

Mr. Bumblebeaux's gaze bored into Megan.

He was still flying upside down, but his eye-lock was nevertheless intense. 'Perhaps. I suspect so, but, yet I don't know.' he said after a trifle few moments, and his eyes were clouding over with a spatter of tears.

Mr. Bumblebeaux looked at Megan, who she saw was looking at her in dismay.

Megan was filled with compassion. 'Then we could put the stone back where it belongs,' she said, most firmly, and smiled kindly.

Mr. Bumblebeaux's bitterness faded gradually. Though Megan could tell it was for whoever, or whatever, stole the stone and not aimed at her.

As Megan's fingers brushed off a hedge, and she rounded a curving bend to the hedging, she saw a tall spire-like object pointing upward. As her feet moved on, and crunched on the light gravel, the hedges on both sides thinned out and revealed an open expanse of green fields. Dotted right in the middle was a monument that made her gasp loudly.

Sticking right out of the ground was an arm, as if someone had been buried and stuck their arm out, but became embedded over. Though this was no ordinary arm. The arm was of the extraordinarily artful; as tall as a skyscraper, and the stone tuniced-arm held aloft a sword in its vice-like grip. This was also as long and wide as a skyscraper. The sword was arrowed directly upwards, whereas the arm was bent slightly at the elbow, as if warded off from a downwards-then-sideways tactical aerial attack.

Megan walked down the decline in the field, nearing the arm as Mr. Bumblebeaux fluttered in his always zany way.

A massive shadow was cast by the arm and sword, and in which Megan stood, peering up and up, staring at the arm and sword running in thousands of feet long, with the blade-tip glinting from the three suns beams.

Mr. Bumblebeaux stood on the side of the arm that was stretching out of the ground.

No flower stems bloomed anywhere in the field. There was only grass, an enclosure of willow trees, and this stone sword shielding a stone arm.

Mr. Bumblebeux's sorrow had gone.

'The rest of the stone body remains buried,' he said, looking down at the ground.

Megan's gaze followed, and she wondered how big the stone statue might be under the grass, if the arm and sword were so monolithic-looking in their massive state of burial.

Megan shook her mind filled with wonders, and did her best to concentrate on the stone.

Her arms circled out as if readying for flight.

'It must be... must be...'

'Big?' Mr. Bumblebeaux said, looking now more like his cheerful Elfish self.

Megan laughed in a thundery way.

Mr. Bumblebeaux's wings thumped past her as he flew from the arm.

The lane of the shadow never moved; the arm and sword remained upright, erect, ever-still never moving.

The manner of the arm and sword were both mightily eery!

From Megan's vantage view, neither didn't exactly blend with the fields.

Megan stared and stared.

She almost willed the arm to wave; the sword to tremble; the flat field to heap-up then rip apart, and up spring a statue the size of all Great Britain. Or... thereabouts in size to a City.

'The sword looks as long as Big Ben,' Megan said, gazing upwards still, with her right hand holding the back of her ringlet-coated neck.

'Who's... Big Ben... when he's at home?' Mr. Bumblebeaux asked, standing on the grass and putting a slight booting to the soil here and there.

Megan hid her giggles. 'B-Big Ben? A clock in my world.'

'Oh, we don't have much need for timepieces here, in The Enchanted Kingdom,' he said, kicking back small clumps of grass that had been dug up. 'Though there is one Land that does insist on employing them... what a load of old twaddle,' he mumbled.

'What are you doing?' asked Megan, joining him in re-turfing the field.

'Blasted Fayes do this.'

Megan stopped. 'W-what's a Faye?'

Mr. Bumblebeaux smiled over. 'Fayes live in Fairy Land. Fayes are cousins of Fairy folk.'

'Fayes?'

'That's it.'

'Why do Fayes do this?' she asked, putting a small mound of grass back into the now nearly unblemished field - if not for the sight of what cast down the shadow, and in within a sheltering Megan was weaving about.

'Fayes like to be... puckish. A very naughty Faye has no regard for elders. Nor any real thoughtfulness. They come here, and play bad games.'

'Games?'

Mr. Bumblebeaux was re-planting grass. 'Wait until I get my hands on the Fayes who did this,' he muttered, 'such sheer disregard.'

Megan waited.

'Games?' he asked. 'Oh, they rip out bits of grass then lob each piece up, but angled just so.'

'Why?' asked Megan, thinking how very dull and boring that sounded.

'To get the grass looping round the top of the sword. An impartial Faye follows the speed and accurate propulsion of the grass, and the Faye-thrower who gets nearest to the top of the sword, wins.'

'Wins what?' Megan was bending over, using the backs of her hands for flatting down the grass that knitted back together with Magic.

'The pomposity of bragging they're the winner.'

'Oh,' Megan said, standing up.

'Never joined in myself, and would never harm grass like they've done here.'

Megan nodded, then went back to placing the last lump of grass back, looking between her legs at Mr. Bumblebeaux, seeming to now appear with flying the right way up.

'There,' Mr. Bumblebeaux said, nodding, turning around in the air, looking pleased and smiling a thanks to a grinning Megan. 'Can't spy anymore hunks of grass. We did well! Thank you,' he said, to her, whilst he flew around in the air doing mini-gambols.

His hands broached down his trouser pockets; he felt the left side filled with the stone, and smiled and nodded. He double-knotted his pocket together again.

'Do Fayes look like you, Princess Blossom, Prince Elfin and Nugget?' asked Megan, wondering aloud.

Mr. Bumblbeaux shook his head. 'Fayes are bright blue.'

Megan's eyes blinked a lot.

'Bright blue?' she exclaimed, confirming with asking.

Mr. Bumblebeaux nodded. He sounded a gruff chuckle, 'Well, let's be putting this stone back to its home.'

Chapter Thirty-Eight

The Nightly Spewing Square

Megan's breath was took away.

A leafless willow tree limped in the breezy wind near to the other trees.

'Oh my,' Megan said, looking sad. 'Is that really real?'

Mr. Bumblebeaux nodded, also looking just as saddened as Megan.

'Fayes?'

'Fayes indeed,' Mr. Bumblebeaux replied.

'How... why?'

'Because Fayes wear the leaves. Chuck all the leaves off then pulp them together too make clothing articles.'

'C-can't The Brim-Tree stop them?' Megan asked, wondering, too, if The

Brim-Tree were near.

'If Fayes had their way they'd rake out all The Brim-Tree's leaves, as well.'

Megan looked even more shocked.

The willow tree with no leaves stirred in the wind.

Behind the bare willow, rows of trees were directly loomed up. The trees look gave them a protective care for the willow.

Megan turned her attention back to the strip-bare tree.

'It looks so sad,' she mumbled.

Megan padded up by the willow.

The vine-branches were flopped on the grassy ground of the field.

Megan felt bad.

One or two long branches crept up in the clean, floating air, and looked like an old crone, nearly balding, was swaying her arms back and forth as she chanted her spell.

Megan, darting a glance back over

her shoulder, saw the ruins of the stone arm holding its stone sword, remaining the same in its upright pointing looking like two skyscrapers, one at the end of the other.

It still looked such an odd sight poking out of the ground, running thousands of feet into the air.

Megan shook her head.

She swung her sight back, and glimpsed the willow.

Megan added her gaze back to the other trees; she remembered once looking down at Prince Oaken, Prince of Gump Land, though these trees didn't uproot and move about like their tree brethren.

Megan had the impression that, if they could have, they would done so to protect the willow from the pesky-fingered Fayes. And maybe, if they were able, issued ear-splitting shouts into the line of the Fayes.

'Pandragon's Key really does have

some of your world's most prized trees. As you can see,' Mr. Bumblebeaux pointed a hand, half-upside down, 'beech trees, cedars, hawthorns, cherry trees, elms, hemlocks, chestnut, maples, sycamores, walnuts and of course all those willow trees.'

Megan totaled there were a tremendous amount of trees.

She nodded along, still feeling fully shocked by the miserable look of the willow, stripped by those deplorable Fayes.

Mr. Bumblebeaux flapped over to the trees. He nodded his head, advisedly. Megan followed. Her feet walked into the emerald-green grass that crept up the trunks of the trees.

Megan didn't feel troubled.

The trees line didn't seem that much remarkable; just like when taking a perambulation about a forested glen.

Her amble threw nothing up of the

extraordinary. Save for being in The Enchanted Kingdom, and taking a perambulating walked turn round The Fairy Key Land.

The atmosphere was warming, but felt just nice.

A non-foggy ray of sunshine swept in from the three suns, which stroked Megan's face.

Eighteen paces ahead, formed around a ring of different-sized trees, was a building.

Four paces to go, Megan looked closer at the one-storey shed.

The squared building was painted in red, like a bright telephone box. At first glance, the building had no obvious doorway. Then a certain door swung out slightly from the breeze. It didn't bang, but its latch knocked the black rusting hook.

Mr. Bumblebeaux held the door open, ajar. 'We're headed in the right way.'

Megan smiled, up.

His wings brushed past the door swinging itself shut behind them. Then the door creaked open again from the windy air.

There was still a slight pong of mildew clinging to Megan and Mr. Bumblebeaux, caused from the shack with the Foretelling by Fhilipsnokie Mooglieschnoogleboo.

As they wove down the brilliantly lit passageway, running into the ground with a slight decline, this was nothing like the shack's black light. The passage had an opening up ahead which flowered into a big gold chamber, the ceiling arcing high above Megan as she walked underneath its arching rafters in gleaming silver.

For a while, nothing was spoke about.

Megan mulled for a bit on Mooglieschnoogleboo's Foretelling.

But she only had the vaguest idea of what such a Foretelling was; and at best, only about some sort of know-how to maybe cast a predication. Her mum's sister used to sometimes talk about astrological signs, and always made sure to grab her daily horoscope in the newspaper. Being born on December the third, Megan knew her star-sign was Sagittarius. She quite liked what her star-system was represented with in the zodiac. Like it was meant to be.

Megan shook her head.

She looked to the far corners of the chambered room.

Empty. All was empty. Empty as empty can be.

Not even a stitch of a cushion nor a swirl of a tapestry was within the room.

There was only Megan and a high-flying Mr. Bumblebeaux. He looked far up like a person walking steadily on a trapeze wire at a circus.

'Oh, would you look at that,' Mr. Bumblebeaux beckoned, fluttering down and pointing.

Megan frowned slightly.

She didn't see anything in the bowl-like room.

Padding nearer, laying flat on the gold floor, was a trap-door, and unseen to Megan, from which a ladder would led down into the dark.

'Would you like me to open... it?' Megan asked, shaking slightly, expecting the answer to be a resounding opposite to a no.

Which really didn't surprise her when Mr. Bumblebeaux nodded excitedly, and looked like he might perform a jig on the spot.

Megan leaned down.

Her fingers searched for some means to grapple the circled handle.

She rummaged around the flush circle; trying to prise it up.

Megan had to kneel more on the floor.

The door could be pulled up by means of a brass-iron black ring.

The handle shivered and in a squeak, she eased the handle so now it stood fully up from the floor.

Megan manged to open the trap-door a few inches.

She half-expected it to clang back. But, she held it smoothly.

Megan sat back on her heels.

She held on to the handle of the trap-door.

Slowly, she teased the handle more and in a wrench, the trap-door fully opened.

Megan took a step back, protectively. She wanted to block out the sight.

When the flap of the trap-door was pried upright, a ladder connected to the back of the trap-door whirled down in slats, pussh-thuuunk, pussh-thuuunk, pussh-thuuunk went the sliding step-ladder, each of its slats stepping out like crashing dominoes.

Megan watched attentively in silence.

Mr. Bumblebeaux looked alert. He turned to Megan.

'We've got to scarper down there,' Mr. Bumblebeaux explained, describing his planned means to move along to the room.

Megan looked even more startled.

'You'll be all okies; you crossed the very barriers of space and time to be here.'

Megan gulped. She didn't reply.

'A ladder into darkness should be... fine,' Mr. Bumblebeaux described happily, standing on the straightened lip of the trap-door, his voice cracked with rapturous joyfulness.

Megan didn't exactly feel tiptop excitement.

The throng of the three-sides of the

trap-door remained stood up. She hoped it wouldn't bang on the top of her head as she started to scramble down, into the darkening abyss.

Megan peered anxiously in.

What she saw wasn't very promising.

Dramatically, there was a silence. Nothing flew in her face. Only darkness poured out. Even though the room like so many others gave off its gleaming glow, the room's light didn't touch the square of the trap-door, with its spreading and unwelcoming darkness.

Megan nearly fainted.

Though she didn't lose consciousness.

Speechlessly, she gazed toward the darkness that trooped out of the opened trap-door. Megan wanted to back out the room.

There was no doubt in Megan's mind that the flung-open trap-door was better off closed.

Megan couldn't believe she was possibly meant to dart down in there.

'Can't you carry me down?' she asked, standing motionless. 'Like when we went up the stairs in the tower by the Berkeley Baxley Arch?'

Mr. Bumblebeaux looked at her. He shook his head. 'Most unfortunately I am unable,' he explained, looking ashamed. 'You see, I am not as young as I once was and I didn't know I still retained the Magic power and strength to pull you. If I carry you down, there's also the unthinkable risk I might drop you, then et cetera.'

Megan gulped.

Mr. Bumblebeaux looked a little bad.

Megan smiled, 'It's OK. I understand,' she said, reassuring the Elf.

She looked in the dark. It was so dark.

Megan's peeking only showed a dark square hole, with a silver ladder-top running down into the darkness.

'H-hello?' Megan called-out softly.

H-hello. H-hello. H-hello. Her lilting carried on in the gloomy dark.

A deep throaty, delightful cough came from Mr. Bumblebeaux, that was also injected with a note of admiration at her bravery,

Mr. Bumblebeaux looked alert. 'Trust in yourself, Megan,' he advised with certainty to her, answering her understandable doubts.

Megan gulped.

The two sides of the ladder-top were sticking up in the air, then appearing to be lost in the dark as the ladder carried on, shrouded in the gloom.

Megan turned around.

She looked up. Mr. Bumblebeaux grinned back, rallying his encouragement.

She gripped the nearest side of the ladder with her right hand, then a bit nervously but surely, swung her right foot down on to the step.

Megan gulped.

Her ankle disappeared into darkness!

Lying the flat of her hand against the back of the trap-door, clutching the ladder-top with both unflinching hands, she shuffled across and brought down her left leg, so now both were ankle-deep in sludgy darkness.

Megan trudged down the hole.

Step one.

Timidly, she let her foot fall on to the next step in the gloom. As soon as she climbed down, Megan's heartbeat pumped faster.

Step two.

Leaning down, Megan tried her best to ignore the ever-pressing dark.

Step three.

Her pair of cornflower-blue eyes squinted to her sides into the onslaught of the lowering gloominess, which was now rushing up to greet her.

Step four.

'*Cannot believe I'm doing this*,' she whispered, into the ladder.

Quietly, and feeling scared, she again lowered herself down the rung.

Step five.

Megan uttered a cry.

She lost her footing; she very nearly tumbled off.

Her right hand snatched the step above, while her left hand grabbed around the the run of the ladder-side. Her clambering feet fumbled for the next step.

Megan clasped on tighter to the ladder.

Mr. Bumblebeaux hovered above. 'You're doing OK!' he shouted. 'Keep going!' he could see the light that veiled her which was able to guide him.

'Thank-k yo-ou,' she called up, appreciatively.

Mr. Bumblebeaux smiled down. Her light beam cast a two-foot glowing light then hit darkness.

Megan started to slowly winch herself down again.

Step six.

Megan's heart sank.

She took several deep breaths before climbing down some more.

Step seven.

It was so dark. Dark like walking out from a gangplank on a pirate ship at night, and not knowing when the crashing drop into the ocean was to come.

Megan felt as though her breath had all been knocked out of her.

Step eight.

Megan's jaw slightly dropped open.

She carried on descending down.

Step nine.

Megan screwed her face up as though wiped with a vinegar-drenched cloth.

She kept one firm foothold on the step on the ladder, and her right foot groped for landing.

Megan heard her heartbeat thumping in her ears.

Mercifully, a flat surface of a floor greeted her probing foot.

Megan shuddered.

Unknitting her hands, her grip loosened from the ladder.

Chapter Thirty-Nine

Halley's Comet

Feeling happy at last, Megan leaped off the ladder.

She shuddered and shook that violently she had to steady herself on a smooth-feeling wall.

Luckily, at that moment of her cautious landing, lights flared up, uncovering gold floorboards and a room so big and wide, a red double-decker bus could easily tootle on its way being drove around in.

Megan walked in long measured strides.

She had landed on a grand enclosed atrium.

Pink tulle hung in bilious clouds, all congregating from its hanging rails to stretch down into peaks, which ran in gathers on the pink cobble-stoned floor

A familiar sound like a moth beating its wings made Megan smile. Here was Mr. Bumblebeaux. He stood on the ninth step of the ladder, which hadn't slated back up, shutting them in.

Within the gold-walled room, very uneven books were piled on a table.

In a swish, Mr. Bumblebeaux circled the table. He continued to circle it in the air.

Megan stood motionless.

Although the feeling wasn't like when she was in the horrid shack, she still felt like something or someone was spying on her; maybe through one of the keyholes of the golden doors standing unwaveringly closed. Though she didn't want to dwell on what was maybe on the other sides. That plotting, nasally nasty-sounding voice was enough to put her off for life of wondering who, or what, could be on the other side of a firmly closed door.

Megan shivered.

Mr. Bumblebeaux, meantime, was throwing papers to his left and chucking scraps of parchment to his right. The table, at one end, now looked like it was rising in yellowing flurries of snow.

When Megan brought her gaze back to the table occupied with now half-seen books, as well as papers, she saw Mr. Bumblebeaux was still sieving through them, making little mounded piles, like a startled peering mole was gazing shyly out of its homely holes.

Besides the tables strewn with papers, Megan's eyes fixed on the table endowed with a lonesome-looking chair, in crushed-pink velvet fabric running over the chair's frame.

Pulling the chair out, not scraping it, Megan dropped down.

Megan honed in.

Her scope read snatched passages on individual pieces of curling parchment, that stuck out of hardback and cloth-bound books.

Megan breathed-over the papers and leafed through the books. This time putting each one more near to her creased face.

With a hand tucked inside her crossed legs and her chin resting on her balled hand, she read.

She went back to the beginning, picked up the scripts and documented bound-texts, re-read the words, then spoke aloud (from a couple of re-tries getting the wordy and tongue-twisters right), as if speaking the descriptions might somehow make them less cryptic and more understandable. She placed the paper and book back, after she'd spoken of its title on its front cover and related piece of parchment, then chose the next one on the table.

'Ballads...

...Abelard...

... *Time recording of Halley's Comet, Normandy, 1066.*'

Megan shrugged.

She carried on reading, saying the words out loud.

'How Attila did not reach Rome....

... *A Life & Times of Horace von Hoppernickle.*'

Megan dispensed with reading; she knuckled her temples then forehead.

Megan's fingers flexed.

She flared her nostrils.

Megan felt befuddled.

She rested the strap of shiny gold cloth on to the front of the pristine-looking, royal-blue Abelard book.

Megan really didn't have any thoughts on the subjects.

She was stumped. 'I don't understand,' Megan muttered.

'Hmm...' Mr. Bumblebeaux stroked his chin, thinking. 'You really are at a loss? Maybe at the moment you are not meant too understand.'

Megan pointed with her right hand. 'Do you think?'

'Indeed I do.'

Megan squeezed the well-worn, threadbare bookmark back into its place within the centuries old pages of *A Life & Times of Horace von Hoppernickle*, then put *Time recording of Halley's Comet, Normandy, 1066* on to the front of *Hoppernickle's Times*. Both were now in piled order she'd started off with on the stacks.

Mr. Bumblebeaux raised an arm. 'Come on, let's be off.'

'I thought you were looking for something?' Megan asked, uncrossing her leg.

'Hmm. I was, but, seems to be have been... misplaced.' Mr. Bumblebeaux shot up, a bit too quickly for his wings took him in flight to left, then he bounded to the right, then he just about missed smashing into the gold-paneled ceiling.

Below, Megan got to her feet.

The room was proportioned much like one of the courtyards she'd seen, only this one was closed over. Nine doors stood in lines directly from the where she and Mr. Bumblebeaux had entered.

Each door had a nine-foot space between each other.

From sitting on the table, she hadn't really paid the doors much attention nor thought.

Now, though, a feeling of direful dread knotted in her stomach.

Mr. Bumblebeaux was hovering by the third door.

'We have to go through that?' Megan asked, standing still, already suspecting the answer.

Mr. Bumblebeaux nodded.

'I can await here t-t-though?' he

suggested, blowing his nose on a bit of red rag. 'Aaah... hooey,' he coughed, wiping his honk. 'Excuse I.'

'No no. Please come as well,' Megan confirmed, not much liking the alternative Mr. Bumblebeaux had mooted.

'As you wish,' he replied, squaring his rag up in his breast-pocket.

Megan plodded forwards.

Mr. Bumblebeaux inclined his rotating head. 'Try the door.'

'It looks locked... don't we need a key?'

'But that's the point Megan, *you* are the Key. The Fairy Key.'

Megan nodded, feeling totally swept up again.

Mr. Bumblebeaux flew to her. 'Try the handle.' he recommended, with a nicely-meant chuckle.

And, as he spoke of the handle, the handle twitched, as if someone, or something, on the other side was not waiting to get out.

Megan let out a little squeak.

She walked forward. Slowly she placed her right forefinger on the curve of the golden handle. It felt secure. She didn't look behind her, but if she had, Megan would have seen Mr. Bumblebeaux smile to himself like he so often did when around her.

Megan held the handle securely.

Her grip didn't slip. Her left handed fingertips pushed slightly on the door as Megan opened it.

In a creaking skreak, as if the bolts and the nails had not been used in a while, the door gave way and yawned open for her.

The gold floorboards ran into a rounding white alcove, which was within the spread of the square room, that was in size to fit at least twenty cars like her mum and dad's one.

The bay of the alcove had a white tall cabinet nestling inside it.

Mr. Bumblebeaux suddenly flapped ahead, whizzing over Megan's hair, so tendrils of ringlets fell in front of her gaping face.

Draws in the cabinet were stood open.

Mr. Bumblebeaux flitted from each draw. 'All empty,' he said, hanging his head, and looking very sad.

The white draws ran in three rows.

Megan counted down.

One. One. One.

Two. Two. Two.

Three. Three. Three.

'It's my fault,' Mr. Bumblebeaux waved his hands to the empty draws.

Megan wasn't quite sure why the draws being empty was such a mournful state of a thing. 'I'm sure it's not your fault. You didn't cause this.'

'No. I didn't,' Mr. Bumblebeaux mumbled, looking preoccupied, as if attempting to mindfully sift through who, or what, could have created such a deed.

'Well, there are you are then. This isn't your fault. And at least there's one stone to put back,' Megan pointed out, trying to look on the bright side.

'Yes, you're right.' Mr. Bumblebeaux untied his pocket and brought out the stone.

'Won't it be taken again?' Megan asked, fearful for the stone's safety.

'Not now you've been here, and touched the stone. It cannot now be removed, unless by your touch,' he explained.

'Oh, right,' Megan mumbled, not expecting that, and feeling rather overwhelmed. A stone in a draw only being removed by her hand... whatever next!

'Would you like to do the honours?' Mr. Bumblebeaux asked, looking a little watery-eyed, but seeming to perk up.

'Me?' Megan squeaked.

'Of course. You're The Fairy Key.'

'I'm The Fairy Key,' Megan rehearsed, with a note of disbelief, but not quite a questioning tone tinging her voice. She looked about the room, noticing there wasn't any windows.

Mr. Bumblebeax flew over. He passed along the stone.

As the stone left his small fingers and went into her open hand, there was a buzz of surprise coming from Megan. This was owing to the oval-shaped stone had lightened up in pinky lights. The stone vibrated. In Magic. In power. It buzzed merrily to itself.

'The stone recognises you,' Mr. Bumblebeaux announced.

Megan uttered a cry of understanding.

It was only the very same pebble that had once lodged into her palm!

Megan remembered lobbing this off.

Nothing, it appeared, could stop the stone strumming in her hand.

Megan was too shocked to say anything.

She had a volley of questions to pelt Mr. Bumblebeaux with.

When Megan placed the stone back into the black-velvet draw, the stone returned to looking like a normal, everyday stone.

'I'm sure you can find the others,' Megan said, encouragingly.

'All eight, gone,' Mr. Bumblebeaux said, sadly, in a plaintive sigh.

'You'll find them.' Megan nodded, standing back, and they both looked to the draw whirring into life, giving a shake, then the stone-filled first draw closed slowly shut.

Megan continued to look extremely at the other eight draws, all long, and standing open. The other eight draws were identical versions of the one now closing.

As well as the one with the stone, she hoped they might have all closed.

Mr. Bumblebeaux sighed, then flew out of the room.

As Megan went to ask a question (or ten), the door creaked into life again and backed itself closed. The outer wall shivered, and looked more like the door was tightly closed, locked.

Mr. Bumblebeaux flew on in his blustering way.

Megan was mulling over which question to ask first about the stones. She was on the fifth step of the ladder. She moved upward, gripping the next step up and bringing her feet up slowly. Mr. Bumblbeaux had positioned himself on the opened trap-door, using it as a seat, giving a thumbs-up to Megan's ascent.

'There we are,' he said, as she scrambled out, also slowly, not letting go of the ladder-sides until her feet were on firm ground. Moving sideways, she swung off, then in a *wwooosssh-claaaank, wwooosssh-claaaank, wwooosssh-claaaank*, the steps wound back up, then the lip of the trap-door trembled, and in a powerful swing, shut.

Megan was thankfully she hadn't been in the middle of getting off the ladder when the trap-door decided to close.

Megan sighed pleasingly at a job well done.

The trap-door looked like it did when Mr. Bumblebeaux had pointed it out.

Backtracking, retracing her steps up and out the red shed, then on through the trees with the stripped willow, they'd gone by the outskirts by the stony arm and stone sword (Megan was very glad to note the ground there had no pockmarks from Fayes), and they were now in a long spacious corridor, which was overlooking a lower part of the hall in Pandragon's Key, that flourished out into a courtyard.

The *wwooosssh-claaaanking* shouts were still ringing in Megan's ears. For a moment, she forgot too ask her questions on the nine stones, one now found.

The first door Mr. Bumblebeaux opened led to another room with a door, then going through that, Megan forgot her questions as her mind now wondered where they were now going.

Nothing out of the extraordinary divulged itself.

That was until Mr. Bumblebeaux opened a door, using his legs too push against the jamb.

Without a word, Megan helped, smiling up.

Once the heavy-feeling door moaned outward, Megan stepped back. Diffidently, she gripped the frame and pepped in.

Megan's vision took in captions of no meaning. Books were bunked up together which were dotted about un-upholstered chair frames that stood rammed next to each other, so it was rather difficult to discern where one chair started, and another chair stopped.

Tables were rowed with books, pages, and notes taken from passages or thoughts scribbled down, which seemed too look to Megan in either pencil or ink. Megan's fingers stilled over a traced outline.

An extravaganza of gold goblets and other cups of materials in silver were planted on a wide table. A few cups were also encrusted with blazing multifaceted stones, and one in particular was enameled in a pink wash, that also had a pink serving spoon by its stand.

A white table placement folder had the one word: *Cuyp*

'Items from your world,' Mr. Bumblebeaux confirmed the origins.

Megan felt very excited.

A metal helmet in the colour of molten silver was resting on a gold table. A gang of gleaming tiaras and glittering diadems were accumulated extensively around the perching sparkling helmet. The silvery shimmering light deflected back on to an opened, flat-bottomed silver casket.

The dazzling almost nearly blindfolded her. More than anything, the light rivaled the tiara table she'd seen not so long ago.

'Gracious,' disbelief showing in Megan's voice.

Mr. Bumblebeaux gave a jubilant chortle.

Megan held up her left index finger as her hand ran over very early copies of books meanings and names lost on her. Sheets of vellum were sat neatly around some sort of book:

Encylopdia by, Mathieu, illustrated manuscripts, representations of illuminations

Megan looked back to Mr. Bumblebeaux's eyeline; he was staring at white vellum envelopes: a lot were opened like those she'd seen, but piles more were strewn in either orderly towers or dumped, and remained closed with the guarded pink sealing wax warding the inner secrets.

Odder still, piano music suddenly swirled up within the air.

The music was of a strange, almost otherworldly tunes and built up, getting into full swing, the wild music, flowing, was not unpleasant, and caused a rippling feeling in her.

Megan, a little alarmed, searched for the source of the crooning music.

The lollapalooza-sounding music festival was plinky-plonking somewhere else, not seen.

Megan could tell she wasn't going to source the sound. So she simply enjoyed the piano concerto. Megan recalled her mum and dad watching a box-set of a *Pride and Prejudice* marathon, one Sunday afternoon, and the music sounded quite like to what she had heard then, which in piano notes had drifted up the stairs and landing of number Nine, Marlyberry Mews that found Megan re-reading her favourite book, and then later drawing.

Walking over, scarce, derelict-looking books looked so old they could easily have gone out with the printing press. Centuries old books were they that Megan could imagine one or two being read in her bedroom, on a fine winter's evening, cozily reading.

'These books like a quiet life, so they do.' Mr. Bumblebeaux said.

'They look so... so - '

' - Mistreated..?'

Megan assumed the books came like that over time. Not that someone had actually wanted to damage a book.

Megan cared a lot. 'That's horrific.'

'Right enough.'

'Nobody ever cared for any of them?'

Brow furrowed, Mr. Bumblebeaux said, 'Not so as far as I can discern. Some are so badly harmed they will not open up, not even their covers. Whoever heard of treating a book in such a gross behaviour? There's never a reason to prescribe such a state on to a book,' Mr. Bumblebeaux concluded.

Megan nodded.

'Alas, most unfortunately, as far back as I can remember, not all in your world are like Megan Button, who cares for her books.'

Megan looked away.

Apart from the fact she felt now slightly embarrassed, she looked aside in a way to again look at the shelves.

Megan felt plainly very sorry for the teams of books.

They did not look unfriendly (as far as she could tell).

Megan felt a rush of sympathy and sadness for them all.

Then, just when things were appearing to look even more run-over for the worsted books conditions, Megan heard the suddenly silent room cut-off its music-merry making.

Megan looked around in unmistakable bewilderment.

Starting from the corners of the room, as if it were awarding her, or in displeasing objection, the air in the book-room shimmered!

Megan looked like she might zonk out in a swoon.

Chapter Forty

I'm Henry VIII I am

Megan's eyes traveled over the sheets of parchment, scribbled with a quick, heavy hand, that were scattered and left strewn over the table-top as if the writer had departed in a hurry:

Treatise, preparatory study – Baron Bane

Troops, invading regiments of Evil

She was not of an age, but for all time

Allegorical piece of mythological text in verse poetry

Female Principle In Alchemical Change

Quicksilver; a metallic or bodily principal of volatility in Alchemy

Next to all the paper clutter, Megan could just make out embossed copperplate lettering on the spine of a thickly, weighty-looking book, advertising the title:

William's Playes, 1615

Next to this gargantuan tome was a sheaf of papers lying orderly on each other, secured in a folio clasp with the handwritten scrawl on the top sheet, denouncing the words *Henry VIII*

'An... interesting play that... for an earthling to conjure up.' Mr. Bumblebeaux confided. Megan had no idea as to the author, nor its contents, though somewhere in the deep, foggy recesses of her brain, when being sat in History, at school, she vaguely remembered the name of the King, and how the monarch had treated his very unfortunate six wives. Of course, Megan would usually be doodling in the margins and generally drawing secretly, lost happily in her own sketching world.

She looked round the gold swirls beneath her feet and above her head; the room was incredibly gold and dazzling. Megan could almost imagine white-gloved people in frock-coats may come out suddenly, bearing plated bon-bons. Non did. Megan sighed a bit: at that moment, a strawberry bon-bon would have gone down rather well.

Scroll-work was adorned on the walls and looked like croissants had been dripped in gold dip.

Occasionally, Megan glimpsed the

table was also slyly crowded with pointing-out, drawn-shut velvet bags, can-like food tins and powdered stopper-topped bottles.

One such bag had a hand-written card attached to a bit of twine fixed about the closed bag. The severe hand-writing gave an owner to a one: Wil Chapyus. Megan shrugged, then placed the dark-plum bag back on to the table, shoving it back between different-sized bottles.

She rifled on. Words were lined over pages, and Megan's eyesight listed the wordy columns and books that held:

Azgincourt
Love poems
1420's
Presented
Noble
Engulfed
Topographic

Manuscript Book
Monarchical   *Constricted*
Manuscripts
Magic Monarchical Manuscripts

Finishing with those, Megan continued to crane her neck, spying down the books spines she was now nose-level with:

Royal... Henry VIII, illuminating manuscripts... Uniting England, Anglo-Saxon, by G... Flourish of illumination... Renaissance led by thrice kings

I don't really understand these words, Megan thought. But she kept reading ever on. Drawn to the pull of what was in front of her:

1466...A human chap in your world, Coxton... Hand-written... Scrolling penmanship... Artwork...

Illuminators artificial... Edward of York... Inner sanctum... 65 books, not 50 as humouredly speculated

A little later, Megan was still bent-sideways.

She kneaded her neck as she read on:

Mooted Writings of past... Histories... de Bevouavy... Roses, War of Roses... Edward IV... Scholar versus Scholarship.

Megan thought this was going a bit too far.

She had no idea of the bleariest as to what any of the words or names meant.

Again, Megan shrugged off the words.

She gazed to the beamed ceilings that were above opened wooden chests, which contained books.

And there were bookshelves. Many bookcases. Aisles of bookshelves.

Megan dared not think how much it would cost to buy one single book, they looked so old.

Ornate tapestries were hung on the gold-flaming dazzled-stroked walls, with gold-gilt symbols woven within plush red velvet on high-backed chairs.

A heraldic insignia inscription and a symbol of a pink rose was crafted on to a book, which Megan, through her own reflection, was peering down at. The tome was like many others of books that had lavish pink roses on their front-bound covers, and all were displaying themselves within glass-housed stands. The lavishness of the rose books was very fine indeed. Dotted around the see-through stands were crenelated façades that ran into a landscape down the lower-half of the room, which was sectioned with tables, on top of which dwelt jewelry, plates, bound books, thin and thick-looking manuscripts.

Mr. Bumblebeaux, not looking bored, was propping his feet on to a gold-thread table-mat, and was reading a book titled *Lady Fortune, The Personification Of Chance. A Penny*

Megan smiled in a warm way; she knew what it was like to lose oneself in a book, being locomoted away with words.

She went back to her own reading. Slipping out pieces of parchment contained within books of manuscripts.

Each single paper-trail held only one or a few scattering of words:

Posterity
Museums
Fairy tale for fairy tale sake
Scriptoria

Exiled in a mansion, scribbled historical artisan
Court
1483
Bosworth Field
Richard Tudor
Pink greyhound
Pink Dragonn Cometh
Bolster
Mystique
Calldwellder
Red and white roses
History texts
Dense calculations of Planetary Movements and Interplanetary Field Beams
Learning
Gold-gilt, royalty
Astronomy
Astrology
Omens

Thick, three lines running parallel, sideways to each other, were on a clean white parchment piece, and below, the lines were attributed to one legendary name: Merlin

Just at that moment, Megan looked up, feeling shocked again to read about the legendary Merlin. Mr. Bumblebeaux, without glancing up, pointed to the drawn-on fabric hanging in a frame upon the castle wall, bearing a notation underneath the building:

Merlin Tin Hall

The drawn-sculpture in light pencil shades was split into three levels. Merlin Tin Hall was triangular at the top, with a rounder, more longer middle level and the floor beneath was squared.

Megan wondered where Merlin Tin Hall might be hiding.

'It was brought here as an annex to your Pandragon's Key,' Mr.

Bumblebeaux said, not looking up from the *Lady Fortune* book, resting in his lap.

'W-hy?' Megan asked, wondering if she should get up to talk, but following Mr. Bumblebeaux's restful inactivity, she instead stayed seated.

'Because of Camelot crumbling, and fearing the same state would befall his Merlin Tin Hall, Merlin, knowing of the then preparatory plans for your Pandragon's Key, asked if Merlin Tin Hall could be transferred over here, to your Fairy Key Land.'

Megan gaped.

Jolted out of her stupefied silence, 'I-Is Merlin Tin Hall still around, here?' she asked, trying to take all this in.

'Indeed so. The extension is a relatively small Wing,' he explained, still keeping his eyes fixed on the book. 'Compared to the size of Pandragon's Key, it would be like a mouse-hole.'

'Can we, I mean I please go there?'

Mr. Bumblebeaux now looked up. He interlocked his fingers, resting his elbows on the sides of the golden and blue Elf-sized chair. 'Whenever you like. Though you've managed to squeeze in a lot on this visit, so you can go to Merlin Tin Hall now, or when you next say a hello.'

Megan thought, then thought a little more.

Sitting still, she thought it best, on the whole, to postpone a jaunt into Merlin Tin Hall. She was having too much fun, reading.

Leaning back, Megan asked, 'Can't Merlin Tin Hall have stayed in my world?' then as an afterthought, added, 'Not that I mind Merlin's Hall being here!'

Mr. Bumblebeaux grinned back. 'If Merlin Tin Hall had stayed in your world, then come the passing of

Camelot, like that, Merlin's Hall would have fallen.'

'I don't understand,' Megan said, honestly, with her eyes shining.

'Well, it boils down to people in your world forgetting the old ways. Old ways of life. Old ways of living. Just general old ways. True, in your world time works so differently, but still, as people, so many people forgot.'

'The old ways?'

Mr. Bumblebeaux nodded.

'Is that why Camelot fell?' she asked, seeming to think there was more to this.

'It... contributed to that, yes.'

Megan's awe-filled gaze returned back to the sheet in her hand:

Merlin

Megan was flabbergasted.

'Did The Brim-Tree... mind?' she

asked, wondering just how Merlin Tin Hall had been brought over into The Enchanted Kingdom.

'Not at all. The Brim-Tree used its Magic and sought advice from Merlin on his Hall's state, so nothing would be lost bringing it over. As it was, only or two items fell between the gateways.'

'Did you look after this?' Megan asked avidly.

Mr. Bumblebeaux knew she meant the removal of Merlin Tin Hall, and not its pictorial framed reference, nor the sheet of paper The Fairy Key was waving about. 'Oh no, completely before my status. Prince Tumble worked with Merlin, and he with The Brim-Tree, too save Tumble the bother of constant consultation.'

'Prince Tumble knows Merlin?' Megan asked, faltering, her mouth hanging open.

'Most of us here do. So odd again

too think you, all in your world, assume he's simply a mythological myth! Well, a bit like me!' Mr. Bumblebeaux chuckled.

Megan laughed.

Far under the timbre-panelled roof and various coat-of-arms on the walls, both bent heads and went back to their respectful reading:

Astrological Symbols
Divinations, Portents, scribbling
The Coming Of The Fairy Key
Cosmos
1497

A small picture of what looked like a man was violently shaking a spear, the word Bollingbrook was next to the picture diagram:

Beautiful

Henry   VIII,   illuminating manuscripts

Royal Astrologer

Astrology Symbol
Square within a square
Nodule
Guild

Megan cast an exploratory glancing sweep over the the dozens of tiny scraps of parchment now amassing in her lap.

She now looked like her legs had turned into paper!

Mr. Bumblebeaux crossed his hands behind his back.

They were journeying down the Magic, gold-flecked extended side to the room. 'There's a small work by Xeonophob, who was a philosopher. Nice Mer-man, him. Not a rare one!

'Anyway,' he went on, 'we equally have our histories chronicled here, within your All Souls Librarium. From each Land they are, of The Enchanted Kingdom, dating back to the year dot and running up in actions and events to right now,' Mr. Bumblebeaux, nodding, flew right and Megan followed three paces behind. Taking a book out of his left pocket (Megan wondered what else he might have stuffed in his pockets), he said, 'This was recently loaned-out from the the First History Department, C - '

Smiling, Megan interrupted, ' - Compassing Histories Of The Magic,' she said, assuredly.

'Well done!' Mr. Bumblebeaux looked impressed, as if he wanted to punch the air. 'Those from The Ordinary Prevalent History Cycles Of The Provinces, ought to have logged this away, not left it here,' he tutted.

'Is The Second History Department far away?' Megan asked, thinking they could put back the book Mr. Bumblebeaux was carrying.

'*Should* be far, yes. But as with your Pandragon's Key, we may round this oncoming corner, and there we are!'

Megan smiled along.

'I found this when I swept threw earlier,' he explained, sweeping out an arm, 'and was on my way to give a good talking to, when I only flew into you!'

'Ah!' Megan said, remembering.

'The look on your face!'

Megan laughed. 'D-did you know I was here?'

'Of sorts,' Mr. Bumblebeaux said, being elusively evasive.

Megan looked down. She gazed at the white carpet streaming under feet, *should I ask how?* she thought.

She looked thoughtfully contemplative. A part of her mummered in agreement. She was still curious. But, she suspected, for some reason, Mr. Bumblebeaux might not give a clear-cut answer, just like he deflected her palavered questions to get more information out of him, when she probed her guess-gaming of Who Owns The Voice?

Megan shuddered from recalling the sound of that nasally-flat voice.

Mr. Bumblebeaux creaked open the small olive-green book. He flitted over, and, flicking through the rough-looking pages that smelt oddly of salt and hot cocoa, showed Megan the text. 'Here we have an example of Aargon.'

'Who's Aargon?'

Megan made her way over to the table.

A stuffed toy rat was wearing a blue overcoat that was two sizes too small for it. Both were old-looking and fraying about the edges.

Ignoring the rodent, Mr. Bumblebeaux replied, 'Aargon The Argonaut, or, as some rulers here rename the fable, Aagron The Noble, or Aargon The Brave.'

Megan couldn't stop herself from

smiling. 'Why was Aargon so brave?'

Mr. Bumblebeaux peered out from the top of the hardback book.

'Would you say you're particularly brave?'

Megan shook her head. Not having to mull long over this.

'Well, there you go.'

Megan sat on the edge of a plush pink sofa. 'What do you mean?'

'In my experiences, whether a Magic creature of those in your world, any that are brave do not consider themselves as brave-hearted,' Mr. Bumblebeaux surmised, with his bespectacled face gleaming back the lights from the roof, a stray of light reflected from his glasses danced on Megan's shoulder. 'They just get on doing the right thing. But those that self-trumpet and announce how brave they are, but when scratched the pretended face, might not be quite so as they'd want you to believe.'

Megan hadn't really thought about this.

'Honour is built up,' Mr. Bumblebeaux said, then remarked more, 'and usually by big shows of bravery, though also by those smaller ones. Personally, I'm of the opinion it's the smaller brave acts that mean more.'

'What did Aargon do that was brave?' Megan asked, captivated.

'Aargon led a band of his adventurers on many great adventures.'

'Just like Marmaduke did?'

Mr. Bumblebeaux, stopping the rolling-up of the loose papers by the book's back cover, looked startled and wonder-struck, 'My, you are a clever little Button!'

Megan smiled, blushing.

'To answer your attentive-minded question: Marmaduke and Aargon have differences, and yet are similar.'

'How?'

'Well, for one, Marmaduke wasn't a Fauwn like Aargon.'

'A Fauwn?' Megan asked, not quite knowing what a Fauwn was.

'Hindquarters, legs and horns of a goat, and the body of a man from your world. Goat is the right word for the animal description, I think.'

'We have goats in my world,' Megan confirmed, thinking how strange to be talking about goats with an Elf!

'Never seen one?'

'I've seen a goat at a farming zoo, but never a Fauwn.'

'Hmm... not seen a Fauwn?'

'No,' Megan shook her head, 'but I'd like to!'

'Stick with me and you might!'

Megan smiled.

'I think there's a long poem in your Librarium about Aargon being accompanied on his homeward voyage.'

'Who was with him?'

'Much of his crew, but some disbanded.'

'Did you write the poem?'

'Me? Gracious not I. I have modest literary capabilities (Megan didn't think this true), but I believe the poem's writer was a one Innus Virgil.'

'Aargon didn't try to slay... Dragons... in my world?' Megan asked, wondering if this was part of his courage. Though she thought it wasn't really brave too attempt to smite a Dragon. But she could see the courage might be needed - even if that got you burned.

'Dragons never flew in your world,' Mr. Bumblbeaux said.

'Dragons didn't?'

'Nope.'

'Then how do we all know about Dragons?'

'Good question, that. You'll find

out.'

'O-oh OK,' Megan asked, registering the tone of voice again, that wouldn't impart much else.

'If my memory is serving me right, and whilst I don't mean to self-praise myself, though it very usually does, there should be an exhibit near here you might like to see.'

'An exhibit?' Megan asked, knowing what this was: she remembered her supply teacher mentioning how her work from Art class could be displayed in the year's exhibit, in the school's dining hall. Characteristically, Megan had gone red at the very thought.

Mr. Bumblebheaux hooked his hands inside his waistcoat pockets, 'An exhibit,' confirming, he reiterated.

'Of what?' Megan was wringing her hands and twisting her fingertips together.

Mr. Bumblebeaux's eyes flashed

with excitement. 'Come and see.'

Megan was standing on one foot then the other. As if told to stand straight on blistering hot coals.

Mr. Bumblebeaux, turning his back, drifted up like a spinning cartwheel to lead the way on.

Megan felt excited, and with a little dollop of fear spued in.

Chapter Forty-One

The Fangs That Strike

Like when at a natural history museum, a large serpent skin was suspended by thin-looking taut ropes that ended in sharp slashes in the air, somehow holding the skin up as if it were alive.

Megan wanted to instantaneously dash away from the scene.

But, her feet were stood rigid on the gold-embossed marble of the floor. She couldn't drag her eyes away from the giant snake.

But this was no ordinary snake.

It looked to a slightly shaking Megan like peeling onion rinds. But a big onion, because the skin was two-hundred feet from its arrow-pointed tail, running in smooth-impressed snakeskin to its hood of its cobra-like head. Holes of its slanted eye-sockets looked eerie to Megan. She could see right through where the eyes once were to the golden rafters propping up the vaulting ceiling.

'There's the skin of a Kilibass.'

And indeed, in front of the site of the skin, a glassed sign had been hammered-and-chiselled in care with an engraving, giving the name of the creature:

Kilibass

Breathless, Megan gazed from the glass signpost on the top plinth of the pedestal, then she swung her stare back to the monstrous snake it advertised. She felt fascinated and repulsed at the same time. 'Is the... Kil...' she gulped, then trying again, said, 'Kilibass?'

Mr. Bumblebeaux nodded, flicking a bit of sliver and gold Fairy dust from the top-part of the signpost.

'Is the Kilibass connected to Aargon?'

Mr. Bumblebeaux looked over, he nodded.

Megan half-looked at the giant snake. 'Aargon didn't kill this Kilibass..?' she asked, in a low voice.

Mr. Bumblebeaux, taken off guard by her question, nearly fell off the plinth. 'No no! Absolutely not!'

Megan got the impression the answer was a resounding and distinct no.

'Aargon asked Val'ahala, this Kilibass, if he could collect the skin once Val'ahala had shed its pelt.'

In a whisper, Megan went, 'Phew.'

Mr. Bumblebeaux smiling, nodded. 'Kilibass' shed their skins multiple times,' he explained.

'That must take a lot of cleaning!'

Megan smiled.

'You'd think, though the Kilibass have came up an ingenious way for the shed of their skins to depart.'

'How does that happen?'

'The Kilibass, when slithered out of their old skin, have no need for it of course, so then it can stored here, or like this one, be hung for display purposes, or, as most happens, the skin dissolves into Magic, then those disintegrated bits blends within the air. Becoming in the Magic of The Enchanted Kingdom.'

Megan blinked.

'The Chief Librarian before I attempted too manufacture their skins, when slid out, as means for paper, but the surfaces were far too rubbery, and could hardly keep any ink nor pencil lead on it.'

'Why is the Kilibass skin displayed?' Megan asked, hoping this wasn't an obvious question.

'Because a lot of creatures in the Lands of The Enchanted Kingdom don't travel. And so this can be a rare opportunity to see more of their world,' Mr. Bumblebeaux shrugged heavily, 'if they physically don't wish to travel into different Lands.'

Megan looked through the roof of the skin's mouth; the jaw was opened like it was about to strike at a boat-sized cow, then gobble it up.

Mr. Bumblebeaux's hair, like thistledown, drifted about him in spiky strands as he flew around the Kilibass skin.

As Megan marched up to the Kilibass, she was taken to wondering if Unicorns or Anquails, or a tankful of Mer-people, come here, in groups, outings or led by an Elfish tour-guide, bringing packed lunches or Magic bags full of food, only the size of a small sac.

Without a warning, the hood of the

titan-sized cobra shivered, looking like it was about to strike at prey below its massive head and neck.

Megan gave a start.

'I-Is the skin alive?' she cried, not altogether gaily.

Mr. Bumblebeaux popped his spectacle-clad head up, from by the end of the Kilibass's arrow-pointer tail. 'Alive? I think that was me. Just tightening up the rope,' he held a tauter twig-like rope in his balled hands, 'or there is a draft in here, so sometimes the Kilibass might look as if it suddenly may launch itself at you.' Mr. Bumblebeaux looked like he wanted to burst into laughter.

'Aaiieee!' Megan cried, nodding.

Feeling undeterred, she looked up. The mouth, with the endowment of razor-sharp bone fangs, was a hundred-foot high directly above her.

Megan took a step back.

The menacing teeth, the smallest

the size of a fence-gate panel, looked as sharp as a gleaming pinpoint.

Megan had bunched her fists up.

Coldly, she stared hard.

Megan's prettily petal-like lips had became a hard, thin line.

The fangs stayed where they were. Rooted into the jaw of the skin's massive mouth.

Megan wished the fangs were more puny.

Megan and Mr. Bumblebeaux had momentarily made their way out, and were back in the space with the once-tinkerling, plinking-plonky piano music.

The Kilibass skin and the skinny bonds holding it in-place were still burned on her memory.

Upon a slightly more closer inspection, she noticed how each rope hadn't so much split then lassoed the Kilibass' skin, though the binds merely touched it, and somehow held the skin up to present the coiling spectacle.

Must be Magic, Megan thought.

She looked up and, at that moment, caught a gliding Mr. Bumblebeaux watching her. Then he carried on with the chaotic chore of picking up papers, butting the ends down firmly, using his hands to line them, then in the same handful, grasping more up, so he could create ordered stacks. He was coming and going over the tables, moving from the fifth stack on to forming a sixth one.

Megan could tell he didn't need any help.

She stared at him for a bit longer then retuned back to the paper-dump she'd left at the table by the sofa:

Guilders
Gilded
1502
Sage

Squire

Megan gave a little whoop.

She knew what a squire was! Feeling like she wouldn't be thrown to spy Elizabeth the I stomp in, then bossily direct squires to put-out a hog-on-a-spit, and wheel-in great big barrels of frothy, foaming drink, she felt like she'd finally got hold of what the words were telling her.

Feeling resolute, over knowing a squire to be a serving attendant carrying velvet-robes, or just a servant bustling about with an over-crowded tray, Megan, carrying the paper-scraps, wandered to the wooden chests busting with over-piled books.

A rather pummelled-looking trunk-chest had four lots of books piled high, with its lid standing open in a curved-topped.

Heaving the plank-and-slated wooden chest, Megan almost fell on her face.

Hearing the scraping, Mr. Bumblebeaux looked on.

The golden claspes, on the chest's corners, were already scratched-looking and in a *humphf*, the shuddering chest was gripped by a puffing, gasping Megan who let go of hefting the iron-ring handle on the side.

The scrape on the floor ended slightly sharply. Megan gave up with attempting to move out the chest, to try and close its lid. Or at the very least, bring the chest down so the books were covered underneath.

Suddenly, a globed ball with funny-little markings over it dropped, rattled down the book piles then slid through Megan's grasping fingers, and then rolled on the floor. It drummed around in rolls like a hamster was inside.

Mr. Bumblebeaux smiled. He

flapped over, winged down, and picked up the orbed map with both his gnarly hands.

After he passed the old-looking sphere to Megan, she grubbed about the chest, wanting to find a more better nook so it wouldn't bounce out again.

In a full delightful gasp, Megan noticed inside the chest, ditches were fashioned on all sides, by means of a small shelf which could house envelopes or long-necked necklaces.

Ferrying the globe over to her right, she put the football-like map on a balance between the shelf, and a row of tall books nearly butting against it but roomy enough as the cloth-bound books had not been stacked in order properly.

The wooden chests with stored books made for a good backdrop, and handy seat.

Megan was listening quite intently, and felt as if Mr. Bumblebeaux had run-over this just before; though she kept quiet and paid attention. 'Walking about downstairs, in a different level of the castle of your Pandragon's Key, inside here, your All Souls Librarium, there's also The Telling Tudor Farthinghay, which is a sort of display room lodging an accumulation of bits-and-pieces, and has artefacts from that period in your worlds time.'

'Sounds just great!' Megan enthused, nodding.

'The Rare and Repair Squad work most in there.'

Megan sat up straighter from what Mr. Bumblebeaux just said. 'The Rare and Repair Squad?'

Mr. Bumblebeaux was putting an embroidered book with pink velvet on a tiny-looking table that seemed as if it might topple over from its now weighty load. It held.

'The Rare and Repair Squad compile inventories, and remake books back to their intended appearance. We learnt a great deal from your world's Tudor binding accomplishments.'

'O-oh OK,' Megan said, sitting back a bit more, and crossing her ankles.

'Elves here, of The Rare and Repair Squad, work hard to maintain your peoples hand-sitched book binding. We amend the damage, but only with original techniques, looping thread into the pages. Bound right, this beauty will last another three-hundred years.'

Megan gasped.

'Three-hundred years? How can that be?'

Mr. Bumblebeaux continued, stroking his whisker on his chin as he studied Megan's reaction, from being suitably impressed at her surroundings. 'Laying press to firm techniques, we make sure, with Magic, these books last longer than in your world,' he said, carrying three cases up a small flight of stairs that led to a bookcase.

Megan again felt frazzled. 'I'm pleased they're getting on so well!' she said, with her eyes glazing over slightly.

Flying down the stairs, having had cased the luggage-holdalls on an empty middle shelf, Mr. Bumblebeaux moved a bound book, like a large tablet, in crimson-purple velvet.

Turning the book, the very look of it, and its gold-gilt embossed decorations, made Megan think it to be a treasure.

'That looks nice,' she commented, shifting a bit, and licking the top row of her teeth.

'It does look nice,' he agreed. 'And

of course, as we well know, the innards of the words are a treasure.'

Megan nodded from Mr. Bumblebeaux's sage wisdom.

Her eyes darted past the Elf, with his back now to her, bent, rifling through old pages, and she saw spine-bound books scribed in gold or silver slanting lettering. Books were in burgundy velvet. Many books had rope stitching, a scattering of books was strewn with gilded silver claps, burgundy tassels were on much more delicate-looking pink-damask fabric books, and loose sheets showed a thin hand wielding a sceptre. The sheets were grouped by other documents, and assembled by single pieces of smaller parchment.

Megan got up.

Shuffling past Mr. Bumblebeaux, who was mumbling to himself, she spied the sheets were blacked with musical interlocking notes. These sheets were with music-sheet music.

Megan could partially remember the look of the lopping notes, lines and dots, when in Music class and she had attempted to follow the music-sheet, except her recorder sounded like a mix between a hooting moose and a blaring foghorn. Which ensured much snide laugher then pokes from the children who not only found this funny, but used it as a tool too bully her with.

Megan shut the snorting sniggers off from her mind, and returned again to the interlocked notes, which were piled on a bottom-sheet which had an elegant penned note:

Endure The Behest Of Creativity

Peering up, she realised that, just past where she was, she was seeing a corner crook, but only partly. Megan's neck craned round to her right, where she saw a small passage.

The squared small corridor looked tempting to her.

Knowing that Mr. Bumblebeaux was only just tucked outside, she made to go in.

As she faced the entry of the corridor, a radiancy of throbbing golden glows was shining directly at the other end.

Chapter Forty-Two

The Rare And Repair Squad

At first glance, nothing seemed at all out of the ordinary.

That was until going under the cut-through of the walkway, this bloomed into an inner courtyard, ceilinged, with a large boulder on a small-wheeled blue trolley, that was parked to her left, that in carved hammer-blows, announced: 1509, Henry VII

The golden and red enclosed room looked like a massive entombed shrine.

Megan was wondering if the Henry VII was connected to Henry VIII.

In her mind's eye, Megan worked through erasing the last number and pondered in a mull; after a few moments contemplation, she grasped that this Henry must have been Henry the Seventh, and came before the Henry VIII with the six wives.

Megan was feeling proud of finally grasping some part of history that, until then, had gone *whoosh* over her ringlet-head.

Smiling, she gazed toward the boulder that looked like it had been removed from a dirty pit, then moved around. A squatter table was next to a taller one, and had a book; around an embossed pink rose was artwork, which was wavy topped at the edges. Two more smaller silver-clasped books butted up, top to bottom; they fit neatly and seemiesly, as though an indenturing of teeth had been taken from someone's gums, then pressed into the soft edges of the book's sides.

Megan grinned.

The taller table was topped with over-lapping notation spirals, with small-looking words around banners, these paper sheets were coiling about a golden urn.

Going for more of a nose, Megan looked around in satisfaction. If she were a cheetah, she would have purred.

She saw many other musical notes, streaming over longer, narrower sheets, and on on one such piles was a multifaceted book.

Megan picked up a sheet read words:

for I am yours, Henry R

Megan scanned the letters, having no clear idea as to who this Henry R was. She guessed a pined letter that was stuck, in a still swing-up, was in reply:

to be both loving and kind, Anne.

'H-hmm... no idea,' Megan mused, then moved on from the glass-encased framed words.

By the diverse papers, framed in clip-frames or golden-gilt larger ones, a heavy-feeling opus was groaning on a tottery, thin-legged table. The book opus was in a closed-spew, sticking out of pieces of music like someone, with the book, ripping out its pages, had been playing, Na Na... Na Na... Na... You Can't Catch Me!

Creaking opening the green board of the book, a loose manuscript was pressed before the book's first page. Leafing on, musical singing notes had been signed with a: Margaret of York

'Who's Margaret of York?' Megan mumbled, to herself.

She mistily remembered York, being somewhere her aunt had once lived, but, apart from that, nothing.

Megan shrugged.

'Did you say... York?' a voice

asked.

Megan jumped.

She knew who it was but she was so lost in her thoughts, she nearly dropped the book she was cradling in her respectful hands.

Mr. Bumblebeaux was flapping by the boulder.

The golden chamber of that side of the room looked rather blurry as his wings moved about in many directions.

'Yes, York,' a bleary-eyed Megan confirmed, holding the book up, then hugging to pad it against her chest so as the manuscript did not file out, and to stop other loose scraps of papers now wanting to nearly teeter-tottering out.

Mr. Bumblebeaux nodded up. 'The Rare and Repair Squad mended that.'

Megan thought of something. 'Is The Rare and Repair Squad something to do with The Magic

Meli...'

'The Magic Melioration Restoration Repairer?' Mr. Bumblebeaux asked, following her trail of thought.

'That's it!' Megan said, putting the book back on its table, then walked over by Mr. Bumblebeaux, and sat, cocking her right knee over her left one.

'Hmm... again: well remembered!' Mr. Bumblebeaux praised.

Megan's cheeks reddened. She smiled, still a little shyly.

'The Magic Melioration Restoration Repairer is not quite within being a lone sub-division, but as an off-shoot to The Rare and Repair Squad,' he explained.

Megan gripped her thighs. 'What's a sub-division?' she asked, enthralled by the busy goings on inside All Souls Librarium.

'A sub-division is a type of group, but within a larger group.'

Megan nodded, sort of understanding.

'I'm chuffed you were looking at that book,' he nodded over to the long-legged table. 'We, or rather you, boast bespoke artefacts and preparatory sketches, essayed studies, all from writers, artists over your ages, and ours, too, of course,' Mr. Bumblebeaux said, with a shaking Megan not believing, again, all this was hers.

Megan couldn't help but think of everything inside All Souls Librarium, inside the castle of Pandragon's Key of The Fairy Key Land, to be like a giant Russian doll.

Snap one doll open, and then in out-and-out amazement, find there's another doll inside awaiting your wonder-filled gaze.

Megan lifted an eyebrow.

'Oh,' she said.

Mere moments before, when she had walked back through the corridor, expecting to pad into the room she was just in, the walls of the corridor shook.

Nearly falling on her backside, Megan placed her hands on either walls of the wriggly corridor. This felt like a funfair ride that shaked-and-shaked, making you feel like you were trapped in a washing machine.

Mr. Bumblebeax was sat on the floor, with his legs out, the ground under him bumping him up every so often.

The walls shook. Then shook. Then shook no more.

A ray of hope licked Megan's face.

The walls settled into place, and thankfully no ceiling slabs from the corridor had fallen on Megan and Mr. Bumblebeaux.

'Where will... we be.... now?' she asked, shaking from the mini-earthquake.

Mr. Bumblebeaux flew up. He leapt out.

Sticking his head back into the entryway of the corridor, he said, 'Similar place, but different space.'

Mr. Bumblebeaux really did seem the sort of Elf who wasn't easily thrown by the unexpected.

Staggering out, trying not to collapse from the sudden quaking and tossing, Megan then lifted up her other eyebrow.

The entry of the corridor now butted on to the side of a silver-inlaid room. The glares of lights appeared to dim down a bit.

Holding the sides of the corridor entry walls, Megan's knees came up over the threshold of a long, oblong glass table, and she stepped into the silver-doused room.

A gangling table was burnished with manuscripts. Books with

garnished gold-gilt edges were displayed on ancient-looking chipped bookshelves.

Megan held her head erect.

Glass tables, in many blown-flamed sizes, were littered with papers. Browsing through a table on her left, she looked very intently at scraps of linen. Next to these cloths were scrap notes, a gold badge-like plate was threaded through the top sheet, and pasted on the shining label, a fevered hand had scrawled:

For: The remembrance for the portrait, H

Other authors works of papers, and the odd book, sighted on a table-top or stacked from the silver and glass marble floor.

Upon a table nearest to her, she wandered over and surveyed the items. Megan thought she vaguely recognised the leather-bound, mottled-covered book on top of sheets of a manuscript.

Megan faintly shook her head.

A sudden chinking sounded, like two glass gongs were banging off each other.

Megan darted.

She looked up, then under a couple of the tables legs, giving it a try to see where the glass-chinking was emanating from.

'I think the room is just settling down. Some of the tables down there probably moved about, and are now legging back into place, where their favourite spot is,' Mr. Bumblebeaux advised, smiling.

Megan hadn't really looked behind her.

She did so.

The room wasn't just a room. But a building in itself.

Small pulleys and ropes looked like

they could support tables or a wagon. The ground was dishevelled with glass tables, rolled maps, and the walls were lost to sight, seeming to go on, and on, running up into cosmic spaces; Megan would have expected to spy a shooting star suddenly streak across the room.

Snaking upward, droplets pooled out of organs of long metal drainpipes, that were running in stand-alone steams. *Toot toot*, went one, letting out a burp of steam.

'Whe-where are we?' Megan asked, her eyes shimmering.

'Oh, this is just a test place. Ideas just get tried out, that sort of thing,' Mr. Bumblebeaux looked unimpressed.

A squealing spray of steam suddenly spurted from one of the blow-holes, like a whale's, out of an endless copperplate drain near to his flying, and then mixed with him, which created a Mr. Bumblebeaux-shaped small cloud.

'Aarhum... ahuh,' he spluttered.

Walking out of the closing silver glass doors, as big and as long like two submarines were stood on their propellers, then rounding a sharp corner, a pitter-patter of booted feet dashing on stone-cobbled tiles ran after them, then a beat of wings flapped, then both sounds of the sharp, heavy footsteps and flying wings were accompanied by a shout of, 'Mr. Bumblebeaux!'

Both he and Megan looked around.

Kingfisher wings were holding up what looked to be a beaming Elf.

'Mr. Bunion?' Mr. Bumblebeaux asked, turning.

'Tis I!' Mr. Bunion boomed.

Megan stood still. Trying not to gape.

And the loud voice suddenly said, again, 'Mr. Bumblebeaux!'

'Ah! Mr. Bunion!' Mr. Bumblebeaux greeted, looking surprised and pleased, at the same time, to see him.

'The Fairy Key?' Mr. Bunion asked, talking quickly, and looking quite feverish down to a gaping Megan.

'Indeed.'

'From the world of to be or not to be?'

Mr. Bumblebeaux nodded.

Mr. Bunion studied Megan as if looking through cage-poles restraining a rhinoceros.

Megan was finding this now very unusual, to be examined in such a manner.

She looked around the one-lined wall with reflecting glass, from floor-to-ceiling, then to the other three sides of the walls which were in lava-gold.

'Would you look at you!' Mr. Bunion declared, his grey face, with nubs, smiling.

He pulled at the ends of his chalk-dusted jacket.

Megan felt quite uncomfortable.

Though to her credit, she didn't shrink back - even briefly.

'I hope I have the pleasure of conversing with you!' Mr. Bunion requested, and looked a little like he was eyeing a prize to be impaled with a pin, then displayed on his wall. Or in his collector's anthology book.

Megan quietly thanked Mr. Bumblebeaux for placing himself with flying by her; not that he meant to do that, as he knew who this was, but she didn't know if the newcomer was to be friend or foe.

'What are you doing with that?' Mr. Bumblebeaux smiled, nodding to the fine vellum paper haul in Mr. Bunion's long hands.

'Just taking this commissioned manuscript to The Magic Melioration Restoration Repairer,' Mr. Bunion explained.

Megan was still feeling thoroughly flummoxed. But she nodded along as if this was all common to her.

'Mr. Bunion here is part of The Rare and Repair Squad,' Mr. Bumblebeaux explained.

Megan nodded, understanding showing on her face.

'Wait until the rest of the team hear this!' Mr Bunion said, raving, as if he couldn't wait. And not wait much longer.

Picking up their feet, they swarmed down the corridor.

Mr. Bunion still cast sideways-on looks at Megan. He kept yanking an upside Mr. Bumblebeaux and saying, over and over, 'The Fairy Key! Finally here! The Fairy Key's here!' As if Mr. Bumblebeaux was completely oblivious to that.

Although he seemed overexcited, Megan felt relived and thrilled to learn Mr. Bunion wasn't an enemy after-all.

His oddly-formed legs, dangling in the air, showed he wore trousers of one red leg, and one orange-and-pink striped leg. His black-and-white stripy jacket was in different lines to the stripes on his trousers, so as he flew about, flitting up, then zooming down, excited, he was a riot of colour from his long brown straight hair, to the tips of his kingfisher-like wings.

Bringing her eyes back in front of her, seeing the corridor unfolded, Megan asked, 'Did you play the music?' because startlingly, a pink grand piano stood centre place in the spacious room.

Mr. Bumblebeaux and Mr. Bunion gazed at one another. Mr. Bunion looked like he might blow-up from laughter, 'No-o. 'Twasn't I on the ivories.'

A pink-top-cushioned stool was just

under the rim on the piano. As Megan rounded the piano, she noticed its shutter was down and her eyes fell upon paper on the floor, littered about as if someone had thrown them into the air as if in a state of piqued anger, and then left them were they happened to fall.

Lines were scrawled, as were musical symbols and notes, all written in streams.

Megan scrooched down and examining one such paper, she scanned how it looked like a pencil or pen had been applied so heavily that certain areas of the paper were scorched through. Another paper revealed half-blue blobs.

'I wonder if an ink-well tipped on it?' Megan said to herself.

'You can find out over time.'

'How?' she asked Mr. Bunion, who looked like he might burst on the spot from chatting with The Fairy Key.

'It's history. Everything here is connected, translated and studied. Readable.'

'I will do! I'll find out!' pledged Megan, turning to Mr. Bumblebeaux, who nodded back.

'Why, you-could-not-only-find-out-which-pianist-made-such-an -awful-sight-on-a-clean,once-bright piece of paper,' Mr. Bunion's nose flared, speaking, like he did, with almost not taking a breath, 'but,' he continued, 'you'd be able to source when and where the exact location, as-to-origins-of-they-were-obtained-from,' he finished with a flourish, impressively.

'That's unbelievable.'

'Isn't it!'

Mr. Bumblebeaux turned. 'Mind you, I find the thumpingly good classification creature known as squid, in your world, to be equally unbelievable!'

'Ha ha!' Megan laughed along.

Megan saw they had entered a foyer.

The foyer was like no other she'd seen before.

This was like a splayed spider, with eight legs running off the main gold foyer in different directions.

The spider-shaped foyer was as quiet as a frozen tarantula.

Exclaiming at the tunnels, Mr. Bumblebeaux set to work at whatever he was doing; he flew about the lobby, nodding as he past one dark gaping passageway. He stopped in the air at the seventh wide hole. Even though no light petered into showing what was down there, Megan could tell each one would run in for a very long time.

Mr. Bunion coughed.

Megan glanced up.

Mr. Bunion looked like he had done that on purpose. His shut, clenched jaw smiled behind a clasped fist. His stripy clothes was such an eyesore now he was with flying in the gold and rainbow-coloured foyer. It was almost like there was nearly too much colour for Megan to see properly; she felt like she was peering through clingfilm.

'Well, I should bid my leave now,' Mr. Bunion looked completely crestfallen.

Mr. Bumblebeaux flew down, by Megan. 'OK. We had best get on, too. If you take the second tunnel you'll get there much quicker.'

'Thanks,' Mr. Bunion mouthed, still looking like he didn't wish too leave.

'Off you go,' Mr. Bumblebeaux said, then added, 'Megan will be back. I'm sure you'll get to speak once again.'

Megan's shoulders shrank back a little; she looked a bit doubtful. But, said nothing.

Uncertainly, off Mr. Bunion went,

looking begrudged as if he was not privy to a treat he desired, and one he very much wanted to take.

And off Mr. Bumblebeaux went, with a Megan who looked like she could now finally relax.

Once there, she walked a bit behind a trundling Mr. Bumblebeaux, who tried not to career into a wall; he jostled his legs, stopping short of slamming into the golden bricks, then flew into the seventh tunnel's yawning dark mouth, and just before the gloominess of the dark engulfed them, Megan automatically scanned over her right shoulder at the foyer, and caught a glimpse of Mr. Bunion, staring at her, before he turned his back, and flapped into the yawned darkness that was breached in the wall, of the fourth tunneled passageway.

Megan gulped.

He hadn't intended to be seen.

Seeking his own way, looking away from Megan, his withdrawing back and blue beating wings became lost, eaten, drifting inside the swirling darkly blacks of the tunneled-way.

Goodness knows where Mr. Bunion's going, Megan thought.

Squeamishly, she gazed to the wall of perfectly solid black now facing her.

Megan mithered on what might be in there.

Waiting.

Megan swallowed.

Chapter Forty-Three

The Screaming Creature

Lucy coughed.

There was silence.

It felt as though a bull sat upon her gagging chest.

The jolt forced her to open her eyes; through black patches she knew that The Enchanted Kingdom was turning truly bad.

The whistling wind was twinned by the three suns lowering below the horizon, and as the light faded the only glow that was being discharged into The Kingdom, was that of the slight, visible arc from the top of a sun's grey luminescence, which torpedoed outwards.

The three moons-like trembling

glass shone on Lucy, to show she was on cracked, split earth, and in her tumbled walking, she tried to think where she was, but all her mind kept on coming back to was that somehow Abraxus, through meddling with the old Magic, held a dark grip on Aradene who had changed, as Abraxus had manipulated and warped her, so she was enlisted, and as Lucy was linked to Abraxus, in her bond of The Dragon Keeper, it was this that was becoming corrupted.

In the distance, gleaming slivers in the earth exploded, whilst fountains of debris rained down in the gales of wind.

A cacophony of screams and an orchestra of gusts volleyed down assaultingly.

Far above, coming from the black and grey insect-like clouds, was a sound that chilled her bones; screams merged with the wind then became howls once more.

Lucy's bottom lip quivered.

This is all Megan's fault, she thought.

Then she thought more thoughts on her dratted sister.

Far in the distance, her ears picked up the sound of hounds baying, coming ever nearer, until their squalled cries mixed with the noise of a pounding paws on the splitting ground.

Lucy had gone very white.

Fear made her urgently scan round for the last things she remembered seeing: the Dragons.

But of them there was no sight, as she came to realising, she had somehow been moved!

Lucy nearly burst into tears. She couldn't cope any longer; her hope was simply driven into huffy disappearance.

As she sidestepped a dislodging

piece of earth, she cried out, because as her hand still held the leaf, all of her fingers and both palms had the thread-like veins, flitting under her skin.

The screams sounded to her left, and then somehow to her right: her disorientation made it so she couldn't make it out properly.

Lucy dived behind a fallen log of a tree.

She shivered.

Pressing her back against the rough, dead tree, Lucy tried to curl inside the overlapping bark.

Behind her, suddenly, came the sounds of many tiny insects scurrying over some of the crumbly tree. Cracking bones all of a sudden sounded to her left, still behind there. Sounds like bones were breaking, then moving, all the while the bones fractured, making Lucy wince. A scream started low, like a wind-up arm on a mechanical monkey playing the two large metal discs of cymbals. The screaming came out in, *'Aa... ahh... aaaah... aaaah... aaaahh'*, then broke into a full-on scream.

Lucy peeped out to her left, then scanned quickly to her right.

Nails were digging into the log, splinters flew into the stormy air, bones in a hand were breaking.

Lucy cowered.

A blast of the screech, wild with craving, came from behind her, and as Lucy hobbled and turned, a tall familiar sight came into focus.

Her black talon nails jabbed and pointed to Lucy, and the grotesque parody creature of Aradene spitted, 'You will also feel the wing of Abraxus!'

She had white skeleton skin, and where she had once tottered with such gliding elegance, now though, she slithered along the ground; her legs moved like a crab and her arms were arachnid-like.

Aradene jigged as if she were being jostled hither-and-thither asunder, like invisible wires were jangling her about, such as a Marionette doll.

Lucy heard screams and guttural wordless murmurings coming from the thing slap-bang in front of her, but Aradene's face was not visible because her hair spilled lankily forward. Her gown of spider webs trailed out and as it fanned, it crept in any direction, as though groping for prey; it seemed to move on its own!

Aradene looked up to the feeble sight in front of her, and recognising Lucy's now black eyes, her face split into such an evil leer it made Lucy step back.

Aradene was screaming down with the wind, blending her screams with the air so both shot into Lucy.

The deep infection within her was

becoming stronger; she could feel her feet sway as Aradene jolted her angled bones low over the ground.

Lucy finally collapsed.

Images spun fast: such sights of the much nicer times of when she was last here; how The Kingdom had flowed with its good Magic.

The creatures, from The Kingdom, all swam into her fevered mind.

Aradene had now reached Lucy.

Yells, trembling voices, panicking screams and wailing howls all blended with the squalling wind that whistled.

Lucy's eyes didn't blink: she stared blankly at Aradene, who was now peering over her, and her hair continually swirled, like live snakes were hungrily set free, and to mark her triumph, in Lucy's face, over the noise, she then screamed a shouting bellow like a baying. Abominable. Banshee.

Chapter Forty-Four

To Dare Question Mooglieschnoogleboo

Megan was sat down on the cushion of the pink chaise-lounge, cuddling the book carefully.

Leaving the book in her lap, she leant back and reflected on what had just happened.

Some moments before, she'd plucked up the courage and followed Mr. Bumblebeaux's wings as they were quietened slightly in the dark. Using her right hand, she groped along the tiled-feeling wall of the tunnel. It was windy. Twisting one way then shooting off another. Mr. Bumblebeaux's familiar beat of his hectic-sounding wings stayed very close by.

Megan couldn't see the roof of the tunnel, but guessed from the oppressive atmosphere that it wasn't too high.

The tiled tunnel was like the innards of a hefty snake. Slabbed tiles were cemented, which Megan thought they were black; not that she could properly see them, but, hazarding a guess, she thought if they were any other colour, light would have shone out from each tile.

'Hmm... whatever can it be? To *eat?*' a voice said up to her right, which reverberated slightly.

Megan stopped, keeping her flattened hand on the tiles. 'Are you OK, Mr. Bumblebeaux?' she asked, wondering if he had smashed into a wall, or dabbled in splatters on the ceiling.

'Well, look what we have here,' the nasally-flat voice suddenly said, somewhere in the looming gloom of the darkness.

Megan jumped back.

She didn't much like this.

'Mr. Cadava?' Mr. Bumblebeaux said, his voice sounding strong. Sounds of his zippy-beating wings flapped by her head. She pushed her long hair out of her face.

'Indeed. And The Fairy Key as well, I see... how... delightful,' the voice replied, from somewhere within the dark.

Megan tried to have a good look around her.

The darkness suddenly parted!

Megan stared even more.

Out stepped a little man. Looking down his nose and generally with an air that whoever he met was far beneath him, scrapped on his black boots.

Megan gulped.

At that point, in not a very nice

surprise, she couldn't say a single word.

The small man was as tall as Megan's knees, but he looked like he was straining to match her waist-height.

Mr. Bumblebeaux flapped even closer still; his wings brushed Megan's face, which she didn't mind at all.

It felt like as if Mr. Cadava had snuffed-out all the goody good moods anyone could ever feel.

'What are you doing down this tunnel, Mr. Cadava?' Mr. Bumblebeaux asked, in a much kinder voice than he wanted to use, managing to keep himself straight in the air, peering down at him.

Mr. Cadava had a strange look about him.

He made a show as if he was examining the tiles, but kept on darting glances at Megan, licking his lips.

Mr. Bumblebeaux skidded in the air in a halt.

She was thankful that, up close, she could just make out the two of them peeled away from the dark of the tunnel-way.

'Bother. Why did you bring that here?' Mr. Cadava asked, not looking in front of him.

Megan gazed to the tight blue, strangle-looking tie, and went to say something about wanting to be here, and kinder, with how much she was so enjoying herself and what a pleasure it was to meet him, but Mr. Bumblebeaux said, in a warm tone, 'We all want Megan Button here.'

'*All* want *it? Here?*' he said, in not a very loving manner. 'We've flumped into the imponderable now!'

Megan stared in dismay. *Does he... mean... me?* she thought, in despair.

'Could you have possibly meant

Megan, here?' Mr. Bumblebeaux asked, looking very stern indeed.

But he knew he had.

Megan didn't say a word at that. She was thinking really very hard.

Mr. Cadava leered.

Mr. Bumblebeaux looked stern. 'How so?' he asked, stepping in front of Megan.

Mr. Cadava stared angrily. 'How so, what?'

'How exactly have we flumped into the imponderable?'

Mr. Cadava looked around, vague. 'Because you cannot just make a sweeping... statement,' he said, accusingly.

Megan stared at him, frowning.

Mr. Bumblebeaux did something he had never once done before: he sounded like a fogsignal was blasting out.

Mr. Cadava smiled; a cruel, deliciously nasty smile.

Megan was very upset.

Mr. Bumblebeaux looked at Mr. Cadava thoughtfully.

Without another word, he set off.

He flapped down a little, facing him, and stilling his wings, met Mr. Cadava, whose beady-eyed, wicked leering unsettled Megan.

No-one said anything at all.

Megan had a deep sense of foreboding.

Mr. Cadava grinned a quite villainous smile. Megan noticed Mr. Cadava was toothless.

Megan looked from the stumpy legs to the upturned face of Mr. Cadava. *Good gracious! Do I know his voice,* she thought?

Mr. Cadava was looking at Megan. 'Take a long walk, did you?' he asked her, in a hollow voice.

Mr. Cadava waited a little while.

He looked like he'd whipped himself into a real temper.

'On the contrary, it hasn't felt long in the least, has it?' Megan shook her head; Mr. Bumblebeaux didn't looked behind him, knowing she'd quite agree.

She stepped up, taking in his blouse-type shirt in autumnal maroons.

'Nevertheless, the - ' Mr. Cadava went to go in a belligerent tone.

' - They'd welcome Megan just as I have. Simply because you find The Fairy Key too finally be here unbelievable is not of concern,' Mr. Bumblebeaux said in a slightly loud voice.

Mr. Cadava looked as if he'd been hit in the face with a wet fish.

Again, no-one said anything.

Mr. Bumblebeaux broke the silence. 'Is that quite understood?'

Mr. Cadava looked cranky. 'Do you think my brain has been sucked out?'

'Of course not. One could never

underestimate your... brainpower,' Mr. Bumblebeaux said, crossing his crooked arms.

Mr. Cadava exchanged a flinty-eyed look with his Chief Librarian. 'Nonetheless, this won't do!' claimed Mr. Cadava, in an indignant tone, wanting to talk over him, 'I *won't* stand for it!'

Megan felt very guilty for being there.

'It is done. Megan Button The Fairy Key is here, as Foretold... as well you know,' Mr. Bumblebeaux pointed out, hinting at something lost to Megan, who stood trying to tape-over her shaking.

Mr. Cadava looked out-and-out petulant. 'You curmudgeon! You're thinking of Fhilipsnokie's farcical Foretelling,' he said, not asking, but telling.

'Of course I am. Among others.'
'Fhilipsnokie's is ludicrous.'

'That is your opinion. As for my own, Fh - '

' - Misery! Know all! *Here* we go,' Mr. Cadava said, interrupting, and who looked bored.

Mr. Bumblebeaux drew himself up. 'Fhilipsnokie's *non*-preposterous Foretelling is most certainly not. Nor is he. Fhilipsnokie is notable.'

'Yes, only in an overview for the idiotic,' Mr. Cadava laughed, a nasally-flat chuckle.

'There is no doubt whatsoever. Absolutely. Fhilipsnokie's is, as I said, among others of noteworthy, and that, in part, proves it,' Mr. Bumblebeaux's voice had now changed and sounded efficiently brisk. 'This matter has ended. I have warned you...'

Mr. Cadava did as he was told.

Megan peeped down to the top of Mr. Bumblebeaux's head; he was stood, rigid, by her legs.

Mr. Cadava's head was rotating

around. 'So, in theory, you're glad it's here?' he asked, as though Mr. Cadava was not going to give up without a fight.

'Megan Button The Fairy Key is not an "it,"' he said, giving quotation marks in the dark air, 'but a she. Kindly please do refer in that regard,' he sharply said, verbally slapping Mr. Cadava across his face.

Mr. Cadava was cross. 'Certainly, *dear*, but within... reason.' he roared, in outrage.

Megan took a step back, alarmed at the wild look on Mr. Cadava's laughing, skin-tight face.

Mr. Cadava threw a dirty look at Megan and Mr. Bumblebeaux.

Mr. Bunmblebeaux was watching Mr. Cadava sadly.

Mr. Cadava was miffed.

Mr. Bumblebeaux did not say anything. Just stood, very still, and protectively in front of Megan.

Mr. Cadava stared wildly at Mr. Bumblebeaux.

But Mr. Bumblebeaux simply waved his hands and wings. As though wanting to find something wrong, in his weedy voice, rubbing his chin, 'How about you-know-what finding The Fairy Key here?' Mr. Cadava said saucily, looking very pleased with himself.

'I d - '

' - Well! - '

' - Your view is completely invalid. To argue further would be pointless,' Mr. Bumblebeaux said in pointed, clipped tones, 'do not speak of matters that do not concern you, Mr. Cadava.'

'I will, if I so pleases,' he barked, screeching. Nothing, it seemed, would stop him.

'And Megan cannot just run amok here, Mr. Cadava! Not to begin with, anyway.'

Mr. Cadava, sniffing in the air, shot

both Mr. Bumblebeaux and Megan a sneering look.

Glowering, Mr. Cadava protested, 'You lie.'

Megan was stood with her mouth agape.

Genuinely surprised to hear Mr. Bumblebeaux being called a liar, she stood her ground. Megan choked a cry and was going too rush to his defence. Even though she was trembling so much inside, she would have forced herself to speak in an ordinary sort of voice.

She now very much disliked Mr. Cadava. Who smelt so deliciously of toffees.

Mr. Bumblebeaux said, all at once, not whimpering, 'I? A dishonest Elf? A comparative liar?' he looked at the enormous warty face of Mr. Cadava, 'besides, knowing as I know at all costs, I do estimate that there shan't ever be a problem... even if you wished there to be one,' he finished, in a tone that brook no more argued tennis balling, and ending the matter.

Megan, rocking on her feet, had gone a little bit pale.

'I do not agree,' Mr. Cadava said, in a low tone, slightly snarling.

Mr. Bumblebeaux looked even more wise than as his usual, clever-looking Elfish self. 'All the same, fear-mongering will not be prohibited,' he said, in a neutrally calm voice.

Looking out from under his hooded eyes, Mr. Cadava blathered, 'Tosh.' He was very irritated now. Clearly, from his attitude, he felt no need to make a good impression. Mr. Cadava wasted no breath pretending otherwise. His ill-disguised annoyance showed that, too.

'This will be always discouraged, Mr. Cadava. As well you know...' Mr. Bumblebeaux outstretched a hand towards Megan's general vicinity.

Mr. Cadava looked stern.

'As I said.' Mr. Bumblebeaux said in a well thought-out, tepid reply.

Mr. Cadava didn't graciously look as if he attempted to think long and hard about this. 'I will tell everyone what you've done, and those that don't like you will *support* me,' he threatened.

By Mr. Cadava's demeanour, Mr. Bumblebeaux thought that the Magic Historian looked like he wanted to be anywhere else, and most likely, he thought, that anywhere else would be working.

'I don't know how you think you can say that. Anyway, it basically comes down to this: you are not the SpokesElf here, Mr. Cadava.'

Mr. Cadava cast Megan a dark, questioning look.

'Yes, I am well of that most unfortunate fact... Mr. Bumblebeaux.'

Mr. Cadava's face looked yearningly at the evident mention of the position.

There was a sudden silence.

Megan did not know what was going on.

Mr. Cadava threw a dirty look at Megan and Mr. Bumblebeaux.

They looked like they weren't old friends. Or Mr. Cadava evidently did not, anyhoo.

'Do you not think I took others into consideration?' Mr. Bumblebeaux judged, calmly, as if squaring up to a foe.

'No, because it's... she is here.' Mr. Cadava's countenance of his face started to look very annoyed now.

Mr. Bumblebeaux did not look equally happy. 'Megan can do as she pleases,' he said supportively.

Mr. Cadava didn't instinctively move.

There was a definite increase in Mr. Cadava's annoyance factor.

Megan took a distanced step back.

Mr. Cadava looked perilously close to shouting, like he was about to lose his temper.

Megan stared incredulously.

In not a very nice way, he was still looking at Mr. Bumblebeaux, who again kept his features simply looking nonchalant.

Mr. Cadava waited for him to say anything. Do something.

Mr. Bumblebeaux didn't say anything.

Megan's face strained.

A hassled-looking Mr. Cadava's shadowed eyes looked like he wanted to box Mr. Bumblebeaux's ears.

Megan was still frozen to the spot from her appearance meeting such disapproval.

Mr. Cadava gave her a very nasty look indeed.

This did long trouble Megan.

Outside of Art class and her arty

work at home, she never usually felt good anything. Anything at all.

Megan smiled slightly, trying to let Mr. Cadava see.

In reply, Mr. Bumblebeaux cocked his head to one side, cheering her on. This was the sort of thing Megan's mum and dad, and her grandparents, would have done.

Mr. Cadava felt bitter.

As Mr. Cadava became more beetroot in colour, it seemed as if his extraordinarily extra-large head was becoming more than a trifle bigger, as the tips of his ears looked like they were struggling to arrange themselves as his crown grew.

Mr. Cadava put a hand into the breast pocket of his grey shirt.

Megan opted to break the silence. 'I-I like it... h - ' Megan muttered. As soon as she had found her voice.

' - Then. And then... if you please, *do* come here again and get landed, or blown up for all I care,' Mr. Cadava hissed in a nasal tone.

'Look here, Morg,' Mr. Bumblebeaux said at once.

There was silence, blanketing with the dark of the tunnel.

Mr. Cadava showed a rare beaming smile.

Megan had gone very pale.

'She will.' Mr. Bumblebeaux insisted brightly, at last. He hadn't sounded at all doubtful.

Megan very much hoped she would.

Mr. Cadava looked very annoyed. His gaze blazed. 'How preposterously cavalier you are being.' he said rebelliously.

Mr. Bumblebeaux, half-upside down now, drew himself up to his full height.

Megan was mumbling something about not wanting to leave.

She was trying to avoid his eye.

'How really very dull you are.' Mr. Cadava added bitterly and quite nastily, thinking whoever he meant to be extremely dim, choosing too not look at either of them. He stroked his long, oily black moustache that appeared like it had been slicked in a mixer of hot, gurgling tar, but which seemed like it had grown, for now Mr. Cadava's moustache looked longer, like strung slugs.

Megan applied her face into her hands.

Mr. Cadava looked like he was about to explode on the spot.

In midst of all this, Megan was pooling all her politeness that her mum and dad had brought her up with. She was a naturally warm child; her parents only embellished and promoted Megan's caring nature.

Mr. Cadava pulled quite hard at the overlap on his black-fronted, unfastened coat-sleeves. 'Ah!

Humbug.'

He looked at Mr. Bumblebeaux in a contemptuous way.

Mr. Bumblebeaux didn't glare back. 'I would suggest you hence return to your workroom... now,' he said, very quietly and calmly.

Mr. Cadava could tell he was trounced.

Megan's face turned a very fire-engine red.

Mr. Cadava's gaze looked like he was looking through Megan.

He shook with disgust.

Mr. Cadava didn't say anything; he gave Mr. Bumblebeaux a stern nod. In a sombre way, he turned on his heels, hunched his shoulders and flew up, and without much further ado, disappeared straightaway through the ceiling. Megan, suspecting Mr. Cadava not to be an Elf, had expected him to disappear in a way such as that.

Megan looked fraught.

'We will be having an... urgent discussion later.'

'A discussion?' Megan asked, not shaking.

'Of sorts. Mr. Cadava's loyalty has always been... questionable. If he does fracture from Pandragon's Key, our knowledge, or rather yours, could make him a valuable ally.'

'For... who?' Megan worried, feeling agitated.

'Abraxus. Anyway, nothing too worry over.' Mr. Bumblebeaux smiled, whose spectacles were askew.

Megan, regaining a sense of feeling more at ease, had not wept throughout the tempest-tossed feeling, from what was between Mr. Bumblebeaux and Mr. Cadava's hotly active word play. Though it took all her will not to burst out crying of embarrassment from wanting to shelter under a rock, or feeling like she wanted the ground to gobble her up, all caused by a one Mr. Cadava.

Megan now let herself go red.

The darkness carried away her pinked cheeks.

Chapter Forty-Five

Books, Books And More Books

Stealing a glance over her shoulder, Megan discovered again the nets of fabric now falling back into place, like a rippling curtain of heavy drapes.

She'd walked on down the tunnel, shivering now and then from her experience with Mr. Cadava.

Then down the one tunnel, a passage slashed up to the right, which she knew as she could hear Mr. Bumblebeaux's wings flap that way, and, guiding her, he told her where exactly to tread. Leaving the main tunnel-way, she and Mr. Bumblebeaux slanted up the dark side-corridor that fed off the main tunnel, and then walked through the draped walls, spilled in screens from the ceiling.

She pushed past folds, then Megan tripped-up out from behind a tapestry. Clinging on to a stitched picture of a Unicorn, Megan righted herself, then holding the curtains open for Mr. Bumblebeaux, she glanced around; she was on a small raised red and black striped dais, the platform of which was set back from the rising throne.

Now, though, one of the three long runner benches was home to books. Books piled in crazy-looking columns. Books piled in hulks, grouped together on the benches, and made her wonder why none fell off.

'Back in The Great III Hall,' said Megan, grinning, letting the tapestry screens drift back into place, ever-concealing the small dark, lobby corridor that led to the much more darkened tunnel.

Megan felt a shiver of pleasure at spying all the texts. All of the content of the billions of books in the room of The Great III Hall drew on her as if she were a magnet.

She continued along the dust-free piles of books. Some were in pristine condition, others with mottled covers, some well-worn. A thick, tallish book had nubbed corners so tatty one could peep the wooden boards poking through the fabric of the cover.

Mr. Bumblebeaux was smoothing down the tapestry with the Unicorn and she saw, also, the tapestry had high zooming Dragons and dipping Mermaids on the bottom, with the odd Flying Dolphin swirling above the crystal blue and deep purple knitted water. Megan wouldn't have been at all shocked to see the stitches start to gush out from the tapestry. It looked so real.

Something happened that Megan

was quite unprepared for.

'These poor volumes,' said a soft voice, suddenly.

Pale as a ghost, Megan looked behind her.

Megan gasped at once.

A small grasshopper in a red beret (with two itsy-bitsy holes cut-out for his peeping antennas), and a rather fetching camomile-coloured shirt, was buzzing by Mr. Bumblebeaux.

At this point Megan very nearly spluttered aloud.

She carefully placed a hand over her open mouth.

Then stopping her rifling, she stooped back up, and walked down the two aisles of long benches.

'Poor stranded books. Lost!' the grasshopper said, in a loud twirp.

Megan heard the grasshopper zip in the air, becoming more frantic so it looked like it was attempting to out-fly a fly-squatter.

'Volumes. How most unbecoming! Volumes damaged! Pitted! Oh! My heart could doth break!' the grasshopper cheeped, and roared. Or as much as he could roar.

Mr. Bumblebeaux was tugging cautiously at the end of the tapestry, nodded to himself, then smiled too Megan, beckoning to her to come nearer.

'*Neglected*. VANDERLIZED.'

'There there - '

' - But! The bo - '

' - There now.'

'Books!' The grasshopper squeaked. Megan really liked him.

'OK now, Mr. Mood, now now' Mr. Bumblebeaux said, striding in the air, flying by him, holding his hands up and dabbing the air.

'Thank you... Barnibus,' the grasshopper panted, feeling very hot, mid-puff, his wings looking like they were flitting ten-to-the-dozen.

'You're most welcome, Coyd.'

Mr. Mood let out a loud *zzzzzip* hum of agreement.

'The books!' he cried, sympathetically, looking dejected.

'Don't work yourself into one of your tizz states,' Mr. Bumblebeaux predicted, to be sure.

Megan hid her mouth to hide a giggle.

The effort of the temptation too burst a laugh out was hard to stop. Knowing she may well do so, Megan glanced away quickly.

Mr. Mood slid down the leg of the throne, looking completely exhausted. 'Is this the brave Fairy Key?'

Mr. Bumblebeaux, nearly hanging upside down, flew to the foot of the regal-looking chair. 'The one and only.'

'My, The Fairy Key's here. And The Fairy Key is a she,' Mr. Mood commented cheerily, smiling.

Megan, grinning back, stood motionless and looked more relaxed. She was very glad Mr. Mood's greeting wasn't the same as how she was greeted by Mr. Cadava. There was nothing of the musically light about his crackling brittle voice. No sweetness had ever entered Mr. Cadava's tone, there was only a rapturous coldness lagging behind his words.

Megan shivered.

Sitting back on the pink chaise-lounge, she rearranged the lace-and-crochet raspberry cushions, and shivered again slightly from recalling Mr. Cadava. She thought Mr. Bunion was something, but Mr. Cadava was something else entirely.

'Ooo,' Megan said.

Crouching, she leaned forward a bit dizzily, moving off the raspberry blushed cushion.

A coiled pink python within a pink

pyramid was by her chair; it had caught her restful-looking eyes. The book had been left on the bench, all alone with zillions more stacked in plies on the long running seat.

Why didn't I notice this before? Megan thought, liking the look of the wrapping snake within the three-sided triangle. She felt the carved boards of the wooden-bound book, with yellowing papers stitched in the spine.

She mindfully replaced the book; just in case whoever put it there wasn't happy it might have been removed.

Megan set off.

Some manuscripts and books looked to Megan so ancient she fancied if she touched them, even a fingertip breath, then it would wisp away into nothing.

Her left leg brushed against pamphlets and leaflets which cascaded dancingly to the floor.

Topmost was what looked like a Minotaur, with a name scrawled under the half-bull: Trolious

Megan searched her memory, searching for anything remotely right.

Never heard of Trolious before. But I think I know what a Minotaur is, she mused, conjuring the image in her mind of what a Minotaur looks like. *A cow? Hmm...no... not quite a cow, she thought. Ah, a bull!*

This bull was like no other.

Megan scratched her auburn-ringlet head.

She picked up the loose papers and shuffled them back into place on the bench. Leaving the drawn picture of the man with the head of a bull, in a knee-length, tight-fitting skirt on the top of the heap; she wasn't overly sure if ought to be, or if there was a correct order, but, it looked as good as any place - to leave the papers decorated with the Minotaur bound manuscript.

Megan turned, as she felt something watching her.

Mr. Bumblebeaux was pacing up and down in the air, scarcely looking back at Mr. Mood wringing his antennas.

'Ah. Trolious, I see,' he said, zooming down, coming in for a crash-landing. He dropped on to the a neighbouring collection of books.

'Who's Trolious?' Megan asked, wondering if he was going to pop up, or worry over the books like Mr. Mood was again doing, his tiny pair of spectacles reflecting back the Fairy dust, clouding in The Great III Hall, as he fretted this way and that.

'Trolious, the Minotuar?' Mr. Bumblebeaux prompted.

Megan shook her head.

Towing up the sheet of the bull-headed man, she let if drift in her lap as she sat on the crinkly-feeling papers.

'The story is concerning the Minotaur, oh, you know what a Minotaur is?' he checked, dangling out his gangly-looking legs.

Megan nodded, firmly.

'Trolious went through a speciality of his: a trial, but before that stage, he went through a tourney.'

'What's that?'

'A contest.'

Megan nodded, getting the gist.

Mr. Bumblebeaux took a breath, then he hurriedly went on, 'Anyway, come the end of the trial, Trolious has to emotionally let go of his brother, who betrays him. Such a sad story. Yes, he did wondrous things. And is surely a fascinating book, but the volume is devastating. Terrible in its sadness. You should devour the fable with your eyes,' the old Elf recommended the read, to Megan.

Megan looked a bit questioning; she thought she might give that a miss.

'The prose is superbly poetical,' Mr. Bumblebeaux added, in a tone as if that should seal the deal.

Smiling convincingly, Megan nodded. *I don't know what he's talking about*, she thought, her features then partly showing this, too.

Megan looked around at all the books.

A pink, sugary-looking wash was scrubbed over the stone-cobbled walls of The Great III Hall, glinting in lathers with an entrancing magenta phosphorescent light.

The itty-bitty fantastic glitters were mingling, hurtling themselves in the air and off free-standing screens, with blue and gold astrological paintings of graphs and glyphs.

Selecting books and papers, her fingers roved a petal-breath over the tops of them.

Megan's tentative fingers roamed

over the carving of the book's cover, which had a scar in the front cover as if a hand had tried to cut out the words of: G YPHS.

Gyphs? she thought. *Is a scribbled letter missing? Why would a letter be ripped out? Impossible to guess, really... useless thinking on it.*

Moving on down the half-piles, Megan beamed a forensic eye over:

Mythopolgia,
a treatise containing a short description of

But she had no clue or rhyme-or-reason for the description, because the book's front page had been partially ripped off.

What was left in the middle, tucked below the *Mythopolgia* title, was a long-dried wax seal. The circle was with a five-point star pressed into its belly.

The whole place was so imaginative.

Megan shook her head.

Her hands picked up stacks, then she peered at what was revealed on the top of the pile, some of which she was grasping.

A teensy-tweensy square, each quarter divided in straight-looking lines, and in the upper left quadrant was a symbol of a spindly-looking key hanging vertically.

An amulet of a triangle was clamped on to a vellum folio, which was smoored by huge green circled wreathes.

She shook her fingers past the dry-feeling leaves and twined brambles of the bushy rings.

The folio was just a plain, old-fashioned book that was shredded so its bindings showed. It was of board, leather-bound, silver clasps, and read with a title: Minstrel of

The vellum-feeling pages had also been torn-out, in part, just like this book's front-and-back covers.

Minstrel? Where have I heard of that word before? Ah! Aren't they sweets? Megan thought, shrugging. Remembering how her Mum and Aunt could demolish a whole family pack in a catching-up, newsy afternoon.

Megan was feeling more and more astonished.

Mr. Mood was zipping in skips, causing a few pamphlets to pour down, plonking in a jumble upon the pink cobble-stoned floor of the fabulous Great III Hall.

Megan was brawling down the feeling of being unaccountably overwhelmed.

Mr. Bumblebeaux held on to a revolving mechanism of three balls stuck together that could be moved about a chrome-looking small pole.

With a bewildering face, 'I don't feel particularly brave,' Megan mentioned in a mumble, in passing, remembering how Mr. Mood had referred to her.

Megan's forensic beady-eye was already lost on another folio, though she heard the allied words around her, 'You are extremely noble, Fairy Key.

'You brought harmony to where there was only sheer discord.'

'*I* did that?'

'You are gifted, Megan.'

'I-If' Megan stammered, apologetically.

Mr. Bumblebeaux grinned.

'I'm really not trespassing here?' Megan asked, incredibly concerned. Being so immersed in the fluster of the moment, quite forgetting this was hers.

'By Jove! Of course *you're* not.'

Megan shook herself.

'I'm not like Lucy?' she asked,

getting the question out quick in a rapidly firing-fire.

'You? Like Lucy? Certainly not.'

'So there's not been a mistake and Lucy's not The Fairy Key?'

'*You* are The Fairy Key. And Lucy is The Dragon Keeper.'

Megan's eyes gleamed.

She looked away for a moment. Smoky dips suspended over long tallow's, which had been discarded on the tables. Megan knew lighting was considered unimportant as The Great III Hall throbbed with light, and lights spilled in from the beams of the now slightly shining three suns.

Perhaps if anymore lighting was necessary, it was provided by those shortened candle-looking wicks. She suddenly had an image of Mr. Mood lighting one, attempting to peep at the letters much too large for him, then vigorously sweating over if the candle might blow the whole place up.

Megan laughed.

Mr. Bumblebeaux had a questioning look on his face. Grinning from her chimpanzee-sounding laughs.

Megan smiled delightedly.

Holding her rumbling chest, she looked about The Great III Hall, big enough to comfortably fit many Lancaster Bomber airplanes.

'Megan, you do not posses one once of vainglory. Lucy, however, certainly does.'

Although not quite nice to hear her sister described like that, she knew Lucy was the likeliest of both of them to be rude, impolite, selfish and swollen-headed.

Megan's eyes welled up.

'You volunteered yourself,' Mr. Bumblebeaux nodded.

Megan's cheeks flushed a tomato-red.

She hadn't thought of it quite like

that.

But Mr. Bumblebeaux had.

Megan scratched her nose.

'You had an enemy to face.' Mr. Bumblebeaux nodded bravely. 'It took a good deal of courage in your heart to face Abraxus.

'And believing that you stood a chance at winning.

'Not only did you try with your all, you succeeded. *You prevailed.*'

In greatest astonishment, Megan was grasping just what she had achieved. Feeling thoroughly happy with what she had accomplished.

'You are so tender of us here,' Mr. Bumblebeaux nodded, 'you came to help. Your first instinct was in fact not for yourself, or even your safety. You wanted to help Princess Blossom.'

She again hadn't thought of it like that.

Though once more, Mr.

Bumblebeaux had.

Megan felt the distinct impression that nothing was off-limits. 'This really is all mine. I-I... I feel it,' a once-felt sensation of warming fuzziness, making her feel toasty, prickled in her once again.

'As I said, this is the crux, Megan: your belief, and how you never once thought of your own safety.' Mr. Bumblebeaux gave her a celebratory smile.

Megan felt... stronger... somehow.

For not a limited amount of times, she was used to feeling lonely, and always at a loss to know why. Now Megan felt as if someone had shown her a treasure and told it was all for her, and more, that the treasure would forever be hers... and *in* her.

Megan's eyes lazered into Mr. Bumblebeaux's.

'This *is* mine...'

Megan was surprised at the words

coming out of her mouth.

Yet there they were. True and certain.

Little did Megan know why they flew out.

Is this a dream? Megan puffed her cheeks out.

Wake up Megan, she thought.

But it was not a dream.

Megan could not wake up because she wasn't fast asleep.

This. Was. Real.

The brightness in Megan's eyes was undoubtedly a swan-feathered sheen.

'You need to go now.' Mr. Bumblebeaux suddenly announced.

'Go?' Megan said defensively, looking shocked.

'Yes, you are needed, for a terrible battle is taking place,' he said solemnly, standing up, papers falling.

'It's Lucy…. isn't it?' pathetically, something in Megan's heart told her that Lucy was involved.

'The Dragon Keeper is one participant in this struggle, yes.'

Fear dulled Megan's zipping thoughts.

'And needs my help? Then I must go to her... now.' Megan looked very anxious, she was becoming increasingly fretting, in a mounting air of wanting to leave.

Mr. Bumblebeaux sighed. 'Alas, help to the powerful is never needed I find.'

Megan remained sitting, and thought quickly about this. Troubling her, thinking it over, there was something there about the powerful...

After flapping forward, Mr. Bumblebeaux pushed Megan slightly rashly. Mr. Bumblebeaux looked sad and in the simultaneous heave of his crooked-feeling hands on her back, he said, 'I'm so, so sorry.'

Animated, Megan reeled. She felt the abruptness of being forced to leave.

His parting words to her were cryptic, but then Megan found some of what Mr. Bumblebeaux said always made no sense, though most oddly, she had a sneaking feeling, as she got wiser, these words would and make sense - even if, for the time being, they were lodged somewhere not to recall, 'Remember, Megan. The most beautiful experience we can have is the mysterious. It is the fundamental emotion of all beings that stands at the cradle of true art and your human true science.

'Whoever does not know it and can no longer wonder, no longer marvel, is as good as gone, and his eyes are dimmed.

'In essence, you brought us true liberty, Megan.'

Megan had barely never had so many questions in her life.

As Mr. Bumblebeaux was

explaining his explanations, Megan's eyes were distracted by the shutterless windows. But it was not the superior-looking, stained-glass scenes of Fairies, Unicorns, Dragons and Mermaids (and many more other Magic creatures, besides) that held her gaze: it was the raging mega storm clouds that were rumbling and gathering, drowning over The Fairy Key Land and brewing over Pandragon's Key!

BOOM.

Thunder sounded.

Megan gulped.

BOOM.

Went another thunder-clap.

BOOM.

Megan's eyes nearly popped out.

BOOM.

Megan cast one last panic-struck look around.

BOOM.

Everything spun.

Chapter Forty-Six

Fiendish Evil Maleficence

Lucy was lying on the ground as the blackbirds preyed in pecks inside her addled mind.

She suddenly felt something digging into her leg; she attempted to roll over, but couldn't, and she suddenly remembered the doll's head in her pocket, and in that very movement, home and her parents flooded into her.

The warm feelings and images began to slip away, in her mind. Lucy knew, just *knew*, that she had to concentrate on these and push aside what was happening around her body.

She saw how her mum and dad sat on the sofa, eating the cakes that earlier she had baked at school, and how her mum had laughed, and her dad had choked after being told what was inside the crumbling pastry: apple and rose petals - although, her mum's laughing stopped when she realised that Lucy had ripped out the roses in her garden for the cake's batter.

She saw her house, then the scope of her bedroom and remembered how she would practice her dance routines in the back garden.

Lucy inwardly smiled as she recalled, months before, sneaking into her sister's room and snooping in her drawing books.

She smelt the perfume of jasmine that her grandmother wore and how at some weekends, for special treats, she and Megan would stay at their grandparents' thatched-roofed cottage Cleaverbud Gables, that had wild peacocks which would come up from out the woods by their gardens.

Like ghosts they all spirited her vision: but she invoked them out, not wanting too look back at happy memories and neither much longing to add any new ones.

A stirring congealed within her and like a flower bud, it bloomed open until Lucy's body emanated light: electric crackles danced over her body; her outlined form was framed by a shocking shade of purple.

She heard something suddenly scab away from her, hissing words as it did so.

Lucy's eyes shattered open and a purple light shone out from them; like a torch beam they drove at everything they fell on.

She felt aware of everything and knew that she alone could bring about a change, so different to the one Abraxus had intended.

Lucy picked herself up.

Stood, and slowly swiveled her head from side to side: she marveled at how she was full of purple light and how it skipped over her entire body, and she knew before seeing it, that an attack from above would take place against her.

She glanced up, her eyes penetrating and emblazing the furthest cloud, the leaf, still in her hand, burst free of its crumpled rotten shell and shone a white, hot light with rainbow sparks flying over its surface.

The light didn't burn her; in fact, it helped her to fuel the complete belief that she could destroy Abraxus, as she knew what must have to be done.

The heavens parted, and there, from a dot to an ever-greater threat, swooped a blue-and-white Dragon, ROARING his call and looking beautiful in his now evil ways.

She threw her arms out and with all her strength, fully resorted and flowing through her, she torch-beamed such light into the path of the Dragon.

'GO AWAY!' Lucy brayed.

His two front feet were stretched open, the purple lightning reflected off his obsidian claws, and as his wings thrashed down, from his sky lined height with such ferocity, a small part of her was shocked that she didn't puff out the way, and yet another part of her answered that her feet bored down into the centre of The Kingdom, along with her own powerful Magic, so she was calling on all manner of an altogether, another, more wild, deeper magical force.

Pelting rain began to spit and screams escalated from behind him, and as Aradene flew through the clouds, her gown sliding against the lightning, she tried to severe Lucy's light, but her cries increased whenever she came too near to it.

As an act of final brilliance, a bolt of light came from her and coupled also with the leaf, amalgamating together in defiance as it rose to meet the fire, being savagely scorched down from Abraxus.

Lucy screamed.

Abraxus *roared*.

*

Abraxus soared down lower. Ever lower.

Lucy kept on screaming.

As the final blast of the light resonated out of Lucy, its force blew upwards and backwards, knocking her off her feet and she landed overturned.

Planets and woodpecker birds drummed in her head. Lucy's insides felt as if they were jigging to the hokey-cokey, and once they had all disappeared, she hauled herself up, looking round grimly for Abraxus. But of him, nor Aradene, there was no sign. *Have I blown them up*, she wondered? and pocketed the leaf, not even having to look at it, too know that its darkness had been scored away.

Dragons gas muzzled at her feet and arose hazily, and as it floated its curls of glittery pink and gold Fairy dust, it parted in a *pouf* in front of her to reveal someone she knew very well: for, Megan came walking out of the fug!

'Oh, good grief, good grief! Megan said, majorly relived.

Thinking of her Mum and Dad, Lucy half-smiled. As Megan stood staring at her younger sister who had a somewhat vacant air, she went to come forward as if to hug her (but Lucy did not meet her in that sisterly space), and so covering up, Megan said. 'You did it.'

Lucy cartwheeled a dismissive step back, instead of still meeting for a hug. She held her head up, and replied, 'Yes, I did it. You know what? I do believe in Magic, especially mine and what I can do with it,' she bragged harshly, in a blathering way.

As the brume, foggy mist was falling on the ground, the full view shone itself: The Kingdom had been brought back to its original goodness. *Just like before, like when I defeated Abraxus*, thought Megan.

Lighted beams shone down through the clouds: the three suns were back to their full-beamy colourful selves, which caressed Megan's glitter-spittled face, and glassy rainbows dotted the sky.

Green grass stretched for as far as their eyes could see, and a sound of running water trickled to their right.

Megan's mass of auburn ringlets, in the three suns rays, seemed as if strands of her hair were alighted.

Megan felt refreshed.

They looked to one another, seeming to have the same thought, so they followed the sound to its source: a small sparkling stream ran flat-out in its course, they each leaned over the bank and ducking their hands into the crystal blue of the trickling brook. Each sister greedily drank until it felt as if their whole bodies swam with freshness.

The winds breath was blowing on to Megan.

Though there was no real need to sip the water, for the Magic in The Enchanted Kingdom somehow made it so they never felt dry-throated. Still, Megan was enjoying the gulp of water.

Lucy looked to the young lady looking back to her in the brook, and all the dirt from her journey had been somehow cleaned away: her ponytail glistened and she hid a smug smile to herself.

'I can't believe I did that,' Lucy prattled her own heroism.

Megan looked pointedly at her.

Although Megan still felt back-to-front, and upside down, she had been so worried about Lucy and if she was alright, wherever she was.

Megan twiddled a lock of hair wound her fingers.

They sat on the grass, which led to crimps overhanging the bank. Megan ran her fingers through some blades, and enjoyed being sat in a patch of merry sunshine. Fantastic!

For some reason, Megan did not want to confront Lucy.

Then for reasons best known to herself, Lucy feigned an air of idle distraction by plucking at some steams of grass: the atmosphere changed between both girls and at last, when they felt ready to venture their separate happenings, Lucy went first and as Megan took her turn, she pondered on this before replying, and for some inexplicable reason she edited out her journey and discovery of The Fairy Key Land, and putting her head critically to one side, also didn't relay the castle, Pandragon's Key. Megan also discounted sharing with Lucy about Mr. Bumblebeaux. Nor anything of the news of All Souls Librarium.

The Fairy Key Land, Pandragon's Key and All Souls Librarium remained for Megan only.

All Megan told of her tale was to stick to the first part of the truth of her being deposited behind a waterfall: she wound up by saying, '... I couldn't move. I think I was in a cave... do you remember?

'It was like the one last time when

we first came here. I was just lying there, completely still, a small part of me was screaming for my body to move, but it just wouldn't,' she choked - from the retelling of what had happened to her, it brought back all the feelings - then she farmed on, 'I could see everything and hear it all as well, but it was if I was looking behind my own eyes... It was incredibly weird.'

They each looked down to the shimmering running water, and Lucy, out of habit, threw a pink gemstone and a small grey rock into its surface, watching the stones sink down and ripples floating out and she knew, and she suspected Megan also realised, that something between them as sisters, had incontrovertibly altered.

Chapter Forty-Seven

The Dragon Keeper

In the pathway of the willows mammoth clearing, stood two girls, a black Unicorn, a statuesque Guardian, two Dragons and a very much alive Brim-Tree. All held their court, and an edge of even greater space had been crafted, as though it seemed all the willow trees moved back to make way for the Dragons - who were now far into the skyline.

As Megan and Lucy had sat resting on the streams bank, a voice had suddenly echoed out from Lucy's pocket. 'Would you both like too come to where I am? There are some friends here, whom would like to say hello,' the deep voice rumbled with mirth.

Each sister got up, flicked off spangles of soil and as a golden light spun in kernels between them, like bursting lights of confetti, it danced faster and faster; leaves, varicoloured, fluttered and smashed brightly into one another.

Megan's corkscrew hair flew in front of her face, and as the girls opened their eyes, they didn't hear the slow trickling anymore - for they had been moved.

Megan felt a nice wind blowing down on her. When they had stepped into the clearing, The Brim-Tree was awaiting their arrival within the grove, and of the Gumps, Lucy spied none of them, which she was quite thankful for.

When the Dragons had landed, and the whistles sung from one of the Dragons wings, it caused everyone's hair to swirl up, and this is how Megan came to cocking her head to

Lucy, into noticing that under Aradene's curtain of hair, a lone black strand fluted up and was then concealed once more, when her hair fell back into place: this was Abraxus' legacy; the taint of his power would be in Lucy always, and a small part of Aradene would want to dance along with the Dragon's darkness.

Their gaping was interrupted, as she glided over the mounded earth to pay her greeting to The Fairy Key, leaving a trail of Fairy dust in her wake.

Megan did a double-take.

'Oh. My. Gosh.' She felt as if she were going doolally.

Megan's rich auburn, russet ringlets, were dusted with gold crowning speckles, which was being shaken off as she shook her head.

After Megan had gotten over the shock, of slowly realising this Guardian had been her brief schoolteacher in disguise, Aradene leaned down, faced Megan, smiled her knowing smile, then she moved aside and as she said, 'Thank you, Lucy,' placed a hand on top of Lucy's head and as she did so, she drew back hastily. She looked intently into her eyes and mysteriously conspired. 'Be safe and careful, Dragon Keeper,' then turned and went away to be beside Charger, seeming to whisper into his twitching black ear.

Hello... Megan Button... his black, smiley eyes seemed to say to Megan.

Out of the corner of her eye, Lucy surreptitiously cast Charger a most disgusted look. Her attention was then grabbed, as she had recognised one of the Dragons (from the thousands of frozen ones she had seen), for she had stood against its clawed feet: she was sure of it, but thinking herself still shook up, she concentrated on the conversation at hand. '...Where's Princess Blossom, Nugget, Prince

Tumble... are they *all* OK now?'
Megan called out to The Brim-Tree,
which looked truly amazing and
exactly like it did when they had left
last time, after being given their titles.

'Yes, remember, some of your
friends are are rulers of their Lands,
and as such, they are attempting to
restore peace to their Subjects.

'Such despair I know they all feel:
the Prince and Princess' of each Land
face an arduous task, to reassure and
bring about calm as once they all felt.'

Bront leaned his armed head down
to be beside The Brim-Tree and
introduced the scarlet Dragon nestled
into him, as the Princess, and here he
revealed his secret to both Megan and
Lucy: he was the Prince of Dragon
Land!

He had wanted to tell them, and
knew this was the exact time for they
were both together in which to do so.
Now, he explained, in his place, until

he went back, he had delegated to his trusted guards and they were attempting to keep the fury under control, of what had happened to them.

This is the reason, he detailed, as is to why rips and clawed holes are streaked through his pocketed-looking wings.

Princess Mandragora diped her huge Dragon's head and in her loud voice, she told the two humans that when Abraxus had realised that he was not the one who had been elected as Prince, a midair battle had commenced with Abraxus fighting the protective Bront: as he wanted to attack the newly crowned Princess.

Megan dithered on the spot for a moment.

A percolating thought rumbled in her mind. Then, sure of herself and her voice, asked plaintively, 'But why did you not tell us when we first met you, that you are the Dragon Prince?'

Bront sighed, sounding like the echo of a mountain moving its weight. 'I did not know your kind, and if I had told you the truth, I was unsure if you both would feel sorry for Abraxus.' he explained. 'Thus understanding his jealous reaction and that you would then justify his actions, by that from what I first thought.'

'Oh,' collectively came.

A wide, glorious rainbow beamed ahead of the three suns magical rays and swooped high into the air. The Brim-Tree's ever-changing, colourful rainbow leaves, which were so bright it almost hurt their eyes to fully look high at them, reflected off the Dragons scales and wings.

The dusting of Fairy powder, spritzed by Aradene, was intermixing on the calming breeze and The Brim-Tree's deep voice said to all,

'Abraxus has come too the realisation that to be completely free, he has in fact to severe the Magic bonds that lay over him, which spin from you, Dragon Keeper.'

A ruggedness came out from the Tree and it seemed to Lucy that it somehow bent to her, growing in its magnified voice and sized intensity, almost causing her to shrink back from the pressured sight and amplified tone. 'You, Lucy, will have a great onus, for, as The Dragon Keeper, you will maintain the hold over Abraxus in his trapped form.

'This responsibility you must take seriously and be sentient at all times, for, his evil is like that I have never seen before, and is now too far gone to be brought back.

'You must take in the important magnitude of what I am saying.

'His dark ways of Magic do still run through your veins, and far in the future when you have reached adulthood, you may have a personal battle, as too what path you decide to take.'

As before, he told Lucy to look in her hand, and suddenly she felt a weighted form: instead of the statue of Abraxus she was expecting to spy, he was now contained in the same state, but inside a globe, where a phosphorescent luminescent lights of Magic Fairy dust shackled him.

It was a snowstorm: its base was burnt orange with furnished ripples to signify rolling fire, whilst the globe sparked off its glassed brilliance. She felt the Magic boil of out her body, leaking directly to the burnished snowglobe; it was a force-field of protective Magic to still him.

Megan watched as Lucy shook the globe, who in turn, was watching the figure form of Abraxus being suspended upside down; she turned it the right way and within the glass, white and rainbow coloured barbs flew in flakes around him.

'Rather time for you to go, I think,' came within the wind.

Hot tears sprung on Megan's rejoicing face.

Megan had the best time she possibly could have. She clasped her heart; her animated face beamed as she soaked up the pageantry of being The Fairy Key.

Megan felt a start-off of feeling victorious.

Now the whole shebang of the atrociously cruddy business was behind her, Megan felt entertained thoroughly and immensely enjoyed herself immeasurably.

How marvelous!

Megan smiled broadly.

She said goodbye to her friends, old companions and new, and as she turned from both the Prince and

Princess of Dragon Land, suddenly next to Lucy, who was stood alone, a shimmering curtain of white encrusted Fairy dust blasted and hung in the air; running up from the ground, large enough for both Sisters to solider through, back to the comfort of home.

Megan felt revived, in a no-nonsense mood, and her chest burst with the matchless, gayest of all feelings: happiness.

Megan pressed her hand to her heart.

She waved creamily and with that, then strode into the Fairy dust.

Megan again bade them a bye.

ROAR. Megan heard Prince Bront rumble his familiar goodbye.

'Bye Bront, I mean Prince Bront!' she called.

Far in the sky, she heard a deep roaring laugh.

As she disappeared within, Lucy

glanced over her shoulder. From her vantage point, The Brim-Tree, Aradene and Charger were all behind the wall of shimmering, live dust, but she could clearly see the two Dragons. As Prince Bront took his flight, Princess Mandragora felt the penetrative stare and looked down; her scaled head jousted to one side and Lucy turned, out of the paradise of The Enchanted Kingdom, to follow the back of her retreating sister.

Where they found themselves, it took them both but a brief moment to realise they had come back to the exact time, though now in Megan's bedroom.

Megan's eyes batted.

She went and retrieved her leaf, which was now completely white, bordered by crackling-like, bomb-exploding rainbow lights, and carefully placed it down to make sure it turned delicately ordinary: she sat it next to her pink-hued skating-boots on the bureau desk, which had a pair of chrome scissors touching one of its spoke wheels (the mini-sectors had robin's-egg blue handles, and a pink ribbon was tied on one oval-shaped handle), that were butted-up against an empty pint milk glass bottle, into which Megan had implanted a luscious bunch of pink peonies, with refilled water pooling in the bottom taken from the faucet in the bathroom.

Megan caught a breakneck sight of Lucy scrunching her dog-eared leaf into her pocket, and drawing out an obscured something she threw it; the doll's head bounced down on the bed when it landed, and as she tumbled the Dragon snared snowstorm, Megan said with stout firmness, 'You've still got to clean up that mess. You know, downstairs.'

A not-so-pleasant smile curled Lucy's mouth.

'Later... m-maybe,' she yawned, sourly and quite dismissively.

'Lucy.'

'You're such a *moron*, Megan.'

Megan frowned.

Lucy grinned.

'Oh Lucy,' said Megan, letting out a deep, heavy sigh, feeling disappointed.

'Moron Megan!'

'L - '

' - Shut your face!'

'Lucy!'

THE END